BLOOD

AND

SALT

BLOOD

AND

SALT

KIM LIGGETT

G. P. Putnam's Sons

G. P. PUTNAM'S SONS
an imprint of Penguin Random House LLC
375 Hudson Street
New York, NY 10014

G. P. Putnam's Sons is a registered trademark of Penguin Random House LLC.

Library of Congress Cataloging-in-Publication Data
Liggett, Kim. Blood and salt / Kim Liggett. pages cm
Summary: "Seventeen-year-old Ash Larkin finds out her family is involved in a
centuries-old saga of love and murder, alchemy and immortality when she follows her
mother to an isolated settlement in the cornfields of Kansas"—Provided by publisher.
[1. Supernatural—Fiction. 2. Immortality—Fiction. 3. Cults—Fiction. 4. Mothers
and daughters—Fiction. 5. Twins—Fiction. 6. Love—Fiction. 7. Alchemy—Fiction.
8. Kansas—Fiction.] I. Title.
PZ7.1.L54Blo 2015 [Fic]—dc23 2014044670
Printed in the United States of America.
ISBN 978-0-399-16648-8
1 3 5 7 9 10 8 6 4 2

For Maddie and Rahm.
It started with a feather.

1

BODY OF YEARS

THE DEAD GIRL hung upside down over our kitchen table.

Ropes dug into her ankles as she swayed from the chandelier. Blood traced a line from the familiar cut across the palm of her hand to one of her delicate fingertips. The drop quivered before joining the little puddle headed for my twin's cereal bowl. I pulled it out of the way, sloshing rice milk and granola onto the table.

"Ash," Rhys yelled at me, mouth full, spoon mid-scoop. "I'm not finished with that."

Ignoring him, I dumped his soggy old-man cereal into the sink. I knew he couldn't see the blood, but I couldn't bear to watch death touch him.

The dead girl belonged only to me.

"Perfect," Rhys said, pushing his lanky frame away from the table and holding up his milk-soaked sleeve.

"You'll live." I lobbed a tea towel at him.

My mother moved barefoot through the open kitchen, her long chestnut hair swinging behind her as she lit a bundle of sage. "To ward off grouchiness."

She wasn't some wannabe hippie. The sage was a holdover from her childhood. Seventeen years ago, my mother escaped Quivira, a spiritual commune in Kansas, with a ton of gold ingots and the two of us in her belly.

"Coffee works for that, too." Rhys smirked as he poured the last bit into his mug.

"Ooh yes, thanks, love." Mom took it right from under his nose.

I had to press my lips together to stifle a laugh.

Rhys glared at me as he scooped the oily black beans into the machine and stabbed the button.

This was as aggressive as my brother ever got.

I welcomed the high-pitched grinding noise—anything but the sound of that rope.

The dead girl had been with me for as long as I could remember, hanging above my crib, my bed, but her visits had grown further apart with each passing year.

Because of my mom's freaky upbringing, she thought I was born a conduit—meaning that I had a special gift allowing me to tap into the senses and emotions of my deceased female ancestors. So far, I'd only seen the one girl and she never made me feel much more than annoyed.

The grinding stopped. The rope crackled and creaked as it

spun the dead girl around to face me—and it felt like all the air had been crushed from my lungs.

Bracing myself against the cool granite countertop, I stared up at the face I'd seen so many times before. What had once seemed a vague family resemblance had turned into a startling revelation. It wasn't just her wide-set eyes, which had rolled back into her head as if trying to escape a terrifying last image, or her down-turned mouth, stretched open, frozen in mid-scream. With our long dark blond hair and pronounced cheekbones, we could've been twins.

My mom did a flyby, leaving me in a cloud of sage smoke.

"Wait." I sucked in a singeing breath as I climbed onto the table, stretching my fingers toward the chandelier.

When the smoke cleared, the dead girl was gone.

"Please tell me you're not on acid." Rhys's voice startled me.

I glanced down to see my mom and brother staring up at me with the same moss-green eyes—comforting and disarming all at once.

I forced myself to breathe. "I saw her."

"Oh, honey, I'm so sorry." My mom climbed up on the table, placing her hands on my shoulders.

"Are we really doing this?" Rhys sighed, navigating his way onto the table and making the china clatter. He had no spiritual gifts to speak of, but he didn't like being left out.

As a rule, I didn't keep secrets from them, but they both got weird whenever I saw the dead girl. If I told them she looked *exactly* like me now, that somehow in the past year she'd grown into my face, or I'd grown into hers, God only knows what they'd do.

My mom brushed tendrils of hair from my face, and my eyes filled with tears. I had no idea what was going on with me; I wasn't much of a crier. Maybe I was just stressed about what would come next: getting a new mark.

As if reading my thoughts, my mother traced a symbol below my collarbone with her fingertip. "If you'd rather wait, we can do it after school, or—"

"No, I'm fine," I said, patting her arm. No reason to prolong the agony.

My mother had developed a series of what she believed were protection marks to shield me from the worst of the visions, but she believed a lot of things. The Larkin women had a long history with alchemy and batshit craziness, so since I had the "protection marks," there was no real way of knowing if I was a conduit or just another functioning schizophrenic.

"Don't you think she's had enough?" Rhys said, clearing his throat, deep lines settling between his brows. He hated it—all of it—the history, the marks, the gold.

"I won't leave you unprotected," my mother said as she grasped our hands. I felt the hard ridge on her hand pressing against my skin. Like the hanging girl, my mother had a long angry scar covering the length of her left palm. A constant reminder of her past.

"This is going to hurt me more than it hurts you," she said as she helped us down from the table, then led the way up the spiral stairs to her studio.

"I seriously doubt that," Rhys said under his breath.

I tried to play it off, but just the thought of the bone needle brought a vile taste to my mouth.

2

SCAR
TISSUE

YOU'D NEVER KNOW IT by the caustic scent in her studio, but my mother made some of the most exquisite perfumes in the world. She had an elite clientele willing to pay a small fortune for fragrances that were truly unique. She worked on other things, too. Secret things. The smell of sulfur and putrid brine wafted through the air, remnants of her last dalliance with the unknown.

Our apartment had a minimalist modern feel, but my mother's studio was warm and cluttered—like stepping back in time—a private oasis in the middle of New York City. Exposed brick walls were studded with arched windows, fragrant plants and vines grew in every nook and cranny. Still, my mom's favorite part of the house was the small stretch of grass in the center of the room. It wasn't just any grass—the seeds came from Quivira. She seemed truly at home here in the studio, standing among hundreds of mismatched bottles stacked on graduated shelves. As a kid I loved watching her work; I was always fascinated by the layer of fine gold dust that clung to her fingertips as she traced symbols in the air. She had her own language for formulas, a mix of ancient alchemy symbols and Caddo—the language of the Native American tribe who first inhabited Quivira. Supposedly, it was passed on from generation to generation of Larkin women, but my mother never wanted me to learn. She didn't want us to be a part of that world. Even if it was all in her head, it was still kind of beautiful, like a twisted fairy tale.

I spotted the sharpened bison bone needle on the edge of her desk.

"Do I smell wild jasmine?" I asked, trying to distract myself from what was about to happen.

A smile eased across her lips as she placed two drops of clear liquid into a narrow vial. "You're close. It's blue lotus." She stood on bare tiptoes to reach a bottle on the top shelf. She only wore shoes if she absolutely had to—another holdover from her upbringing.

My mother glanced at me appraisingly. "Your nose may be improving. Any chance it's rubbed off on your brother?"

"Highly unlikely," I said. To Rhys, everything smelled like Play-Doh, cinnamon, or feet.

"You know it's rude to talk about people in front of them," my brother called out as he meandered around the studio, squeezing through the apothecary shelves with his hands held high in the air, trying not to touch anything. He thought

7

alchemy was just a fancy word for witchcraft, but my mom always said it was about transformation. It could be herbs, metals, chemicals, or even the soul.

"I wish you'd teach me," I said as I watched her work.

"You know everything you need to know," she replied as she pulled bottles from the shelves.

"Just what anyone could pick up from a textbook." I removed a glass stopper to take a whiff. Sharp and metallic.

She smiled, but there was a tinge of sadness in her eyes. "You have your whole life ahead of you . . . a beautiful life, free of all this," she said as she took the bottle away from me. "You're not responsible for the sins of your ancestors."

Rhys made a throttling motion behind her. He hated when she talked in riddles.

"I know what you're doing, Rhys," my mother said without turning around.

Busted, I mouthed with a grin.

A deep flush reached all the way to the tips of his ears before he skulked off to look out the windows.

"You know, you have Katia's eyes," my mother said to me.

The dead girl. "Wait . . . did Katia look *exactly* like me?"

"No." She gave me a puzzled look. "There's a family resemblance, though. Why would you ask that?"

"Just curious." I feigned interest in an old marble pestle.

Katia Larkin, my great-great-great-whatever-grandmother, was a powerful alchemist in the 1500s. So powerful that the king of England, the king of Spain, and the Catholic Church all wanted to burn her at the stake. Apparently, she could turn common metals into gold and heal the sick. But the real kicker: They said she was immortal.

How she ended up in the middle of Kansas in 1541 is a sordid tale. Katia and her four children escaped to the New World with the conquistador Coronado. In exchange for their safe passage to Quivira, Katia agreed to make Coronado her immortal mate, but of course, she'd fallen madly in love with one of his soldiers, Alonso Mendoza.

Shit hit the fan when Katia tried to go behind Coronado's back and make Alonso her immortal mate instead of Coronado. Legend has it that Coronado killed Alonso and forced Katia to blood bind to him. The only way to break the bond was to find vessels, whatever the hell that meant, so she could be reunited with her one true love. It was all very *Days of Our Lives*, and my mother believed every word of it.

"Are you ready?" she asked, cradling the elixir in one hand, the bone needle in the other.

I nodded and walked to the center of the room, to the raised bed of grass.

Rhys sidled next to me. "You don't have to do this."

"Don't worry." I shooed him away. "I'll be fine."

Rhys perched himself on the far edge of the grass, looking at the wall so he wouldn't pass out. He wanted to be there for me, but he didn't do well with blood.

I removed my blouse and lay down, feeling the crush of soft blades against my back.

My mother kneeled beside me. Pushing aside the strap to my camisole, she traced the symbol with her fingertip directly below my collarbone. "Today, I will give you a circle with a dot in the center. Closest to your heart."

"The symbol for gold and sun," I said, taking in a jittery breath.

"Someone's been paying attention," she said as she leaned over me, her chestnut hair spilling onto her shoulders, obscuring her face.

She breathed slow and deep and began to meditate, or pray, or whatever it was she did. Sometimes Rhys and I would come home from school to find her that way, and we'd wonder if she'd been in that state all day. She always said she was *practicing*, using the energy of her surroundings to hang on to her soul as the world collapsed around her. Needless to say, we didn't ask about it often.

Rhys tapped his shiny loafer on the tiles. "Can we just get this over with?"

She dipped the fine bone needle into the murky tincture. "*Uhurahak a u' a,*" she whispered. "That means 'let go and let yourself fall.'"

Concentrating on the narrow shaft of sunlight streaming in through the open skylight, I inhaled deeply as she pressed the needle into my skin. It stung. You'd think after seventeen years I'd be used to it, but it still hurt like the very first time.

This was an ancient method of tattooing—the ink made from rare essences and metals—part of a series of archaic protection spells that left no visible mark after the pinpricks healed. The tattoos covered my entire body now. I didn't know if they did any good, but it made Mom feel like she was helping me. I'd trade a little pain for her peace of mind.

As she held my shoulder down, I felt my mother's scar tissue pulsing against my skin.

"The dead girl has a scar just like yours," I said.

"It's an honor." She eased her hand away, closing it into a fist. "She must've been chosen to walk the corn."

"Here we go." Rhys shook his head. We'd heard these stories a million times, but unlike Rhys, I never tired of them.

"It's tradition in Quivira," my mother continued, her features relaxing, her eyes taking on a dreamy quality. "The chosen couple walks the corn on the summer solstice. That's when Katia tests our blood, searching for the vessels. Nearly seventeen years ago, I walked the corn with your father, Thomas."

"But he didn't make it out of the corn," I said as I tore my eyes away from the patch of blue sky to study her face.

"No, we were separated," she answered in quiet resignation, pausing to admire her work on the outer rim of the circle. "But Katia led *me* out of the corn, and allowed me to leave Quivira to raise my children."

Rhys hunched over, resting his elbows on his knees. I knew it was killing him not to say anything. He thought our entire family history was a crock of shit.

"Katia didn't get that opportunity," my mom said after a

series of quick jabs with the needle. "Coronado killed her only daughter."

According to Mom, Coronado was desperate to stop Katia from finding her vessel. When he learned of her plans, he vowed to wipe out our entire bloodline.

"Why did he hate Katia so much?" I asked. "Just because she didn't want him?"

She paused, the needle hovering above my skin. "Love—hate—sometimes it's a fine line. Falling in love with Alonso was Katia's undoing. The Larkin women fall too hard, too fast, and too fierce."

"I'll never fall in love." I exhaled a tremulous breath.

"Sweet Ash." She looked down at me tenderly, stroking my cheek. "When you fall in love, you will carve out your heart and throw it into the deepest ocean. You will be all in—blood and salt."

Something about her words felt wrong—like putting pressure on a deep bruise.

She dipped the needle into the vial, then started on the dot in the center of the circle. "To an outsider, Quivira looks like nothing more than unkempt fields, but really it's a utopia, totally cut off from the world. Katia placed a protection spell over Quivira to keep it that way. It's beautiful."

"It's a cult," Rhys said.

"The land itself is sacred," my mother said defensively. "Descendants of the families who came to Quivira with Katia remain to this day. The Mendozas, the Grimsbys, the

Hanrattys . . . even Coronado's children stayed behind. Generation after generation . . . waiting . . ." Her voice trailed off.

"What are they waiting for?" I asked, taken aback by her strange tone.

A bird soared above our skylight, sending a shadow across her face. "Crow," she whispered as she dug the bone needle into my flesh. "And so it shall be . . ."

I clutched the grass with my fingers. "Mom." I winced, blood trickling down my chest, seeping into my camisole.

Her eyes went wide and dark, like the Atlantic after a storm. "The day has come. Can you feel it? Can you feel her presence?"

"What are you talking about? You're hurting me." I held her wrist.

She blinked a few times and then gasped. "I'm so sorry." As she pulled out the needle, she accidentally stabbed her thumb. Pressing her hand against my wound, she tried to slow the bleeding.

"Is something wrong?" Rhys leapt to his feet, eyes still trained on the wall in front of him.

"Everything's fine," I assured him as Mom scrambled for the first-aid kit.

"I don't know what came over me," she whispered as she bandaged the wound.

I felt uneasy as I put my blouse back on. She'd never been that careless with the needle before. The bird passing overhead had definitely spooked her. In alchemy, the crow had many meanings—including being the harbinger of death. I

13

wanted to ask her about it, but not in front of Rhys—he'd had enough for one day.

"You can look now," I announced as I stepped off the grass onto the terra-cotta floor.

Rhys searched my face for signs of trouble. He seemed satisfied until he caught sight of a piece of bloody gauze resting on the grass. His face turned an unnatural shade of gray. "We're going to be late," he said as he headed for the stairs.

I started to follow, but my mother pulled me in for an unexpected hug. "Everything you'll ever need is inside you."

"Ouch," I whispered in her ear.

"Oh, oh!" She laughed as she pulled away, taking the pressure off my chest. "I love you both very much."

"We know." I smiled and squeezed her hand before I went downstairs.

Rhys was holding the elevator, straightening his tie in the mirror.

I slung my bag over my shoulder and stepped in next to him. "You're the only person I know who actually *likes* his school uniform," I said in an attempt to lighten the mood.

He brushed his dark blond bangs from his forehead. "Yeah, Ash, we know, you're so cool."

As the elevator door closed, I caught a glimpse of the chandelier. I could almost feel the rope scraping against my ankles—feel the slit in the palm of my hand, dripping blood.

What if the dead girl was *me*?

3

AND SO
IT SHALL BE

IN THE SUBWAY, I swiped my MetroCard and went through the turnstile, while my brother swiped his card over and over again to no avail. People piled up behind him, grumbling and sighing.

"I told you we should've taken a cab," Rhys said.

I reached over and swiped his card for him. As we made our way to the platform, I peered down the track to check on the train. I felt something graze the back of my neck. I whipped around, looking for the creeper who'd touched me, but there was no one there, just the nameless, faceless throng of commuters.

I slipped my hair out of its messy bun, letting it fall over my shoulders and back. "Did Mom seem weird to you?"

Rhys shook his head and laughed. "I don't even know how to answer that."

I scanned the crowd. "Weirder than usual."

"Other than the fact she believes she's part of an invisible cult where our five-hundred-year-old ancestor is performing corn rituals and Coronado from my eighth-grade history class is terrorizing the world in an attempt to keep his immortality . . . not really."

I pulled my brother down the platform to get away from a drunk guy who reeked of urine and was belting out "The Star-Spangled Banner." "He's not terrorizing the world, just *our* family."

"Wait." Rhys drew away from me. "You're not starting to believe all that? It's bad enough you still let her stick you with needles. It's sick."

I smoothed my hand over my blouse, feeling the bandage underneath. "You're not the one seeing a dead girl."

"Power of suggestion. Think about it." Rhys slathered his hands in antibacterial gel. "If I'd been told since birth I was seeing a pink elephant, I'd see a pink elephant. It's basic psychology. Mom's paranoid. She always gets spooked around the summer solstice. June twenty-first will come and go, and everything will be normal again." As the light from the approaching train came into view, the crowd pressed forward. "Well, you know, *our* normal."

The train screeched to a stop; I elbowed my way onto the already packed car. Rhys stood on the platform, letting everyone and their pet rat on before him. Classic. The doors started closing. He gave me that pathetic look, and I lunged forward, pushing a businessman out of the way and jamming my body between the heavy doors.

"Come on, sweetheart," someone bellowed from the other side of the car. "You'll see your boyfriend at school."

I grabbed Rhys and pulled him into the car.

"You didn't need to do that," Rhys said, his cheeks ruddy. "I would've been fine."

"You would've been *late*."

Rhys closed his eyes in resignation.

He hated it when I got all alpha, but I couldn't help it. Maybe it was a birth order thing. I was born four minutes before him, weighed a full pound more at birth. He claimed I tried to eat him in the womb.

My brother was way too polite for this city. He was quiet, too, which created the perfect blank canvas for girls to project whatever they wanted onto him. I'd always felt that he belonged to a different era, a gentler time, like a character from a Jane Austen novel.

As we got off the train, our paths merged with that of another girl who wore our school uniform. She tucked her shiny black bob behind her ear and smiled up at my brother with a shy, kittenish gaze. "Hey, Rhys," she practically whispered.

My brother pretended he didn't see her, his eyes glued to the erectile dysfunction ads plastered on the walls.

I watched her shrink back into the crowd.

"What's wrong with you?" I nudged him as we made our way up the steps toward the sunlight. "She's cute."

He shook his head. "She got a sixty-four on her biochem final."

"So?" I steered him across the street to avoid a pack of stroller Nazis.

Rhys bit the inside of his right cheek like he always did when he was trying to stifle a smile, and then a huge grin engulfed his face.

My brother and I might have been polar opposites, but our love lives looked exactly the same: arctic.

While Rhys was just incredibly picky, my aversion went well beyond that. I was interested in boys, *very* interested, but my body had a different idea. Every time I got close to a guy, in a romantic way, this overwhelming revulsion bubbled up inside of me. It wasn't a boys-are-immature-and-sweaty kind of thing. It was more like an I'm-going-to-puke-all-over-your-shoes kind of thing.

My mother said physical attraction and mate selection all came down to scent. I'd never smelled anything remotely appealing on any of the guys in my school. Every now and then, a nice cologne caught my attention, but as soon as the top note burned off, all I could smell was clogged pores and desperation. I used to think I just hadn't met the right guy, but I was losing hope.

As we got closer to school, I yanked my blazer out of my bag, brushing unnaturally orange crumbs from the lapel.

Rhys shook his head in disgust. "I can't believe we're related, let alone twins."

A jet-black bird jutted between his ankles to get at the crumbs. Rhys leapt out of the way, nearly crashing into a group of hipsters.

"It's just a bird," I said, putting on the jacket.

"Do you know how many diseases birds carry?" he said as he darted in front of me to enter the school gates. "Over sixty."

I glanced up at him, ready to dish out something snarky when I stopped dead in my tracks.

Blood.

A pool of crimson, followed by a wide swath leading from the gates, through the open courtyard, as if someone had been dragged.

People jostled me from behind, maneuvering around me to get inside.

"What's your problem?" Rhys asked.

"Don't look down," I warned.

"Did I step in something?" He groaned and looked at the bottoms of his shoes.

He didn't see it.

I watched a group of girls trudge through the blood, kicking up tiny drops of spatter, which dotted their crisp white ankle socks.

A shudder ran through me like cold acid in my veins. Was it the dead girl?

"Ash! Are you even listening to me?"

"Go to class," I murmured as first bell rang.

"I'm going in the same direction as—"

"Just go," I said a little too forcefully, and then took a deep breath. "I have to stop by the admin building first—they gave me the wrong size cap and gown."

"Okay?" He raised a brow as he backed away, giving me a low wave as he disappeared into the sea of blue blazers.

As the last of the stragglers rushed off to class, I followed the trail of blood to the library, which used to be the chapel when the school was a monastery.

My bag vibrated, making me jump.

I dug the phone out. It was my mom. I knew I should pick up, but I had the strangest feeling . . . like everything I needed to know was on the other side of that door.

A chill swept over my skin as I pressed down on the heavy iron door handle. It was unlocked.

I turned off the phone and stepped inside.

4

BLACK SILK RIBBON

"HELLO?" I CALLED OUT, my voice reverberating around the vast space.

I didn't expect an answer. The library was closed on Fridays. No one really came in here anyway—they got what they needed from bookstores or Amazon. It was a beautiful library, as long as you didn't look at the giant stained-glass window of a bleeding Jesus glaring down from the cross. Normally, I liked the library; the scent of old books with millions of fingerprints on them. Some had coffee stains; others had stains you didn't even want to think about, but they all had history.

It was harder to see the blood against the dark hardwood floors, but I could just make out the glistening streak that led into the stacks.

A faint creaking sound penetrated the silence. My body went rigid. Anyone else would think it was the ancient floorboards, but that particular sound was etched into my consciousness. Rope. Not just any rope—the dead girl was bound by a papery material that crinkled like old skin.

But it wasn't the thought of seeing the dead girl that made me catch my breath. There was a hush of footsteps—and a slow and metered breath, not my own—accompanied by a light dragging sound, as if someone were skimming a finger along the spines of the books in the next aisle.

Carefully, I shimmied a few books from the shelf and peeked through.

That's when I saw her.

Long, lustrous black hair grazing the waist of a simple white sundress. High cheekbones, wide-set eyes. Her only adornment was a long black silk ribbon tied around her throat. Her feet were bare.

She moved in a feline way, with a fluidity that seemed to have no beginning and no end, but I knew she was real. *Alive.* I could even smell her perfume . . . it was heady and sweet.

"I've been waiting for you," she said, glancing up at me as she passed my hiding spot.

My skin exploded in goose bumps. Pressing my back against the shelf, I squeezed my eyes shut, wishing I could make myself disappear. My heart was beating so hard, I was sure she could hear it. I held my hands over the top of the bandage as if I could dampen the sound of my heart thrumming in the tattoo.

Swallowing hard, I forced myself to open my eyes. There

were probably less than twenty steps to the door, but I couldn't make myself move. It felt like there was an invisible thread connecting us—every beat of my heart drawing me closer— as if I'd been waiting for her, too.

I stepped out from the safety of the stacks to face her. She was so arresting, I hardly noticed the dead girl swinging gently behind her.

The mysterious woman took in a tiny gasp of air, as if she was just as stunned to see me up close as I was to see her. Her eyes grazed the length of my body, lingering on the exposed skin of my neckline.

Self-consciously, I buttoned my blouse all the way to the top.

"You've become a very beautiful young woman." Her voice had a gravelly edge that didn't match her dewy face and bright gaze.

What did she mean I'd *become*? "Do I know you?" My voice was so faint I hardly recognized it. I had the distinct feeling that I'd seen her before, but I couldn't imagine where. Maybe in a dream.

"You're strong, too. It's all in the eyes. We have the same eyes, you see. The color of the Sargasso Sea, with the black ring. Quite unusual." She was right. She had a thick black ring around the deep blue iris—just like mine.

My mother said Katia and I had the same eyes. Could it be possible?

"You're Katia." I exhaled a shaky breath.

She gave a nearly imperceptible nod as she stepped toward me.

"Your mother, Nina, will be fulfilling her destiny soon. It's time to come home . . . to Quivira. You and your brother will be welcomed. I can protect you there."

The hanging girl's naked body twisted behind Katia to reveal her face . . . *my* face, contorted in agony.

Katia stepped into my line of sight. "What is it? What do you see?"

"There's a dead girl hanging behind you," I whispered. "She looks like you and *exactly* like me."

Katia's jaw clenched. A shroud of sorrow seemed to wash over her face, but she never looked behind her. "Of course," she murmured softly. "You're tied to her. Because of your gift."

"To who?" The words caught in my throat. "And what do you mean *tied*?"

She pulled the edge of the ribbon from her neck, freeing it from the tidy bow. I cringed in anticipation of the ribbon revealing some hideous scar, but her skin was flawlessly aglow, as if bathed in candlelight.

"A young woman like yourself needs a beautiful ribbon. Something to hold her in place." She coiled the black strand around my wrist.

The glossy sheen, the slick sound, the feel of it creeping across my skin. It was the same feeling I had in the subway when something grazed the back of my neck, the same feeling that came over me when my mother dug the bone needle into my flesh.

"No. That's okay . . . really . . . I . . . I d–don't . . . want it . . . ," I stammered, trying to slip my hand free.

Violently, she twisted the ribbon, jerking my hand toward her.

A glint of gold in her hand.

A metallic whisper.

Searing pain, followed by numbing warmth.

The musky copper smell snaked its way into my senses.

I looked down in terrified awe to see that in one swift movement she'd cut both of our hands open with a golden blade, and entwined our fingers.

My knees buckled as I felt her warm blood press up against mine.

5

FIRST
BLOOD

I STRUGGLED TO BREAK free of her, clawing at nothing but air.

The world tilted; flashes, images, and sensations burned beneath my eyelids like overexposed film. I felt her presence rise inside me like a fever, burning away my will to fight, to live, to feel anything other than what she wanted me to feel.

"Uhurahak a u' a." I heard her whisper to me from some deep sacred place, the same phrase my mother always said to me. "Let go and let yourself fall."

Her words filled me, and with them came images from another life.

Remnants of charred flesh linger in the air. The faint roar of the crowd chanting my name—Katia. The heavy scrape of armor thunders in my ears as the guards pull me from my prison cell. Instead of leading me outside to the savage pack, they take me to the depths of the prison, to the watergate where a small vessel awaits. Coronado steps forward to meet me, his dark brown eyes smoldering in the lamplight. "I understand you seek passage to the New World."

"Please, I'll do anything you—"

Coronado plunges his sword through my chest. My bodice blooms crimson like a rose opening to meet the sun. I'm gasping for air, but my lungs only fill with blood. I'm drowning in it when a tingling spreads across the surface of my skin, settling deep inside of me. The air comes back all at once, flooding my body with relentless life. Coronado shoves his fingers inside the tear of my bodice, feeling my newly healed flesh. He knows what I am.

"What do you want from me?" I recoil from his touch.

He smiles, beautiful and cruel. "Immortality."

I dropped to the hardwood floor, feeling cold and empty. For a moment, I still believed I was Katia, trapped in that cell, Coronado's shark eyes boring into me.

I sprang to my feet, my head pounding like a tribal drum. I staggered around the library searching for her, but found no one. Had she really been here? Or was it just another vision, like seeing the dead girl?

My hand, I remembered. I studied my palm, but there was no mark, not even a hint of blood. I cupped my hands over my mouth, trying not to scream. Her scent was all around me—inside of me—both repulsive and intoxicating, like the narcotic scent of undiluted tuberose—utterly carnal—buttery sweet.

I pressed my hands against the bandage on my chest. Something must've gone wrong with the last protection mark. Instead of weakening the visions, it seemed to have made them stronger. Is this what it felt like to be a conduit?

I snatched my bag and ran into the courtyard to find the sky had darkened, everyone gone; the school gate was already locked. Somehow the entire day had passed me by.

Without another thought, I began to scale the stone wall next to the gate. I'd never climbed a wall before, but my fingers found the grooves in the rock easily, as if I were born to it. I could smell the ancient layers of oxygen and minerals in the stone, even the lake where the clay that formed the mortar had come from.

Something was happening to me.

Crouched on top of the wall, I jumped down to the sidewalk, scaring the crap out of some poor lady walking her dog, then took off running toward home. I ran until every thought in my head was snuffed out by the sound of my own heartbeat. Until I knew I was still here. That I was still me.

6

GOLDEN

AS SOON AS the elevator door opened to our dimmed apartment, I knew something was off. Usually, at this hour, Mom would be flitting around the kitchen, cooking dinner. Rhys would be camped out on the sofa doing homework, looking thoroughly disgruntled. Tonight, the apartment felt barren, with an odd musky scent in the air.

"Rhys?" I ran to my brother's room to find his bed perfectly made—nothing out of place. My mother's room looked much the same.

I glanced at the clock on her nightstand and my heart stuttered. I'd been MIA for over ten hours now. They were probably worried sick about me.

My phone. I ran back to the living room, frantically digging through my bag. As soon as I turned it on, it vibrated. I had messages.

My hands trembled as I dialed voice mail.

"Ashlyn"—my mother's voice was low and urgent, making my hair stand on end—"the time has come for you to let me go, but I will never truly be gone. I will always be a part of you." The way her voice wavered nearly gutted me. "On the summer solstice, your father and I will walk the corn for the last time. We've been chosen as Katia's and Alonso's vessels. This is my fate." She let out a short ragged breath. "Take care of your brother, as he will take care of you. I didn't leave you unprotected. You'll know wh—" A horrible screeching noise interrupted her, cutting off the call.

"Mom?" I whispered into the receiver as the phone slipped out of my sweaty hands, crashing to the hardwood floor. If she'd gone back to Quivira, where was Rhys? Fighting back the tears, I slumped to the ground trying to piece my phone back together, when I caught a glimpse of a familiar figure near the terrace.

I crawled toward it. Staring back at me was the dead girl, the black silk ribbon billowing from her neck. Reaching out for her, my hand grazed the glass, and it dawned on me. I was looking at my own reflection.

Cautiously, I reached up to my throat and felt the shock of silk.

I untied the bow and slipped it from my neck. Although the long black strand looked refined and delicate, it had a significant weight to it, a heft of durability. This was proof that she was real, that it really happened, but as I studied the palm of my hand where the wound should've been, I felt crazy all over again. The ribbon seemed to coil around my fingers like it belonged there.

What the hell's happening to me?

I crammed the black strand into my pocket and went to the kitchen to splash cold water on my face.

A glint of gold caught my attention. There on the kitchen table lay an open stainless-steel briefcase, filled to the brim with gold ingots nestled between stacks of cash and a few documents.

I picked up one of the small gold bricks, and a strange vertigo gripped me. A tingling sensation pulsed beneath the surface of my skin. The ingot morphed into the golden blade that Katia had used to cut my hand. "Oh God." I tried to drop it, pry my fingers loose, but I only seemed to clasp it tighter.

A wave rose up inside of me. I struggled to hang on to the present, but I could feel the past crushing me from the inside out.

As I lead the Larkin girl and Mendoza boy through the corn to the sacred circle, I sense their bond . . . their connection. They're deeply in love. The girl is beautiful, with long chestnut hair, eyes like shaded moss. The boy has Alonso's handsome fine-boned features and lean build. The girl holds out her hand to me—the promise of freedom trembling in her veins. I use my golden blade to slice through her skin and then my own. Our palms meet. I feel her life unfold in my bloodstream like a poem. Every dream she's ever had, every fear she's ever known. Just when I begin to give up hope, a tingling warmth explodes deep inside of me, deeper than anything I've ever felt before.

Tears spring to my eyes as I embrace her. "Nina," I whisper. "A vessel at last."

The memory receded, leaving me in confusion and despair.

My hands shook as I dropped the gold ingot to the table.

The young girl from the vision was my mother, Nina. I'd never felt her presence so intensely, so intimately. And the boy must've been my father, Thomas. The resemblance to Rhys was undeniable.

I wasn't exactly sure what it meant to be a vessel, but I knew it couldn't be good.

A faint fluttering, scraping sound came from my mother's studio. Staring up the wrought-iron spiral staircase, a feeling of dread settled in the pit of my stomach. I crept up the stairs and opened the steel door. The dank smell of mold and perfume overwhelmed me. But it went deeper than that. Beneath the mandarin-inspired perfume was the metallic scent of the soil in which the fruit had grown. The salt breeze seemed to wrap around the sweetness of the pulp. I could even smell the sweat that came from the workers who harvested them. Burrowed deeper was the sinister gamy odor of rot and algae.

My nose was never this good before. My mother always told me the Larkin women had exceptional olfactory skills—it must be another side effect of being a conduit.

I turned on the lights and a shuddering breath escaped my lips.

The studio was filled with black birds. At least twenty of them—perched on shelves, chairs, tables—all staring at me unflinchingly. It wasn't just the sheer number that gave them a menacing presence. With their muscular bodies, dagger-ish beaks, oily black feathers and sharp talons that scraped against the worn wood of my mother's apothecary shelves, I had the distinct feeling they were studying me . . . waiting for something.

I wondered if they were real or if this was another vision, but when a bird swooped down from the open skylight, its stiff wing scraped against my shoulder blade, making me gasp.

A flash of movement beneath my mother's work desk caught my attention.

"Who's there?" I called.

"Ash, is that you?" my brother's voice answered.

"Thank God." I pressed my hands against my stomach.

Rhys hated birds. I knew he'd never make it out of here on his own. "I'm coming to get you."

I kept my eyes on the desk, but I felt them watching me as I passed.

"Where have you been?" Rhys tried to get out from under the desk, but his limbs were folded in awkwardly.

"I'm sorry." I pulled him to his feet.

"I tried to call you." He held on to my arms. "I tried to find you at school. I was completely freaking out, and then I came up here to find Mom and all these—"

A shrill cry pierced the atmosphere, making my brother flinch.

I looked around and saw that the number of birds had multiplied. There were at least fifty of them now, all over the studio . . . watching us . . . waiting . . .

"They're just birds," I said, trying to keep my voice as even as possible, but I couldn't stop thinking about how weird my mom got this morning when the crow passed overhead. We saw another one at school . . . and now this. It had to mean something.

Rhys's bony elbow accidentally knocked over a bottle of ambergris oil, which shattered against the terra-cotta floor. The sharp sound agitated the birds—eyes darting, wings flapping, the grating sound of claws digging into wood and glass. One of the flapping birds took flight, swooping behind us. Rhys and I ran for the door. As I slammed it shut, crows bashed against it, sharp beaks crashing into metal, followed by a series of dull thuds as they dropped to the ground.

Bright red blood seeped beneath the door.

Rhys backed into the banister, a sheen of sweat covering his sallow face. "That could've been our skulls."

I knew he was right, but I needed to keep him calm. "Birds fly into windows all the time," I said as I pulled him down the stairs. "We have bigger problems right now."

"Bigger that *that?*" He pointed toward the studio. "We need to call the police, or animal control, or something."

"We need to pack," I said as I went into Rhys's room and took a duffel bag from his closet, tossing it onto his bed.

"Where's Mom?"

"We're going to meet her." I snatched a pair of tennis shoes from under his bed.

"Fine, but I'm calling the police first." Rhys took his phone from the blazer hanging behind his door.

"And how would we explain all this?" I dropped the shoes and pried the phone out of his sweaty hands, putting it in my pocket. "Um . . . hi, our mom ran off to be a vessel for a cult. Oh, and by the way, she has a secret lab full of demonic crows?"

"See!" Rhys shouted. "You just admitted it . . . they *are* demonic."

"We can't call anyone. We're seventeen." I pulled a stack of perfectly folded shirts from his drawer and shoved them into his arms. "You want social services to get involved? Then we'll never get her back."

I heard him ranting to himself as I went into my room and started digging through the clothes that littered my floor.

After a few minutes, Rhys appeared in my doorway, duffel slung over his shoulder. "Wait . . . did you say *ran off to be a vessel for a cult?*"

I pretended not to hear him as I jammed random articles of clothing into an old backpack.

"Ash!" He took a bold step into my room, nearly tripping over my lacrosse stick. "You need to tell me what's going on."

"Mom." I zipped my backpack. "Ran off to Quivira."

"How . . . how do you know?" His breath hitched in his throat.

"She called me." I pushed past him into the kitchen.

"What?" He ran after me. "What did she say?"

I rummaged through the junk drawer for the car keys. "She said she's going back to Quivira with Thomas so they can become Katia's and Alonso's vessels."

"Perfect." Rhys let out a burst of nervous air. "Our mother's completely lost her mind. Maybe we just need to call the psych ward."

"And she left something for us." I nodded toward the open briefcase on the table.

With shaking hands, Rhys looked through the documents resting on top of the cash and gold. "Last Will and Testament, the deed to the apartment, our passports?" He sank down in one of the chairs at the kitchen table. "She's not planning on coming back," he whispered.

I felt a stab of fear as I prepared to tell him more about what happened today.

"The dead girl. I saw her again at the library . . . she looked just like me . . . and she wasn't alone."

"What do you mean?"

I stared him straight in the eyes. "I met Katia."

He lowered his chin, taking in a deep breath through his nose. "Katia, as in our five-hundred-year-old ancestor, Katia?"

"She talked to me. She cut me," I said, rubbing my palm.

He leaned forward with his head in his hands, looking like he was going to pass out.

"No. It's not like that. Look . . ." I sat next to him and held out my palm. "There's nothing there. I must've blacked out or something."

As Rhys reached out to touch my hand, an icy current ran from my fingertips all the way up my wrist, almost as if my blood leapt away from his touch. I pulled my hand back and the feeling subsided.

He crossed his arms. "So it was some kind of hallucination?"

"I think so." But when I put my hand into my pocket, I felt the ribbon resting there. I wanted to show it to him; I wanted to tell him about the memory of Mom and Thomas, but I wasn't quite ready to share any of that yet. And I was pretty sure Rhys wasn't ready to hear it.

My brother skimmed his hand over the gold and cash. "Do you think she stole this?"

"I don't know, but maybe we can use it as a bargaining chip to get her back from Quivira."

His jaw dropped. "Quivira? Is that where you think we're going? Have you lost your mind? We need to call the police or the FBI—we can't handle this by ourselves."

"If we call the cops and this is stolen property—Mom will

go to jail." I forced myself to sit up straight. "We can do this. We have to try."

He leapt from the chair and started pacing the kitchen. "You think we're just going to be able to waltz in there and take what Katia needs to break her blood bond to Coronado?"

I stood, blocking his path. "I thought you didn't believe in any of that?"

"I don't." He swallowed hard. "But *they* do. It's a cult. They're dangerous."

"Katia told me we'd be welcome." My eyes veered toward the chandelier as I thought of the dead girl. "That we'd be protected there."

"Oh, okay," Rhys snapped. "I guess it's fine because you heard it in your *imagination*." He smoothed his hair away from his face and took a deep breath. "Even if we decide to get her, which I'm not saying we're going to do, you think we can just put Quivira in the GPS, and it'll take us there?"

I pulled his phone from my pocket and typed in—Quivira, Kansas.

"Eighteen hours and thirty-four minutes," the distinctly British female computer voice replied.

"Let me see that." He snatched it back from me. "Look . . ." Rhys brought up an aerial photo. "It's in the middle of no-where—it's just a bunch of farmland."

"Mom talked about the corn. This has to be it."

His breathing became heavy as he studied the photo.

"Today's June fifteenth," I said. "There are six days until the summer solstice—until she thinks she's going to walk the corn with Thomas so they can become vessels."

"See . . . that's just crazy." Rhys shook his head in disbelief and started pacing again. "Even if we found Quivira, what would we say to these people?"

"We're Larkins. If it's anything like Mom said, we tell them we've come home. Gain their trust. Talk some sense into her, and get the hell out of there. They can pick a different vessel."

"And if that doesn't work?"

"Maybe we can buy her freedom. Cults need money, too." I had cautiously picked up the gold brick I'd dropped earlier to place it back in the briefcase when I felt something embedded on the back of the ingot. I turned it over to find the circle with the dot in the center—the same mark I received this morning.

I ran my hand over the bandage near my collarbone. Either I was going crazy, like Mom, or I was really a conduit. And what did that even mean? She didn't prepare me for this.

I shut the briefcase, securing the latches.

My brother's arms were prickled with goose bumps. "I have a terrible feeling about this."

"I don't know how to explain it," I said as I touched the imaginary scar on my hand, "but I know we have to go there ourselves. It's the only way to save her."

But it went deeper than that. Somehow I knew I needed saving, too.

• • •

I said my silent good-byes to the city as we crossed the George Washington Bridge in my mother's SUV.

Armed with enough cash and gold to float a small country, we were headed to Quivira.

I watched my brother drift off into an uneasy sleep, his breath fogging up the side passenger window. Even though he was sitting right next to me, I'd never felt so alone.

Pulling the black silk ribbon from my pocket, I draped it around my throat.

7

EVOLUTION

THE SUN ROSE, flooding the car with hazy lemon light. I knew it was stupid, but it felt like nothing bad could happen to us as long as the sun was shining.

As the light skimmed my brother's face, he jerked awake as if he'd just come out of a nightmare. Raking his fingers through his hair, he let out a deep sigh. "Pennsylvania?" he asked as we passed a horse-drawn buggy with bright orange reflective triangles on the back. Inside the buggy, kids about our age stared back at us with the same kind of alien fascination our faces must've held.

"Ohio."

"I'm sorry." He stretched out his legs. "How long was I out?"

"Six hours."

"I've got the next shift."

"We need gas, *again*," I said as I pulled off the highway.

Up ahead stood an old white house with a sweeping front

porch that had been converted into a gas station/bait shop. The paint was peeling off in sheets, and it seemed like one stiff breeze could blow the whole thing to smithereens.

I pulled up to the gas pump. Rhys swung his door open just as a pickup truck peeled into the parking lot behind us, nearly clipping him. Two husky men got out, dressed from head to toe in camo.

The bigger one, with the reddish goatee, slammed a beer and let out a gag-worthy belch. "Did you see that dumb look on his face when we stood up from the blind?"

"He was, like, *Oh, shit, man.*" His friend laughed so hard, he had to stop to catch his breath. "And then we went crazy on his ass. BOOM."

They gave each other a series of sloppy high fives before strutting inside.

"I get that there are people who hunt to feed their families," I said to Rhys. "But these guys have a brand-new truck with tricked-out radials and, oh my God, a Nickelback bumper sticker. They aren't living off the land. Whatever they killed, it's going on their wall."

"Don't go all PETA on me. Not here," Rhys said as he peeled a crisp hundred-dollar bill from one of the stacks and stuffed it in his blazer pocket.

"Seriously, how can they call that a sport?" I asked as I popped the gas cap.

"Yeah, I really don't want to be on their wall, either, so keep it down." Rhys headed inside.

As I pumped the gas, I dug around in the backseat for something that would pass for breakfast. I finally settled on a warm Dr Pepper. While opening the can, I accidentally slit my finger on the sharp aluminum edge.

"Damn." I'd stuck my finger in my mouth to slow the bleeding when I noticed a long wisp of honey-colored hair hovering in the wind above the bed of the hunters' truck.

I dropped the can. As the wet hiss of soda seeped into the gravel, a sick feeling twisted my insides, refusing to let go. Animals didn't have hair like that. *I* did.

Cautiously, I walked toward the back of the truck. As I pulled up on the shiny chrome handle to lower the door, my body went numb.

There, lying on her side, was the dead girl.

I stared in dark fascination. I'd never seen her lying down before. Her back was turned to me, but her left arm was stretched beneath her, exposing the deep slash in the palm of her hand, seeping blood. I followed the rope knotted around her mottled ankles to find the rest of it coiled next to her, like a cobra waiting to strike. The bottoms of her feet were caked in fresh soil.

A mass of dark blond waves covered her face, but I knew it was her—the same girl I'd seen my entire life. *Me.*

Without another thought, I climbed into the bed of the truck, accidentally brushing my leg against the pile of rope. That eerily familiar crinkling sound sent a chill marching up my spine. Just the feel of it against my skin made my blood bubble in revulsion. I kicked free of the rope, but the dread never left me. Every particle of my being told me to run, but I had to see her face. Katia said I was tied to her. I needed to understand what that meant.

My hand trembled as I reached out and grasped her shoulder, gently pulling her toward me. Her skin was cold, but I'd never felt so warm. I felt life surging through me—pure power tingling just beneath the surface of my skin right before I was ripped from my consciousness. I fought to hang on, but I felt myself disappearing into another time.

"Give me your arm," Coronado commands as he pulls a blazing hot iron from the embers.

The breeze catches Alonso's hair, whipping it around his face. He steals a glance at me before stepping forward to comply, his face so beautiful it makes me want to weep.

As Coronado drags the tip of the iron across the tender skin on the inside of Alonso's forearm, I cringe. The sickeningly sweet smell of burning flesh overpowers my senses. I clench the folds of my gown, but keep my face expressionless. If Coronado discovers my true feelings for Alonso, he won't hesitate to throw him overboard.

"I claim you as one of the Arcanum. You belong to me now." Coronado finishes the mark, then pours a bucket of seawater over his handiwork. I hear Alonso's skin sizzle. The pain from salt in his wound must be excruciating, but Alonso stands like a statue, staring out over the endless ocean separating us from the New World.

As Coronado and his soldiers retreat to the lower deck for another night of drink and tall tales, Alonso sinks to the ground, cradling his arm. I go to him, touching his wrist. He flinches.

"Do you trust me?" I ask.

"Yes," he whispers, clenching his hand into a fist.

I reach out for his arm again, gently rolling up his dirty shirtsleeve.

Swiping my finger against the sharp edge of his dagger, I coax my blood to the surface. I hold my finger above his cut; he stops me.

"What will your blood do to me?" He looks up at me through long wild strands of sun-kissed hair.

"Take the pain and make you scar more quickly, but you will bear his mark forever."

He pulls me closer. "It won't make me immortal?"

"No," I answer, stunned by how painful I find the notion of Alonso remaining mortal.

"You'll be blood bound to Coronado." I feel his warm breath pulsing against my cheek.

"I would rather die one thousand deaths," I whisper, meeting his gaze.

He presses my cut finger into his wound.

He sucks in a shallow breath through his teeth and I see the broad muscles in his shoulders relax as the pain is extinguished. His flesh heals into a thick rope, revealing Coronado's signet, a winged creature, crudely etched into his skin.

I run my now-healed finger across the brand. "Your body is only a vessel. You belong to no one."

"You're wrong," he says, his golden brown eyes settling on mine. "I belong to you."

The creak of the screen door wrenched me back to the present.

"Ash!" I spun around to see my brother hurrying down the steps. "What do you think you're doing?"

"You see her?" I whispered.

"I don't know what's going on with you," he said as he approached me with his hands raised in front of him as if he were trying to soothe a wild animal. "But you need to get out of the truck . . . *now*. Those guys could come back any second."

"I can't leave her like this."

I reached back to touch her and felt short rough fur beneath my fingers. I whipped around to find my knees nestled against a white diamond-shaped patch of hair just above the rib cage of a young buck, its torso riddled with bullet holes.

The deer's leg twitched.

I scrambled out of the truck, knocking my brother to the ground.

The deer got to its feet in the bed of the truck, blinking big dark eyes at us. It shook its antlers, as if shaking off death, then leapt across the road majestically and disappeared into the thick woods.

The screen door creaked open. Rhys and I took off running back toward the car. My heart was pounding, which meant my brother was probably about to have a coronary.

The hunters strolled down the porch steps toward their

truck with toothpicks dangling from their lips, looking totally content—until they saw the empty space where their trophy used to be.

"What the Sam hell?" the guy with the goatee yelled as he looked under the truck.

"Son of a *bitch*!" the other one screamed as he paced the lot. "Did somebody steal him?"

Rhys slipped in on the driver's side and I got into the passenger seat.

My brother's hand was shaking as he pressed the ignition button.

"Do you need me to drive?" I asked.

"No," he snapped as we pulled away.

I watched the woods in anticipation, hoping to catch a glimpse of the deer. I wanted one last look to know it was real.

"What just happened?" Rhys yelled as he merged back onto the highway. "How did you know it wasn't dead? Why would you *touch* it?"

"I saw the dead girl."

"Where?" Rhys looked around in a panic, momentarily swerving into the other lane of the two-lane highway.

"Back there, in the truck."

"Wait." His knuckles blanched as he gripped the wheel. "You're telling me you thought the *deer* was the dead girl?"

"She seemed so real," I whispered as I rocked back and forth in my seat, trying to figure out what the hell was going on with me. "Rhys." I turned toward him. "I think Mom was right. I think I might seriously be a conduit, and the protection marks . . . they're not working anymore."

There was a long silence that neither of us knew how to fill.

"Can you at least clean the blood off your hands?" Rhys finally exhaled, looking like he was going to vomit.

"I'm sorry, I didn't realize . . ." I dug the first-aid kit out of the glove box and ripped open an alcohol pad.

I braced myself for the sting of the alcohol on my index finger, but it never came. Wiping off all the blood, I found nothing there. Not a scratch. I could've sworn I sliced my finger on the edge of the aluminum, but I could've sworn a lot of things lately. I guess this is what it meant to be a conduit. We needed to find Mom soon so she could fix me. I didn't know how much longer I could take this.

I crammed the first-aid kit into my backpack, then pressed the side of my head against the glass, watching the woods blur into an endless stretch of brown and green. Rhys had slowed down to pass another buggy when an old wooden billboard caught my attention. THE RAPTURE IS COMING was written in large block lettering. Perched on top of the sign were two black birds. Crows. The harbinger of death.

One for each of us.

8

WRECKED

"YOU HAVE REACHED your final destination." The voice blared over the GPS, startling us both. We'd been on desolate back roads for so long, I think we'd forgotten what technology sounded like. We moved forward another ten feet, then the GPS signal died. It wasn't a gentle wane; it was abrupt, like we'd just fallen off the face of the earth.

"No. No way," Rhys said, squeezing his phone like he was strangling it. "This is a joke." He squinted through the bug-smeared windshield.

I pulled over into a makeshift lot full of old rusted-out cars.

Beyond that stretched nothing but corn. Miles and miles of corn.

Rhys flung his phone at the dash. "I told you we wouldn't be able to find it."

"This has to be it," I said as I scanned the area. Obviously, it hadn't rained in some time, giving the landscape a muted palette, much softer than I'd expected. There was something so familiar about the surroundings, but I couldn't put my finger on it—maybe something from a dream or a Wyeth painting.

"I need to use the restroom," Rhys said.

"Be my guest." I glanced over at the towering stalks as I picked up his phone and tried to find a signal.

"No . . . I mean *really* use the restroom."

I dug out some paper napkins from the discarded bag in the backseat and handed them to him.

He eyed me skeptically. "Are you serious?"

"Everybody poops, Rhys. There's even a book about it."

"Just don't *talk* about it," he hissed as he took the napkins and got out of the car, slamming the door behind him. He walked off toward the corn, shoulders hunched, looking completely mortified.

I cut off the engine and found myself staring at hundreds of abandoned cars—every decade was represented. It seemed odd to have a car graveyard in the middle of nowhere, but I guess it was as good a place as any.

I rummaged through the center console, hoping to find gum or a breath mint. My mouth felt like the inside of a Dumpster. *Tic Tacs . . . score.* I popped a couple and looked through the rest of the contents—a pair of sunglasses and a tin of lip balm. And I thought I was low-maintenance.

I dabbed the balm on my lips and glanced at myself in the rearview mirror to see if it made any improvement, but all I found were dark blue irises lined with thick black rings—like Katia's—like shackles.

I put on my mother's sunglasses. They looked glamorous on her, but they made me look like a bug.

We'd been driving for nearly twenty hours, and my body felt welded to the seat. I was exhausted, but still felt the adrenaline pumping through me—that and a ton of caffeine.

The instant I got out of the car to check on my brother, my hair began to frizz and stick to my neck. I had pulled the black silk ribbon from my pocket to tie my hair back when a rogue breeze kicked in and blew it from my hands. I watched it hover in midair, graceful as a dancer, weightless and free. The black strand swooped in front of me before drifting into the maze of abandoned cars.

I hurried after it, my footsteps kicking up clouds of dust as I moved in and out of the stacks of twisted metal.

I took in a deep breath. The smell of rust, rubber, and oil filled my lungs, but there was something deeper underneath, something infinitely more appealing. Dark fertile earth, sandalwood, fresh rain, strawberries, a hint of tang.

I maneuvered around a column of hubcaps, following the ribbon as it plummeted like an arrow into the waiting hands of the man standing before me. He wasn't really a man, maybe about eighteen or nineteen, but he was the kind of beautiful that made me think I might still be hallucinating.

"Does this belong to you?" He held out his hand. The ends of the ribbon curled around his wrist like a secret caress.

He had gorgeous olive skin and refined features, with thick, almost black hair that grazed his shoulders. It curled up slightly on the ends in a sexy, haphazard way. His almond-shaped eyes were so clear, so full of light that it was impossible to tell exactly what color they were. Blue, green, and brown flecks set adrift in a sea of gold.

I reached out, taking the ribbon from him, my fingers lingering on his. I waited for the usual wave of repulsion to hit me, but instead my pulse quickened as if I were standing on the edge of a precipice. A dizzying flash of heat rushed to my cheeks. This was something new.

Whatever was happening must be a physical malfunction of sleep deprivation or some kind of residual conduit feeling. Still, the urge to feel more of his skin overwhelmed me.

"Do I know you?" he asked, rubbing the back of his neck. "Maybe from a fashion magazine or something?"

At first I thought he was trying to be slick, but there was something distinctly genuine about him.

"You read a lot of fashion magazines?" I asked as I tied my hair back with the ribbon.

"No, I guess not," he said.

He started to step away from me; I actually prayed to any god that would listen to make him stay. I'd never felt such a strong physical attraction to anyone.

Even if it was just for a fleeting moment, he seemed to make all my problems disappear. I wanted to bottle that feeling and carry it around in my pocket. The thought of kidnapping him crossed my mind.

He smiled back at me. "Are you looking for something . . . a particular part?" He had an amazing mouth. Perfect lips with a tiny dimple on the right side of his cheek.

"Not exactly." I flashed a grin as I walked through a labyrinth of stacked tires.

He joined me. "Are you just passing through, then?"

"You could say that." I stole another glance at him as I pretended to inspect the treads.

He cocked his head to the side, studying me. "This place is pretty far off the beaten path. Are you lost?"

"I don't think so."

He bit down gently on his bottom lip. I could tell he wasn't completely satisfied with my answer. I followed his gaze to my attire. I must've looked pretty psycho in my school uniform skirt, dusty motorcycle boots, and bloodstained blouse.

"Oh, it's not my blood," I said with a nervous laugh.

He looked at me quizzically.

I was giggling at blood. What the hell was wrong with me?

"There was a deer," I tried to explain, but I was only making things worse. "The deer's fine. I mean, he got right up and hopped off into the woods . . . happy as a clam."

Oh my God, Ash, shut up.

"So, I guess you know a lot about cars?" I asked, desperately trying to change the subject.

"A little." I swore I saw him blush. "Just from the manuals."

"You don't look like the typical junkyard-worker type."

"I guess I left my undershirt and overalls at home today. That's what you were expecting?"

"No," I replied sheepishly as I registered his worn linen shirt and pants. "But I didn't expect you to have all your teeth."

He let out a warm unself-conscious laugh.

Standing just a handful of inches above me—at about six feet—he had surprisingly good posture, which made him seem taller. It was clear even through his clothes that he had a well-toned body. Not overly muscular, but athletic, maybe soccer or swimming—a sport that demanded a strong core. Everything seemed effortless for him—the way he moved, the way he spoke.

"It's too bad you can't stick around. I could show you the sights," he said, stepping closer.

"There are sights?" I teased as I turned down a narrow pathway lined with orphaned fenders.

"Sure." He smiled broadly as he followed close behind. "The sunflower field at sunset, maybe we could split a bottle of dandelion wine."

I looked down at the ground, attempting to hide my idiotic grin.

"Then I would take you to Windy Point to watch for shooting stars."

"Would we make a wish?" I glanced at him over my shoulder.

"You can if you like, but I don't need to." He offered that smile again with the tiny dimple.

"Sounds like you've thought this through."

"It's not over yet." He grabbed my waist, stopping me in my tracks. My pulse pounded beneath his touch. He dragged his thumb across the top of my hip bone, and my stomach lurched as if the ground were caving in, sending me into a free fall. "At dawn, we could take a swim at Crystal Pond."

"And then what?" I managed to ask.

He pulled me close, whispering in my ear. "You'd never want to leave."

I felt giddy.

He removed my sunglasses. I thought he was going to kiss me when he suddenly dropped his hands.

"What's your name?" he asked as he took a deliberate step away from me, his eyes narrowing into slits.

"Ash-Ashlyn—"

"Surname," he interrupted tersely.

My mind went blank. What was my name? "Larkin," I answered breathlessly, still reeling from his touch.

His eyes went wide before his face turned into a solid block of ice. The muscles in his jaw and shoulders tensed. "It's you," he murmured as he slowly backed away from me, then took off running into the corn.

9

INVITATION

"WAIT!" I RAN after him, not caring how pathetic I looked.

Just as I reached the corn's edge, Rhys stepped out of the towering stalks, nearly giving me a heart attack.

"If you mention this to anyone I'll never speak to you again." He made a beeline for the car.

Completely stunned, I stared off into the dense field. Rhys should've run right into him.

"Ash," my brother snipped behind me. "Do you mind telling me why some guy's taking off our hubcaps?"

I turned, my heart pounding with anticipation. Was it him? How'd he slip by me? I pushed past my brother to get to the car.

When his head appeared over the side of the SUV, my heart fell. An old man, red-faced, wisps of white cotton-candy-like hair shellacked to his skull with sweat.

"There you are," the man said, as if he was greeting a friend. "I was afraid I'd lost you."

Rhys looked at me for an explanation, but I had just as many answers as he did.

The old man flashed a grin. "Tanner . . . Tanner Beaumont," he said as he bent down to put the hubcap back on. "I've never seen a spinner like this. Escalade, huh?"

Stained wifebeater, overalls, missing teeth. "You've got to be kidding me," I said under my breath. This must've been my mystery man's boss. "I think I just met your colleague," I said in relief as I leaned up against the car.

"Goober?" His eyes lit up.

"That's his name?" I winced. He didn't look remotely like a Goober.

"Yeah, he's a good boy. He didn't give you too much trouble, did he? Sorry if he drooled on you."

"No, um . . . no, he didn't," I answered as I stared off into the corn.

"What can I do for you?" He stood up and I swear I could hear every one of his vertebrae grind into place. "I got a bunch of Hondas . . . I even got one of them Priuses."

"Where did all these cars come from?" Rhys asked.

"Well, we call this here the Kansas Triangle." He motioned at the land surrounding us. "You know, like the Bermu—"

"Yeah, we get the reference," I interrupted. "But the cars are all here."

"Oh, it's not the cars that disappear. It's the people."

"What?" My brother went ramrod straight.

"This land here's cursed. Used to belong to the Indians. See, people come here looking for Quivira. They come from all over the place . . . weirdo spiritualists, reporters, geologists, historians, even a few of them ghost hunters, and they all disappear. Haven't had anyone in a while, though, not since that 2012 Camry over there."

"What do you mean they *disappear*?" Rhys asked, shifting his weight nervously.

The old man leaned forward like he was telling us a secret. "They go into the corn, and they don't never come out."

"Have you called the police?"

The man grinned, digging his thumbs into the straps of his overalls. "I *am* the police."

Rhys pressed his lips together and then let out a nervous burst of laughter. "Okay, time to go."

"How do we get there? To Quivira?" I asked.

"I suppose you're lookin' at it. There's at least forty-five miles of corn. No roads." He looked up at the sky, dreamlike. "Sometimes at night, you hear the crows. All them flapping wings sound like helicopters, only there's no lights. Just like Nam . . ."

An enormous balding Saint Bernard jumped out of the back of an old white Cadillac, knocking Tanner to the ground. A huge line of drool dropped from its jowls onto the man's face.

"Goober." He let out a high-pitched giggle.

"*That's* Goober?" I said. "I was talking about the boy . . . the man I met here earlier."

He looked up at me in confusion. "How long you been out here, missy? Kansas heatstroke ain't no joke."

There was no boy or man or man/boy. *Awesome.*

On the plus side, at least the figment of my imagination wasn't named Goober.

"You weren't planning on going in there, were you?" he said as he got to his feet, squinting into the corn. "'Cuz if you do, save me the trouble and leave the keys. This car would make a fine convertible. I could cut off the top. It'd be good for haulin' trash."

"Give us a minute, please." Rhys dragged me toward the back of the car. "We have to get out of here and call the police . . . the real police," he whispered. "You heard him . . . people go into the corn but they don't come back. Look at all those cars, Ash."

I stepped in front of him to try and block his view. "Maybe those people wanted to disappear. Mom said it was some kind of utopia."

Rhys tried to grab the keys out of my hand. "But he just said—"

"The guy had a Vietnam flashback right in front of us. Since when are you so gullible?"

He stared out over the corn, a deep crease settling in his forehead.

"The summer solstice is only five days away now," I said

as I put my hand on his shoulder. "The sun is getting ready to set. If we're going to find her it has to be now. We have to try. We can always come back and call the cops if we have to."

Rhys gave me a nearly imperceptible nod.

I grabbed the bags from the car before he could change his mind again and set them down in front of the junkyard guy. "Can we park here for a few days?"

Tanner twitched his head to the side to spit through the gap in his teeth. "Not for free you can't."

I peeled off a bill from one of the stacks and stuffed it into the bib pocket of Tanner's filthy overalls. "Here's a hundred. I'll give you another when we come back."

He fondled the cash from outside his pocket. "Sure thing." He grinned.

I put on my backpack, then tossed Tanner the keys.

Rhys begrudgingly picked up his duffel and the briefcase.

"Hey, what's your name?" Tanner called after me as we walked toward the corn.

"Larkin," I answered. I didn't have to think about it this time. I felt it all the way to the marrow of my bones.

The old man's face went slack as he turned and scurried away from us up the dirt road.

"What the hell," I murmured. I was starting to get a complex.

As Rhys and I stood at the edge of the corn, the sun began to melt into the horizon, casting a golden glow across the field.

A breeze blew in behind us, forcing its way through the stalks, revealing a path.

Like an invitation.

I heard my brother swallow.

"It's good to be afraid," I said. "It means you still have something to live for."

I took his hand and we stepped into the corn.

10

CORN

THEY SAY THE FIRST STEP is the hardest.

But it's really the third—when you're too far in to turn back and not far enough to completely commit. Either way, you're kind of screwed.

"This is a bad idea. A really bad idea," Rhys said as he led the way through the narrow path in the corn.

I wasn't going to argue. It wasn't worth it. There was no stopping him when he got on a roll like this.

Tuning him out, I focused on how dense and lush everything was. It was like stepping into a different world; the world before man. The twelve-foot-high stalks had a thick bamboo-like quality. The leaves, brilliant green, had a beautiful translucence—creating a lacy display of shadow and light. The scent was sweet and earthy—like spring, but with a slight hint of decay.

Other than my brother's incessant complaining, it was

eerily quiet. No insects, no wind, not a sound other than my boots sinking into the rich soil.

With each step forward, I had the strangest feeling of déjà vu, like I'd walked this path a thousand times before.

I closed my eyes, dragging my fingers along the stalks, and tried not to imagine what the sunflower field would look like in this light or, more importantly, what *he* would look like in this light. My junkyard crush. Obviously, my name had set him off, but what made him ask in the first place? It had to be the eyes. What did he and Tanner see in me? Were all the Larkins something to be feared?

And in that brief moment of reflection, I found myself alone.

There was no trace of my brother.

I heard the ground cover depress somewhere behind me. I turned, finding nothing, and everything all at once. I felt an undeniable presence, like the corn was watching me, but that was crazy.

Fighting back panic, I looked up at the sky to get my bearings, but felt completely disoriented. North, south, east, and west didn't exist anymore—only corn. Dizzy and confused, I spun around, feeling for a way out, but it seemed as if the stalks had closed in around me.

Something slammed me from behind; I stumbled forward, feeling that strange vertigo again. My hands clenched in the soil, trying to find something to hold on to, but the dirt sifted through my fingers. Even though I was already on the ground, I felt myself falling, the same sensation I'd felt in the library with Katia. A gasp escaped my lips as the crush of memories fell over me like a heavy velvet curtain.

Leaving his armor behind, Alonso makes his way toward me. To-night, on the cusp of the summer solstice, he will become my immortal mate.

Using my golden blade, I cut the length of his palm. "A kisctsa rauuir tiaticaa kaukuu'." I then cut a deep slash above my heart. Just as I'm about to place his palm against my chest to bind our fates, Alonso's head jerks back. Coronado's deep brown eyes are full of starlight and malice as he sweeps his blade across my lover's throat. Alonso's blood falls across my face like rain.

Coronado turns his attention to me. I stagger back and start running through the corn. The towering stalks whip my skin, leaving a trail of blood in the moonlight. I don't know which way to turn. Coronado catches up to me and lunges for my arm. I hit the earth and then he's on top of me. I lash out with my blade, but he grabs it and uses it to slit his own palm. I can feel my traitorous blood reaching out for his as he presses his wound against the gash above my heart. I writhe and scream, trying to break free, but it's too late—I can already feel his black soul penetrating mine. I feel his blood coursing through mine and mine through his. We are one, bound in hate, bound in blood.

"Ashlyn."

I lifted my head. The devastation I felt was overwhelming.

My mother had told me what happened to Alonso, but seeing it . . . feeling it through Katia's memories was something else entirely. A strange ripple of energy rushed over the corn, followed by the scent of ozone. I heard my brother calling my name. Fighting against the gravity that wanted to keep me there, I grabbed the stalks, pulling myself up and through the corn, toward the sound of his voice. I careened through the field to find my brother kneeling in a twenty-foot-wide patch of scorched earth, the bags strewn around him.

"Wait," he called out with a slight tremor in his voice. "It might be hot."

I studied the alien ground surrounding him. I didn't feel any heat, but it wouldn't have stopped me anyway. I couldn't leave him there, all alone, in that black chaotic void.

Charred soil crunched beneath the weight of my footsteps, but it was cool. It reminded me of volcanic ash.

As soon as I put my hand on his shoulder, he collapsed into a sitting position.

"Oh God." The color drained from his face when he noticed the blood from the scrape on his knee.

"What happened?" I asked as I pulled the first-aid kit from my bag and bandaged his knee.

"I don't know." He let out a huge burst of pent-up air as he held his head in his hands. "I turned, and you were gone. The corn kept opening up in front of me. It felt like I was running in circles. I couldn't find you and I tripped and fell. The corn just . . . disappeared."

"Disappeared?"

"Like, disintegrated." He glanced up at me before I had a chance to hide my shock. "I know! It sounds crazy. I think I might be losing it right along with you."

"We're both . . . overwrought." I chose my words carefully. Maybe Rhys was seeing things, too. "Look, all we have to do is find Mom and get out of here."

"Ash," my brother said as he stared off into the corn. "Something's wrong with this place. Do you feel it?"

"I don't know what I feel anymore," I said as I helped him to his feet, trying not to give in to the fear gnawing away at me. "But we should try to find her before dark."

Suddenly, bringing him here felt wrong, like I'd led him straight into the devil's mouth.

"Which way?" he asked as we stood in the center of the barren patch of earth.

As if answering his question, the breeze whipped through the field, revealing a path and a clearing in the distance.

Rhys and I walked faster. I think we were afraid the corn would swallow us whole.

11

QUIVIRA

AS WE STEPPED out of the corn, it took me a minute to catch my breath.

The sun had already set, but the sky was full of life, painted in broad brushstrokes of peach, purple, and pink.

The scent was heady—honeysuckle, new and fermenting mulberries, and the remnants of a cedar campfire hung heavy in the humid air. But there was something else, too—an appealing mineral smell nipped the edge of my senses.

Beyond the huge expanse of deep green grass scattered with fireflies was a picturesque lake with an unearthly opal hue.

Rhys and I moved toward it, looking around cautiously, but there wasn't a soul in sight.

Unlike the tiny towns we'd passed through to get here, Quivira seemed to be untouched by drought. Moisture clung to every dark blade of grass, and the air felt lush.

Nestled around the lake were five large structures. My mother once said she grew up in a lodge, but this wasn't what I'd pictured at all. I'd expected a desolate place littered with dilapidated shacks and millions of shirtless, dirty kids with unusually tiny ears.

Each of the buildings was architecturally unique. One was a Tudor—cream, trimmed with dark brown accents. There was one that looked like a giant gray clapboard box. On the far end of the lake stood an enormous A-frame that blended into the surrounding woods so perfectly I almost missed it. On the left side was a beautiful Spanish Colonial made of tan stucco and dark wood, but the grandest of all was a stone mansion with a red-clay-tiled roof. It was like seeing a vintage photograph in full color.

It *was* a utopia.

When we reached the shore, I leaned over the low stone wall, scooping up the water in my hands and tasting it with the tip of my tongue. It was the color of sea glass, but brinier than the sea.

"It's a salt lake," I marveled.

"In the middle of Kansas?" My brother skimmed his hand across the water. "That's impossible. How could they've kept this place a secret?"

I looked over the dense woods nestled between the structures. None of this was visible to us from within the corn. "Mom said Katia put some kind of protection spell over Quivira."

Rhys shook his head. "Maybe you really *are* having a heat-stroke." He started to splash water on his face, but halted. "Do you hear that?"

The lake was still, except for the occasional ripple breaking against the wall where dozens of canoes and rowboats were tied. The boats clinked together softly, the gentlest of wind chimes. Other than that, it was eerily quiet. No lawnmowers or cars, not a sound, except for a faint, high-pitched lament that grew stronger by the second. Someone was singing, if you could call it that.

Rhys stood next to me, pointing to a speck of bright yellow at the far end of the dam, jarring against the muted greens, blues, and browns. It came slowly toward us like a wayward ray of sunshine, finally revealing itself to be a girl in an ankle-length yellow cotton dress, skipping alongside the stone wall. She was about our age, with peaches-and-cream skin, long strawberry-blond hair, and a pert nose.

"'Tell me why-ee, ain't nothin' but a heartache,'" she sang. "'Tell me why-ee, ain't nothin' but a mee-stake. Tell me why-ee, I never wanna hear you say, I want it *that* way.'"

Rhys and I stood there, mouths agape.

The girl glanced over at us and did a double take.

"Oh God." Rhys grimaced. "I hate that song."

"Stick to the plan," I whispered. "We're going to become a part of the community until we can get Mom out of here, got it?"

The girl bounded toward us with a huge grin plastered

across her pleasant face. "Oh my stars, it's you." She crashed into me with a crippling bear hug.

I stood there, stiff as a board, waiting for it to be over. "Um . . . do I know you?"

"Oh." She let go and slapped her palm against her forehead. "I completely forgot myself. I'm Beth. I live in the Grimsby lodge." She pointed to the Tudor-style compound on the right side of the lake. "And that's the Hanratty lodge, the Larkin lodge, the Mendoza lodge, and the big one past those woods on the left is the meeting house."

"I'm Rhys, and this is my sister, Ash—"

"I know who you are, silly. Everyone knows." She studied me. "It's uncanny, though."

"What's uncanny?" I asked, hoping for a clue about the dead girl.

She smiled. "The resemblance . . . to Katia."

"You've *seen* Katia?" Rhys asked with a raised brow.

"Every year, on the summer solstice, she comes out of the corn to heal the sick with her blood and give us her blessing."

"Ah, okay." Rhys shot me a knowing look. "So, she *lives* in the *corn*."

"Yep." Beth peered into the fields behind us. "How'd you end up way over here? They've got a whole welcome party waiting for you over on the east side. Boy, is Spencer Mendoza going to be irked," she said with a mischievous smile. "I can't *believe* I got to meet you first."

70

"How do you know our names?" Rhys asked. "How did you know we were coming?"

"Oh, no one knew you existed until a few days ago." Her dark brown eyes sparkled in the fading light. "Katia told us you'd be coming home in time for the ceremony."

"So, our mother's here." Rhys squeezed my elbow, letting out a huge sigh of relief. "She's okay?"

"Oh, she won't be arriving for a few more days. Katia's taken them to see Aiyana in New Spain."

"New *Spain*?" Rhys asked. "What . . . Mexico?"

I stepped in front of him. "Who's Aiyana?"

"Aiyana's the original immortal from the Quivira tribe. She taught Katia everything she knows. Aiyana will help prepare them for vesselship."

"What do you mean 'them'?" Rhys asked.

A giggle escaped her lips. She pressed her hand to her mouth like she could stuff it back in. "Your mother and your father, of course."

"Our father?" Rhys sputtered. "*Thomas?* Has he been here this whole time?"

"What on earth do you mean? He's been with Nina. With you."

Rhys and I exchanged an uneasy look.

"We've never laid eyes on him," Rhys said.

"Hmm . . . that's curious." Beth blinked furiously as she looked out over the corn. "I see." She nodded to no one. "Let's just keep that between us for now," she said, pasting a smile back on her face.

"Can you take us to her . . . to *them*?" I asked, my pulse racing at the thought. Could our father and mother really be together right now?

"First things first." Beth looped her arm through mine. "We have to get you cleaned up for the wreathing ceremony." She wrinkled her nose. "No offense, but you smell funny." She tugged on my arm. "Come on, everyone's waiting."

"What's a wreathing ceremony?" I asked as my brother lagged behind with the bags.

"It's very special." Beth led us along the lakeshore. "It only happens once every seventeen years. A week before the ritual, the chosen daughter from the Larkin bloodline picks a boy from the Mendoza bloodline to walk the corn with on the summer solstice. Your bloodlines have been specifically bred for each other. For this occasion. It's *so* romantic." She took in a giant breath of air like a two-year-old. "Normally, you'd get to choose your own intended, but since you don't really know anyone, Katia chose for you. You're so lucky," she said to me, sighing dreamily. "Wait till you see him."

"Hold up, you mean *I* have to do this wreathing thing?"

"Oh, don't fret. You don't have to actually walk the corn. The vessels have already been found. But since Nina's away, we thought you could stand in for her, experience your heritage. Tradition's important around here. Wouldn't want to miss a chance for a celebration. Your mother and father will walk the corn on the summer solstice before becoming Katia's and Alonso's vessels."

"What does that even mean, being a vessel?" Rhys called from behind.

"Oh my stars! You don't know?" She yanked me to a stop, waiting for Rhys to catch up.

"On the summer solstice, Katia will transfer her soul into Nina's body so she can break her blood bond with Coronado. Then the Great Spirit will return Alonso's soul, placing it in Thomas's body. They'll be together at last. They'll finally be free. We all will," she added wistfully.

"Uh-huh . . . sure." Rhys shot me a weary sideward glance. He still thought all this was some kind of a hoax, but I was beginning to wonder. Maybe the legends were true. All of them.

Beth started walking again, pulling me along with her.

"But you can leave Quivira, right?" I asked. "It's not like you're being kept here against your will."

"Why would anyone want to leave?" She waved her hand around. "We have everything we need. The community was sealed in 1861."

"Sealed?"

"Because of the Arcanum." She nodded, matter-of-fact.

"'Arcanum'?" my brother asked.

"Coronado's guards are called the Arcanum." Beth lowered her voice, as if someone might be listening. "In 1861, Coronado brought the Arcanum here, and threatened to slaughter us all. That's when Katia enraptured the corn."

Rhys shook his head in dismay as he looked out over the fields.

"Oh, don't worry, they can't get in. The corn protects us."

"The corn protects you?" Rhys burst out in a fit of nervous laughter and then dropped the bags at his feet dramatically. "So, you're telling me Katia and Coronado are alive, like, living, breathing, alive, and immortal?"

"Of course, silly goose." She bounced on the balls of her feet a few times.

"And you think our mom and Thomas are some kind of magic vessels." Rhys pinched the bridge of his nose.

"Whew." Beth pretended to wipe her brow. "For a minute there I thought you might be a little touched," she said as she continued to pull me up the cobblestone path.

"Touched?" Rhys called after her as he regathered the bags. He looked like he was about to have a nervous breakdown. He pumped his legs harder to catch up to her. "What's your deal?"

I shot him a look to be nice, but Beth didn't seem to mind.

"I'm a seer. Seers can see into the future. But I'm broken. See?" She flipped her stick-straight strawberry-blond hair over to one side to reveal a large scar running the length of her skull. "I took a fall. I don't remember anything. I guess it made my third eye clog and I was seeing all kinds of cuckoo banana things. I saw the two of you coming months ago—the path that will lead us from darkness—but then I also saw a monkey eating a walnut and I thought to myself, Beth, don't be daft, we don't even *have* walnut trees."

"So, you're saying you have monkeys?" Rhys's voice cracked under the pressure.

Beth swirled a finger next to her temple making the crazy sign. "Apparently, I'm not the only one who hit their head," she said, smacking his arm playfully. "I'm joshing you. No, we don't have monkeys. But that would be grand, wouldn't it?"

"Yeah, that *would* be grand." Rhys looked around for an escape route.

Beth grinned. "You're weird, but you're cute. Are you intended?" She smoothed her hair down, tucking it behind her ears.

"What, like engaged? No." Rhys jutted his head back, like he was disgusted by the idea. "Why, are *you?*"

A soft blush settled into her delicate skin. "Oh, I'm unintendable."

"Well, I'm only seventeen," Rhys replied.

"There's no shame in being a late bloomer."

She either had the best deadpan I'd ever seen or no sense of humor whatsoever.

As we turned down a narrow wooded path, Beth pointed things out, like where to find the best boysenberries, where to dig up arrowheads, how to make birdcalls, anything and everything that sprung into her head, which was *a lot.* "Up there, on top of Dead Man's Hill"—she pointed to a simple shingled structure—"that's the schoolhouse."

"Dead Man's Hill?" Rhys asked. "Why do they call it that? It's not even that steep."

"Oh, some people, when they get old, they just go up there and sit. And die," she added with a sweet lilt to her voice as she spun around, making her yellow sundress billow.

My brother looked at me with wide eyes.

As we neared the end of the path, the enormous stone mansion came back into view. With its arched doorways, heavy leaded-glass windows, and grand entryway lined with brass lanterns hung from iron stands, it looked like something straight out of a gothic novel.

"The meeting house," Beth announced.

With each step, my throat got a little tighter and my heart picked up speed. What if this didn't work? Fooling Beth was one thing, but what if they figured out we didn't really want to "come home"? What would they do to us?

Beth opened the heavy double doors and led us up a set of stairs to a long hallway.

"Boys on the right side, girls on the left," she said as she steered me toward a tapestry curtain.

Rhys stepped in front of her. "She's not going anywhere without me."

"Okeydokey," Beth chirped, and without a second thought she took his arm. "Rooster in the henhouse," she called out as she opened the panel and led us into an enormous parlor full of half-naked women.

12

TRADITION

ASSAULTED BY A GANG of warm, soft bodies, Rhys and I were quickly separated by a flurry of hugs, tears of joy, and bursts of exaltation. Before I even knew what was happening I was corralled behind a flimsy screen.

"Well, she's a Larkin, all right." A sprightly woman with dark brown spiral curls came in close to study my face. "Just look at those eyes."

"No need to be shy," a burly woman said as she stripped off my blood-smeared blouse. "Can't go to your wreathing ceremony looking like that."

"We're happy you're home." A woman glanced up at me shyly through light blond eyelashes as she crushed a soft gold substance in a pestle with gardenia-and-orange-blossom-scented oil. "You must be so proud of your mother and father."

"Off we go." Someone peeled off my camisole.

"Wait . . . ," I sputtered as I clasped my arms around my bare chest.

Two younger girls crept behind the screen, giggling like hyenas as they pried off my boots and socks.

"Okay, if you can just hold on a min—"

"This is a happy day indeed." A small birdlike woman with brown frizzy hair reached in and ripped the bandage off my collarbone.

"Hey!" I yelled, but they weren't paying any attention to me.

"Is it really her?" A young girl approached, a spray of freckles across her nose and cheeks, trying to see around the ample rumps surrounding me.

"Ooh, look at this fancy clasp," another woman said as she unbuttoned my skirt.

"What the fuck?" I screamed as my skirt dropped around my ankles.

The room went deathly silent. They all looked at me in shock—like I'd just given them a universal slap.

I peeked my head around the screen to find Rhys biting the inside of his cheek, desperately trying not to laugh. I was on my own.

I stood there in my underwear, covering up the best I could with my hands, trying to figure out what to do next, when Beth sidled up to me with a tense smile. "It's part of the ceremony, Ash. Tradition," she whispered.

Why was she helping me? Did she know what Rhys and I were up to? She was a seer, which meant she could see the future. Granted, she was a broken seer, but it seemed like I should keep an eye on her anyway.

"What she *means* is she's excited," Beth announced to the crowd. "Right, Ash?" She nudged me in the ribs. "That's the word they use for excitement where she comes from."

"Yeah." I managed a shaky smile. "I'm . . . excited."

All the tension disappeared from Beth's face, and the women picked up right where they left off.

Stripped of all my clothes, I was bullied into a copper tub full of warm water and rose petals. Not the roses you'd find in a cheesy honeymoon suite. These were real roses—wild roses—the kind that gave off the scent of some forgotten time.

I didn't even like changing clothes for gym. Being bathed by a creepy cult was not on my favorite-things-to-do list.

The same woman who removed my bandage reached forward to untie the ribbon from my neck; I seized her hand. "The ribbon stays."

"Let the girl be, Agnes," a soft voice beckoned.

I released Agnes from my vise grip. She backed away from the tub looking more than a little terrified. I had no idea what made me react so strongly.

"Your ribbon's lovely." The woman with the kind voice settled next to me on a wooden stool. She had a shock of long white hair, and the skin around her cornflower-blue eyes looked like weathered parchment. "I'm Lucy, but my friends call me Lou."

I pulled my knees in tight to my chest, half intrigued, half horrified by the scene playing out before me. The women looked fairly normal, considering how isolated they were from the rest of the world. Maybe a century or so behind the times, fashion-wise, but they seemed healthy and happy. There were three distinct looks. Some had thick black hair and olive skin. Others were sturdily built megawatt blondes, and then there were redheads with spindly limbs and wide smiles.

"Ash," Rhys called out meekly. "If everything's okay, I might just wait outside." I peeked through the crowd of women to see my brother inching his way against the far wall, trying to make his escape. Beth caught his arm and swung him back into the thick of it.

"Ladies, this is Rhys Larkin and, yes, he's unintended."

The room erupted into a fit of cackles and catcalls. The look of horror he shot my way as they pawed him was priceless.

"May I?" Lou asked as she held up a pitcher of water.

Reluctantly, I tilted my head back and let her pour the water over my hair.

"I remember when I prepared your mother for this very occasion seventeen years ago," she said. "You look so much like her."

Just the mention of her brought up so many feelings—fear, hope, but above all, love. "When can I see her?" I asked, trying to bury my emotions, but the quiver in my voice betrayed me.

"Soon." Lou smiled, her eyes twinkling. "This must be overwhelming for you," she said as she worked tea tree oil into my hair. "Especially since you're a conduit."

I inhaled sharply. "What do you know about that?"

"I can sense auras. I definitely feel another presence with you, but Spencer already told us what you are."

"Who's Spencer?" I asked, sitting up straight, sloshing water over the side of the tub.

"Spencer Mendoza. He's the spiritual leader of the community—Katia's eyes and ears." Lou snapped her fingers, motioning to the water on the floor.

Beth, who was talking to my brother, fetched a rag and maneuvered through the gathering.

"Sorry about that . . ." I winced, peering down at the puddle.

"No bother," she said with a shrug as she mopped up the floor.

Lou leaned forward and whispered, "They say being a conduit is a curse, but you control it very well."

Not well enough, I thought to myself. "My mother helped me."

"I can see that," Beth chimed in with a reassuring smile.

I ran my fingers over the last tattoo, wondering if it really was a curse. There was no pain when I touched it. I looked down to see that it had completely healed. And then I remembered my mother had pricked her finger with the bone needle when she was working on me. How she'd pressed her finger against my wound. As Katia's vessel, maybe she was already immortal. Could she have healed me like Katia healed Alonso? She'd never been sick a day in her life, never been to the hospital, and she always looked so young.

Maybe that's the reason the protection marks weren't working anymore. Maybe her blood healed me before it could take effect—maybe it messed everything up.

As they scrubbed the grime of the outside world from my body, they told me stories about Katia. They spoke of her wisdom and kindness and the horrible injustice of Coronado killing Alonso and then forcing Katia to make him her immortal mate. But the biggest tragedy was when Coronado killed Katia's seventeen-year-old daughter, Marie.

"To make matters worse," Lou said as she leaned in close, "they say Marie was in love with Coronado. She was just a young woman, but first love is often the hardest. Can you imagine? Marie thought Coronado hung the moon, and then he killed her. Like his signet, a crow, wings outstretched, a star in one claw, a moon in the other, Coronado is a trickster. He's capable of all kinds of treachery and black magic."

A shiver of recognition rushed through me when I remembered my mother's studio filled with those black birds. Was Coronado looking for her?

Lou placed her hand on my shoulder, startling me. "It might seem like a bunch of hooey to you that we're going ahead with the wreathing ceremony this year when there's no need, but it's tradition. We didn't even know until a few days ago that Nina and Thomas were the chosen vessels. Katia kept it a secret all this time to protect them from Coronado. But now the chosen vessels are coming home to walk the corn once again," she said with a childlike grin.

"What does that mean, 'walk the corn'?" I asked, peeling a rose petal off my shoulder.

"At the wreathing ceremony, the Larkin girl chooses a Mendoza boy—the boy of her heart. Then, at high noon on the summer solstice, Katia leads the couple into the corn, to a barren sacred circle of earth—the spiritual heart of Quivira. There, Katia tests the girl's blood, hoping to find her vessel—the perfect match, so she can be free of her bond to Coronado and be reunited with Alonso."

"But what will happen *this* year? To my mom, and my . . . dad." Just saying the word *dad* out loud made my heart ache in a way I hadn't expected.

"Nina and Thomas will walk the corn—for the last time. Katia will take them to the sacred circle. As Katia's soul enters the vessel, she'll shed her body, like a cocoon. When that happens, Coronado will be forced out of his own body. Without a vessel of his own, his soul will be forced to wander the earth alone, always searching, always longing. The Great Spirit will deliver Alonso's soul into the Mendoza vessel and they'll live happily ever after."

I couldn't help thinking of the dead girl, the wound on the palm of her hand. "What happened to all the Larkin girls and Mendoza boys who went to the sacred circle before my mother and father?"

Lou's fingers stiffened in my hair. A look of regret seemed to pass over her face. "People don't speak from beyond the corn," she said in a hushed tone.

The woman with frizzy brown curls came near and Lou's whole demeanor changed. "The unchosen Larkin girl and the Mendoza boy leave the safety of the corn to live their lives in the outside world. But *this* year is special." She leaned back, resuming her scrubbing duties. "After the ritual is complete, we'll be one big happy family. Forever."

I couldn't help thinking I was missing something. Why was this such a big deal to them? What were they getting out of it?

An explosion of giggles pulled my attention to the center of the room, where girls of every age were scrambling around trying to get ready—brushing one another's hair, doing last-minute mending. I think that's what made it so unsettling; it was all so ordinary, like they were getting ready for a school dance, not preparing for a cult ceremony.

"What exactly do I have to do at this wreathing thing?" I asked as Lou began to work my tangles out with a wide-toothed wooden comb.

"Girls, bring the basket, please."

Lou made room for Beth and another girl to step forward and kneel in front of the tub; they were carrying a large basket brimming with dark green leaves from the cornstalks.

"This is Lauren Mendoza, and you know our Beth." I liked the way she said *our Beth* like she belonged to everyone. There was something so endearing and goofy about this girl.

Beth extended the basket to me. "Please, take a leaf." I noticed a scar on her inner wrist—an unmistakable c branded into her delicate skin. I looked around for the same mark on the other girls, but only Beth had one.

"The girls will show you how to make the wreath," Lou said as she dried my hair with a cloth.

The other girl, Lauren, was stunning—olive skin, long dark hair parted in the center, showing off her widow's peak. The last bit of light streaming through the window seemed to bend to her face as if it wanted to be there. But there was no warmth in her; she gave off the acrid scent of mourning.

"Take three leaves and braid them together, one after the other," Beth said.

I tried to do it, but my wet fingertips slipped and fumbled.

Beth was patient and encouraging, but Lauren countered that with a lot of heavy sighing and eye rolling.

"When the ceremony starts," Beth said, "we'll cover your eyes with a sash and I'll lead you to the line of eligibles. The Larkin women have a heightened sense of smell. Under different circumstances you'd use your senses to recognize your soul mate." Beth leaned in as if she were going to tell me some deep dark secret. "Katia chose for you. Number nine."

Lauren accidentally crushed one of the leaves in her hand. Beth gave her a wide-eyed look of horror.

"I'm sorry." Lauren whispered so quietly, I wondered who the apology was for.

I went back to work on the wreath, but it felt like the leaves were wrestling against me.

Beth kept glancing back at my brother, who was being

doted on by a girl with two long coppery braids. She had taken it upon herself to clean and re-bandage Rhys's skinned knee. He looked like he was going to pass out.

"Who's that?" I asked as I leaned forward in the tub, trying to get a better view.

Beth turned back to me, her cheeks flushed with embarrassment. "Oh, that's my half cousin Betsy Grimsby. She's unintended, too."

Clearly, Beth had a little crush on my brother. "So, tell me about number nine," I said, trying to distract her.

"You're still not braiding the leaves right." Lauren glared at me through her shiny black lashes.

"Then why don't you do it for me." I pushed my shoddy work toward her.

"Believe me, I would if I could . . . but I can't." She forced it back into my hands.

I had no idea what I'd done to piss her off, but she made me anxious. And I hated being this bad at anything.

"We *can't* help," Beth patted my arm. "It has to be your own creation. It's tradition. You're doing really well for your first time." She could barely say it with a straight face. "I mean . . . it's more symbolic than anything."

I looked down at the limp massacred leaves in my hands and laughed. "Poor number nine."

Aside from Lauren's sour mood, the atmosphere was jovial. Everyone seemed excited and full of life. It was contagious. I had to remind myself that these people were total freaks who wanted to steal my mother's body.

"She's ready," Lou said with a flourish of her pruney fingers.

The women helped me out of the tub and began to smooth the warm, gold-flecked oil into my skin. It took everything I had to make myself stand there and let them do it. There wasn't anything sexual about it—in fact it was just the opposite, it seemed almost reverent, but I got irritated when people even brushed up against me in the subway. The plan had been to gain their trust, but I didn't expect the process to be this hands-on.

"You look perfect," Lou said as she slipped a sheer white cotton sheath over my head. "Just as I imagined."

I ran my fingertips over the delicate lace scalloping the neckline, wondering if it was the same gown my mother wore on the night of her wreathing ceremony.

Lou led me to a full-length mirror. I couldn't help but smile. I looked like a painted tintype from another century. I knew the girl standing before me, but she looked like a better version of me. My loose waves were threaded with tiny white sweet alyssum blooms. Skin smooth as silk. The long willowy lines of my body seemed more powerful now, the downward curve of my mouth that had always felt childish had become sensuous—even my eyes appeared more striking, like deep water that had been set afire.

A drum outside began to pound slow and steady, like a

dirge. As the women formed a line, I realized it was a signal that the ceremony was about to start. Beth led me to the back of the line.

Rhys joined us, looking like he'd just been through the wringer.

"Don't be nervous." Beth squeezed my arm like a blood-pressure cuff, which only made me more nervous.

My body battled between anxiety and excitement. I wanted answers. I wanted to remain indifferent—see what this was all about, but the community seemed perfectly harmless, as far as cults go—and, dare I say, charming.

Beth gave me some last-minute advice. "Remember, all you have to do is walk down the line, stand in front of number nine and say, 'My body, my soul, I commit to you.' He'll re-move your blindfold and you'll put the wreath on his head. It's that simple. And have fun with it. Make it suspenseful. Wait till you see him." She leaned on me like a crutch. "He's so hump-able."

"'Hump-able'?" I repeated in disbelief.

"You know," she whispered. "*Hump* is when you kiss a boy you're not intended for."

"Oh God, Beth. That's not wh—"

The doors opened and Beth hurriedly tied the sash over my eyes. Rhys made sure it wasn't too tight. The gesture made me breathe a little easier.

With Beth on one side and Rhys on the other, I clutched

my sad wreath, and they led me down the stairs toward the entrance.

"You don't have to do this," Rhys whispered.

"It'll be fine." I squeezed his arm. "We need to play along for now."

But for me, it was more than playing along. Something about being here in this moment felt right. And that scared me more than anything.

13

WREATHED

SLOWLY, BETH AND RHYS led me outside. The heat from the lit torches kissed my shoulders; I felt an overwhelming calm wash over me, a lightness in my soul.

I stepped onto the cool damp grass, feeling it between my toes. Every step I took seemed to root me deeper into the soil, like a memory being reawakened from deep within my cells. The wind found me, pressing the soft cotton sheath against my body. Even with the susurration of the crowd, I'd never felt so comfortable in my own skin.

The women spun me around fast, at least a dozen times, and then set me loose. They giggled as I stumbled around the field like a drunk. I steadied myself and took a deep breath, shutting out the rest of the world and letting my senses take over.

A breeze blew in over the corn. The stalks rustled like endless layers of a stiff taffeta dress. I knew the choice had already been made for me, but there was a part of me that still wanted to know how I would've felt, who I would've picked had the choice been mine.

I stretched out my hands in front of me, my fingertips grazing the chest of the first eligible in line. A flutter of excited whispers swept through the gathering. I walked down the line, skimming my fingers across their chests, counting as I went. Each and every one of them smelled pleasant and harmonious. Earthy, mellow tones. Nothing like the boys I was accustomed to.

Number five smelled especially good, notes of cardamom and freshly oiled saddle leather. Intriguing.

I reached number nine, the one I was supposed to choose. This was the most appetizing yet—oak and honey—a scent that could envelop me like a thick wool blanket on a chilly night.

This was it. The moment had come.

I opened my mouth to say the words when the wind shifted. Something gripped me. My blood seemed to throb in my veins. At first, I thought I was going to fall into another conduit memory, but it was deeper than that. An inexplicable urge swept through me like a fever.

Locked into something nameless, I moved away from the line, weaving through the sea of people. Everything in me seemed to reach toward the scent—my blood, my skin, my bones, my spirit.

I brushed my fingers against a man's chest—he flinched.

Every part of me felt like a frayed wire just waiting for a spark—aching for it.

I whispered to him.

> *"Wii cuu'at ukuk huka aciksta*
> *Takaarahak karitki hukaawikii'ac kictiirahk*
> *Cuu'at hurii kituu'u' huka*
> *Paatu a ka'it."*

As soon as the words came out, I clamped my hand over my mouth. Caddo—I had just spoken Caddo fluently.

The crowd erupted into panicked murmurs.

I couldn't stand not being able to see. I pulled down the sash that covered my eyes.

My heart leapt into my throat. It was *him*. My junkyard crush. For a moment I forgot about our bitter parting. His hair was pulled back. I could have gotten lost in the lines of his face, but his eyes held none of the warmth from earlier. He was like a stone wall. Impenetrable and cold, as if we'd never met.

Beth rushed to my side. "You can't choose Dane," she said as she tried to ease the sash back over my eyes. "He's ineligible."

"Dane." I repeated his name. That was so much better than Goober.

"He's a Mixed," she whispered.

"What does that mean, *Mixed*?"

"Anyone with traces of Coronado's blood is considered a Mixed," she whispered as she tried to steer me back to the line. "A Larkin with a Mixed is forbidden."

"Is that why you ran off earlier?" I asked, searching his face for answers, but he only gritted his teeth.

"She's ruining the ceremony," a woman hissed behind me.

I glanced over my shoulder, scanning the stunned crowd, my eyes settling on a line of very anxious-looking boys.

"You've met?" A girl's voice startled me as she sidled next to Dane. Lauren. She snaked her arm under his, hanging on to his bicep.

"Yeah, I met him today at the junkyard and—"

"She's a conduit," Dane interrupted me. "She doesn't even know what she's saying. She's confused."

The way he said the word *conduit* felt like an insult, like another word for crazy.

I wanted to argue, but there was something in his eyes, a pleading look that made me hold my tongue. I could see it was important to him that our meeting stayed secret. But why?

"He's right," I said, tightening my grip on the wreath. "I *am* confused."

A look of relief washed over him, briefly softening his features.

"Poor girl," Lauren said loud enough for everyone to hear. "You shouldn't have to go through with this in your *condition*."

"Leave her alone," Dane murmured.

I tore my eyes away from Dane, but when I looked down and saw his hand, all I could think of was his thumb dragging across my hip bone.

A flush swept my cheeks.

And then I realized, it wasn't just my name . . . or my eyes that made him turn away from me at the junkyard. He belonged to someone else. I felt completely gutted.

"Ash, he's not meant for you," Beth whispered as she placed the sash back over my eyes. I let her do it this time. I didn't want anyone to see how hurt I was. How could someone I'd just met wound me so deeply?

"No harm done," Beth called out to the crowd in a strained singsong voice as she led me back toward the line of eligibles. "Trust me. Number nine is perfect for you," she said under her breath. "I'll lead you right to him."

Suddenly, I forgot how to move my legs. Beth had to half carry me down the line.

"I didn't know you spoke Caddo," she said as an aside.

"Neither did I," I exhaled. I knew bits and pieces from my mother, but the language had just . . . come to me.

Beth nudged me in the ribs and we came to a stop.

"My body, my soul, I commit to you," I said in monotone. Even though it was just for show, it felt strange saying the words aloud, like I was betraying myself in some way.

Oak and honey eased the sash from my eyes.

I was stunned. Blond, towering, and broadly built, with dark gray eyes. He looked like a Nordic prince. He bent his head forward and I placed the wreath there. When he straightened, one of the leaves flopped down in his face.

"Sorry about that." I sighed as I reached up to tuck it back in. "Apparently, I suck at wreath making."

"It's an overrated skill," he said. "I'm Brennon Mendoza." His smile seemed to beam from every pore. "I know this must be very strange for you," he confided. "But we don't have to walk the corn. All you have to do is smile every once in a while, dance with me. Make the old folks happy."

"I can manage that." I smiled up at him . . . and I meant it.

Brennon took my hand, and we were flooded with good wishes and congratulations.

I stole a glance at Dane, but his eyes stayed focused on Lauren.

I knew he couldn't be mine, but when I touched him, every cell in my body reached out to him like I'd known him for a thousand years. Like I'd finally come home.

Then I thought of my mother's words. Maybe this was what she meant by blood and salt.

Salt in the wound.

14

PUNCH DRUNK

FOLLOWING THE CEREMONY, we moved into the meeting house, to an elegant ballroom on the third floor that dripped with garlands of wisteria and honeysuckle. Candlelight flickered off the wood-paneled walls, casting long shadows across the coffered ceiling.

Banquet tables full of mystery meats and pickled everything stretched in front of us. There were giant bowls of punch so high in alcohol content that the liquid burned my eyes before even reaching my mouth. A lady with a mountain of wild curls was scolding some little kids who were hiding under the table trying to sneak punch. A band made up of gutbuckets, mandolins, washboards, fiddles, and spoons played folk music—a raucous marriage of English and Spanish styles. It was like going back in time. This could've easily been the 1800s.

I spotted Rhys dancing with Beth. Well, not *dancing* really, just kind of bouncing around like a pogo stick. But he seemed to be enjoying himself, that is, until Betsy Grimsby, Beth's half cousin, glommed on to him again and pulled him away, parading him around like a trophy.

The room buzzed. So what if they believed in some weird shit? I could picture my mother here so easily. Maybe coming here was the right thing for all of us.

As Brennon led me through the gathering everyone patted him on the back, shook his hand. I was surprised no one was asking him to kiss their baby. He seemed to be the golden boy of Quivira.

"First dance . . . first dance." A woman pushed forward, dragging a tall, weary-looking man with her. "I'm Patricia Mendoza and this is Gerald." She eyed me up and down, appraising me, her expression frozen in place. Her smile was a little frightening, like a cross between a beauty queen and a jack-o'-lantern. "We're Brennon's parents."

"Oh, it's nice to meet y—"

Before I could even finish my sentence Mrs. Mendoza took my hand and pulled me onto the dance floor.

"Okay . . ." I laughed.

"Sorry." Brennon shook his head in mock embarrassment as he followed close behind.

As we came to an abrupt stop in the center of the dance floor, she maneuvered Brennon so he was facing me.

"What's going on?" I asked, feeling the crowd press in around us.

"It's tradition." He smiled.

I raised an eyebrow. "There's more?"

A tall man with a twisty mustache, wearing a brocade waistcoat, turned toward the band, whistling through his teeth, and the band struck up a different tune—a slow and delicate piece.

I knew where this was headed.

Mrs. Mendoza placed my hand on Brennon's shoulder and his hand on my waist.

"Oooh," the crowd roared lasciviously.

"Wouldn't it be easier to tell us to dance?" I whispered.

Brennon cracked up; his mother shot me a look of warning. Apparently, this was her big moment.

Together, she and her husband placed my other hand in Brennon's.

The audience burst into cheers, making me flinch.

Brennon squeezed my hand. "Remember what I said."

I nodded. *Dance. Make the old folks happy—I've got this.*

With tears in her eyes, Mrs. Mendoza latched on to her husband and backed away.

Brennon gave me a reassuring smile before he started moving me around in circles on the crowded dance floor. I think he was leading me in a waltz, but I had no idea what I was doing.

Soon, the onlookers lost interest, and it finally felt like I could breathe again.

Brennon was a gorgeous distraction, but my thoughts still wandered to Dane. I spotted him talking with a group of men across the room—and that tingling sensation spread over the surface of my skin, settling deep inside of me.

He was more than handsome. I'd been around my fair share of pretty boys. This was something else . . . something chemical. I'd never doubt my mother's theory of attraction again.

I watched Dane as inconspicuously as possible as he moved through the party. Even though he was Mixed, people treated him with a certain amount of deference. All the girls took special notice of him. Clearly, I wasn't his only admirer. Why was I being so ridiculous? He wouldn't even look at me. Come to think of it, Dane seemed to look at everyone *but* me.

The music changed to something more upbeat, a jig of some sort, and Brennon lifted me up and twirled me around. I couldn't help but laugh. There was an easiness about him. I tried to imagine what it would be like, picking someone to spend the rest of your life with based on their scent. Brennon wouldn't have been a bad choice. Fireworks didn't go off in my chest when he touched me, but maybe that was better—who wants to spend their whole life getting burned? And Brennon didn't make me want to hurl when he touched me, which was still kind of a novelty.

As we danced, Brennon filled me in on the Quivira gossip. "The Hanrattys stick to their own." He nodded toward a grim-faced group huddled up on the right side of the ballroom. "And it's best to steer clear of the cheese balls. The Hanrattys always make the cheese balls."

"Got it. Hanrattys are weird. Don't eat their cheese balls." I smiled.

"The Grimsbys are good folk . . . like Lou, she's a peach, but there are a lot of seers in that bloodline."

"I'd never met a seer, until today."

"Consider yourself lucky. My friend Pete over there"—he nodded toward a tall, rail-thin boy watching a group of girls dancing and carrying on—"he's a Grimsby. He can't even entertain the idea of calling on a girl without one of his aunts telling him how it will end in tears."

I looked around the room. "What other kinds of spiritual gifts do people have?"

"There are a couple of dowsers—people who can find water sources—a few finders, folks who can locate missing objects or sense their history. Comes in handy when Ruth Hanratty loses her teeth, which happens about once a day," he said, chuckling. "But the gifts are diminishing with every generation. Except for the Mixed, of course."

I perked up. "What about the Mixed?"

"When Coronado left Quivira, his children stayed behind. They say there's black magic in their blood, and their gifts only seem to get stronger. But *you* are one of a kind," he said with a grin as he spun me around fast. "You are a Larkin, the first twin in your family, *and* the first conduit of your bloodline."

"Are there any other conduits at the party?" I asked, my heart quickening at the thought.

"Of course not." He pulled back slightly, with a sour look on his face.

A bitter feeling welled up inside of me.

He lowered his head, his tone softening. "I hope I didn't offend you. It's just . . . you're very different from the other conduits. You're very fortunate."

"Am I?" I felt my throat constrict. I tugged at the ribbon tied around my neck, but that wasn't the cause. I couldn't help wondering what it really meant to be a conduit . . . what I'd become if the protection marks weren't working anymore.

A guy bashed into me; he twirled his partner around—it was Lauren. The way he scowled at me made me think it wasn't an accident.

Brennon quickly moved us away, toward the far right corner of the ballroom.

"What's *their* problem?" I asked as I peeked over Brennon's shoulder to find them glaring at us.

"That's my cousin Lauren, just being Lauren, and the one with the black eye is Tommy. He's a little off-kilter, but he's a third cousin removed. He's got a little too much Hanratty blood, if you know what I mean."

"Yeah, well, from the looks of him, I wouldn't be surprised if that black eye was self-inflicted."

"How did you know?" Brennon laughed. "And over there . . ." He nodded toward a distinguished-looking man, impeccably dressed with thick dark hair, a dab of gray at his temples, who was holding court near the buffet table. "That's my uncle, Spencer Mendoza. He's a big deal around here."

Spencer's eyes locked on mine.

I staggered back a little.

"Are you okay?" Brennon shot his arm around my lower back, supporting me.

"Yeah." I inhaled sharply as I regained my footing. "I just got a little dizzy." I watched Spencer excuse himself and leave the ballroom. As he passed, I got a whiff of parchment and eucalyptus, but there was something foul underneath. I had no clue what just happened—I'd never set eyes on him before, yet I hated his guts.

A commotion came from the center of the dance floor and the band went quiet. Betsy Grimsby, my brother's admirer, seemed to have passed out. Rhys crouched next to her as Beth asked people to step back and give her some air. I wouldn't be surprised if she was faking to get my brother's attention. The girls of Quivira seemed old-school like that.

After making sure I was okay, Brennon excused himself to help. It was a relief. With all the attention elsewhere it was the perfect opportunity to find Dane. Before my mother arrived and we left Quivira for good, I wanted an explanation for why he ran away earlier, and why he was so cold to me at the wreathing ceremony. I felt I deserved that much.

I spotted him walking out of the ballroom. I slipped through the crowd, into the hall, down one flight of stairs, where I discovered Spencer Mendoza and Dane talking quietly in the archway of the men's parlor. I ducked behind the tapestry curtain of the women's parlor directly across the hall from them.

"The boy has no power," Spencer said. "But the girl's a conduit, a direct link to Katia. She's dangerous."

"She's not the vessel and the summer solstice is almost here." Dane glanced down at his feet. "I don't see why it matters anymore."

Spencer seized Dane's arm. "Who are *you* to say what matters anymore," he spat. "Have you forgotten what you are? Your duty?"

"How could I?" Dane pulled away from him, rubbing the inside of his wrist.

Spencer took a deep breath and tugged down the hem of his button-down vest. "Do as I say. And consider yourself warned," he said before turning and storming back upstairs to the ballroom.

Dane dragged his hands through his dark hair. He turned to head down the next flight of steps, but hesitated, like he wasn't sure if he should stay or go. I wanted to see his face. I wanted to know what he was thinking. He descended the stairs, and I couldn't help but follow—almost as if I'd never had a choice.

15

SAVAGE

I SEARCHED FOR DANE, but I'd lost him. Even with the meeting house lit up like a jewel box, it was still incredibly dark outside—the kind of dark that pressed in around me like a lead veil.

I walked to the shore, watching the ripples fade to black. The clouds obscuring the moon sailed past, giving the water an odd veneer, like the film on an old dog's eye.

"You shouldn't have come here." Dane's voice slipped from the shadows.

The blood seemed to flutter in my veins.

I should've been embarrassed, but I wasn't. I'd already made a complete fool of myself. What was one more twist of the knife?

I stepped across the lawn, toward the sound of his voice, straining to catch a glimpse of his face. But what I saw chilled me. Standing a few feet deep in the corn, he watched me through the heavy stalks, his dark eyes glistening with a focus that unnerved me.

I crossed my arms over my flimsy garment, afraid he could see right through me.

"What was all that about . . . with Spencer Mendoza?"

His jaw tensed. "You and I can't be seen together. Alone."

"We're just talking. Besides"—I stepped forward—"I don't care about any of that. About me being a Larkin and you being a Mixed or whatever," I said as I fidgeted with the end of the black silk ribbon.

"*I* care." His voice had a menacing edge. "We take tradition and honor very seriously in Quivira."

"I didn't mean it like that. I just . . . when we met . . . and then you left . . . and I saw you again . . . it's just . . ."

I took another step toward him. As soon as my foot hit the soil at the edge of the corn, a current ripped through my body, flinging me back at least ten feet in the grass.

Stunned, I got back up. He stared at me unflinchingly.

I tried again, but the moment I stepped into the corn I was thrown back with an even greater force.

"What's happening?" I struggled to get to my feet, feeling more than a little dazed.

"The only way you'll leave Quivira is if the corn wants you to leave."

I couldn't stop thinking about Tanner's warning. *People go into the corn but they don't come out.* Could it be true? I held my ground a few feet away from the edge of the field. I could feel it now—an invisible energy force keeping me there.

"But how are you—"

"I'm a Mixed. I have Coronado's blood." He pulled up his left sleeve, showing me the brand on his inner wrist. "All of the Mixed have certain *quirks.*"

"Beth," I exhaled, remembering the scar on her inner arm, her strangeness. But her mark looked different from Dane's. "Can all of the Mixed go into the corn?"

"No." He looked at me with a pained expression. "And you're the only person who knows I can. If anyone found out, they'd kill me."

"*Kill* you?" I whispered as I glanced back toward the meeting house.

"I need to know I can trust you," he said as he brushed his hand over the scar tissue on his arm; I had an overwhelming urge to touch it.

"I know how to keep a secret," I managed to whisper.

He walked toward the edge of the field. "There *is* a way you can walk in the corn," he said, extending his arm. "Take my hand." He glanced nervously behind him. "But we need to hurry."

When I looked out over the field, a dark feeling rose inside of me. The stalks hulked and swayed in the breeze, like a churning sea, but the thought of touching him overruled every other thought in my head.

As I reached out for his hand, something violent quaked inside of me, a dull ache grinding me into the past.

I tried to hold on to the present, but it felt as if someone had a death grip on my rib cage and they were trying to pull me through a sliver in the earth's crust.

I drag Alonso's corpse through the corn. A sadness unlike anything I've ever felt washes over me, as if my heart can't bear to beat without him. I call upon the Great Spirit, begging her to break my blood bond to Coronado and return Alonso's soul to me, but she refuses.

Then a whisper rustles through the crops, tickling my ear. "I can bring him back to you."

I stumble back—there's no one there, but I can feel a presence all around me.

"Who are you?" I demand.

"Without darkness, there can be no light." The whisper swirls past me this time, circling Alonso, moving his hair about his face, making him appear . . . alive.

I know who speaks to me now—I can feel him trying to slip under my skin.

The Dark Spirit.

I should block him out, refuse to listen, but when I look down at Alonso's mutilated body, I know what I have to do. The Great Spirit has turned her back on me. She's made her choice, as I must make mine. "What do you want of me?" I ask. "I'll do anything to bring him back."

The whisper then seeps inside my throat. I breathe his power into my lungs. The Dark Spirit etches the terms across my heart.

"Let him go," a voice behind me pleads.

I turn to see Aiyana. Her long plaited hair, eyes shining like wet shale. "The Great Spirit knows best. You must accept your fate."

"I can't," I scream, tears running down my face. "I love him."

"There are other ways to break the blood bond."

"But not ways to bring Alonso back to me."

"If you turn your back on the Great Spirit, I will be forced to turn my back on you." Aiyana's words cut right through me.

My entire body trembles. I cannot let Coronado win . . . cannot let Alonso go. I will have my vengeance.

Ripping the stalks from the field to form a circle, I cut my wrist with my golden blade and walk along the rim, letting my blood sink deep into the soil. I call upon the Dark Spirit. "A'ckista ra'u taku nistka'au'a."

"Katia, stop!" Aiyana races toward me, but she's unable to enter the sacred circle.

I dig my hands deep within the soil. The ground grumbles in defiance until it finally gives way, taking Alonso's body down with it, forming a deep crevice in the center of the circle. A gateway to the Dark Spirit.

I feel the light leaving me and the darkness taking hold, consuming me.

I know what must be done. Every great deed requires great sacrifice.

And so it shall be . . .

• • •

"Ashlyn."

I was thrust back into the present, standing at least thirty feet inside the corn, Dane bracing my wrists.

"You walked straight into the corn like you were in a trance," he said, his voice low. "I've never seen anyone do that before. How did you do that?" He shook me.

People began to pour out of the meeting house, screaming and crying.

Dane's eyes darted toward the commotion and then to the corn behind him. He looked down at me, lips parted, eyes blazing. "What are you?" he whispered, letting go of my arm.

As if a spell had been broken, I was torn from his side. A tremendous force of energy pulled me back toward the perimeter, spitting me onto the grass of Quivira.

Rhys and Beth spotted me. As they ran across the lawn to reach me, I peered back at the corn, searching for Dane. The look of savage beauty on his face nearly shattered me as he stepped back, letting the dark green stalks envelop him.

16

ADRIFT

RHYS COLLAPSED TO his knees beside me on the grass, gasping for air. I couldn't tell if he was trying to catch his breath or if he was going to throw up.

"What's going on?" I asked, still in a daze.

"He's come back," Beth said as she stared off into the corn.

"Who?" I pulled myself into a sitting position.

"Coronado."

"How do you know that?"

"The crows," she replied.

I looked up to the sky and saw the faint outline of black birds flying high above.

"These people . . ." Rhys panted. "They think the crows belong to Coronado . . . some kind of animal spirit."

"They're called familiars." Beth blinked slowly, like she could push them from her vision. "The crows attacked during the slaughter in 1861 when Katia sealed off Quivira. They returned the night Nina and Thomas walked the corn. Their presence has marked the disappearance of so many Larkins over the years. But this is different—his magic's getting stronger."

"Ash, we have to leave," Rhys whispered as he pulled me to my feet.

My stomach coiled up into tight knots as I looked out over the corn. He still didn't know we were trapped. Rhys would absolutely freak if I told him. "We can't leave." I shook my head. "Not without Mom."

"Look at me." He turned me toward him, his hands trembling. "Someone just *died*, Ash. She died right in front of me."

My mind stuttered, trying to grasp what he was saying. "Who?"

"My cousin Betsy Grimsby," Beth said softly as she looked down at the ground.

"The girl you were dancing with?" I asked, my mind spinning. "I thought she just fainted."

"There was so much blood." Rhys winced. "Coming out of her nose . . . her mouth . . . her eyes. She just bled out right in front of me. She must've had an aneurysm or something. I tried to get them to take her to a hospital, but they looked at me like I was crazy. They think Coronado's 'black magic' had something to do with it."

Brennon ran up to us. "Thank heavens you're okay." There was blood spattered on his white dress shirt.

Rhys must've noticed it, too, because his knees went weak. Beth helped me hold him upright.

"What's happening?" I asked Brennon as I looked past him, toward the crowd gathering in front of the meeting house.

"I'm not sure, but Spencer will know. Come." He motioned for us to join the others.

The people of Quivira were huddled in sections, seemingly sticking close to their respective families. Children clung to their mothers' skirts, while the elders stared out over the corn with blank, glassy expressions. One man was down on his knees, tears streaming down his face as he looked up at the sky. But they were all eerily quiet, like they were holding their breath. It made me hold mine, too.

"Friends," Spencer Mendoza announced as he stepped into the center of the crowd. "Rest assured, the vessels are safe. Katia and Aiyana will protect them until the summer solstice."

The crowd let out a collective sigh of relief.

I looked around in confusion. One of their own just died, and this was their highest concern?

"It's Coronado, isn't it?" a woman blurted, her cheeks mottled and damp with tears.

Spencer nodded dramatically. "We know, all too well, what the appearance of the crow means. Because of the sudden and violent nature of Betsy's death, we must assume Coronado had a hand in this. Through black magic, he may have found a way to worm his way into our minds . . . our hearts."

The gathering erupted in panicked murmurs.

"Betsy wasn't a Larkin. Why her?" A man with thick sideburns pulled his children close.

"Is it because Katia's away?" Lou asked with her palm pressed against her chest. "Has the corn weakened in her absence?"

Spencer held up his hands, quieting the din of agitated whispers. "The corn will hold," he said sternly. "We are being tested." He tugged down his vest. "Unfortunately, because of the nature of Betsy's death, we must set her soul free with fire."

A woman next to me gasped, her slender fingers trembling as she attempted to cover her mouth.

"That's a terrible insult to the Grimsby family," Beth whispered as she hugged herself. "Only the Mixed are burned."

The woman then began to sob openly. A man placed his arm around her, holding her tight.

Spencer glared at her. "We cannot risk Coronado's influence taking root in Quiviran soil. But take comfort. Everything we've hoped for, everything we've dreamed of is within our grasp. Nina and Thomas will be joining us soon, friends."

I wished he would stop saying *friends* like some kind of creepy roadside preacher. And what did he mean, everything we've *hoped* for? Why did they care about Katia getting her dead boyfriend back?

"Tomorrow, we'll meet on the fields for the annual social," Spencer announced. "A little levity will do us good." He clasped his hands behind his back and walked around the circle. "But for now, we must return to our lodges. If Coronado's black magic is at play, only the weak of spirit shall succumb.

So hold fast and pray. And be ever watchful, for the night near the summer solstice is full of wicked things."

A palpable hush swept over the people of Quivira as they stared straight ahead at the corn . . . like zombies . . . like a cult.

Spencer stretched out his arms, as if to embrace the crowd. "And so it shall be . . ." He bowed his head.

My skin erupted in goose bumps. *And so it shall be.* The same thing my mother said when she dug the bone needle into my flesh. The same thing Katia said when she formed the sacred circle.

The community answered his call in unison. "And so it shall be . . . at the harvest of the end of the world. The reaper will come forth and sever the wicked from among the just; and she will make us immortal."

It hit me like a tidal wave.

For five hundred years . . . *this* is what the families have been waiting for. All their hopes and dreams were pinned on this event. They believed *they* were the *just* among the wicked of the outside world.

My heart felt heavy, my fingers, numb as I reached for my brother.

"Immortality," I whispered.

"What the hell's going on?" Rhys said through his teeth.

"They think Katia will make them immortal after the ritual. That's what this is all about."

A group of men pushed through the crowd, carrying a wood stretcher bearing what looked like a mummy, wrapped in a white sheet.

The mob silently followed the stretcher toward the boats lining the dam.

Rhys held me back. "We can make a run for it," he said as he stared off into the corn. "They won't come looking for us in there . . . they're too scared."

"Rhys . . ." I swallowed hard. I wanted to tell him about the corn, but I couldn't make the words come out. "We'll be safe here until Mom gets back."

"Safe?" He grasped me tighter, his eyes welling up with fear. "Look around, Ash. This is a cult. That girl just died and no one batted an eye, and now they're building her a freaking funeral pyre."

Beth pried my brother's hand off my arm. "It's best if you come with me," she said.

Rhys and I looked up to find the entire community staring at us.

"Your belongings are already on the boat." She looked at me and I knew what she was trying to tell me. This wasn't the time to cause a scene. They were watching us. If we had any chance of seeing our mother again, we were going to have to lie low a while longer.

My brother must've felt it, too, because he let Beth lead him toward the dam.

"Where are you taking us?" he asked as he walked stiffly through the crowd.

"Home," Beth whispered.

Brennon was waiting for me by the dam. He scrunched what was left of the wreath onto my head and kissed my hand. "Till tomorrow."

He got into a canoe with his family, and his mom waved at us, flashing a tight smile. I wiped the back of my hand against my dress. I don't know what made me do it. The words . . . the ceremony . . . the dance . . . for some reason it all felt a little too real.

Rhys and I stood perfectly still as they carried the stretcher past us to the lake and placed it in the water. It was some kind of raft.

The other families climbed into the boats lining the dam. Beth helped us into a battered canoe painted with bright yellow daisies. In one fluid movement, she settled herself into the hull, pulling the paddle from the bottom of the boat to row us "home."

As the fifty or so boats traveled together across the lake, a young girl's voice rose above the rhythmic strokes of the oars pushing through the water. She sang a hymn I didn't recognize—a song of lost love, sacrifice, and redemption. I was glad the others didn't join in. Her lone angelic voice was perfect in that moment—hauntingly beautiful.

At the darkest point, in the center of the lake, they set

Betsy's body adrift. Spencer threw a lit torch onto the raft; her body was swiftly engulfed in flames.

We sat there for what seemed like an eternity, watching her body burn. The orange flames stood out with perverse clarity against the midnight sky.

17

SPIRIT

AS THE CHARRED REMAINS sank beneath the surface, the boats began to split off—some to the east, toward the Mendoza lodge; some to the west, toward the Hanratty and Grimsby lodges—ours was the only boat that headed due south, toward a tiny speck of light at the tip of the lake. The Larkin lodge.

"Believe me . . . I'm not complaining"—Rhys let out a shaky breath as he scanned the lake—"but why are we the only canoe headed this way? Where are the other Larkins?"

"You're all that's left," Beth said, her warm brown eyes gleaming as she continued to row, slow and steady.

My brother's spine stiffened. "What happened to them?"

"Coronado," she replied as she looked skyward. "He took them."

"Killed them?" My brother rubbed his arms, like he was trying to warm himself up.

"No one knows," she said serenely. "But it feels like I *should* know . . . like the answer's right on the tip of my tongue." She stopped rowing, closed her eyes, and stuck her tongue out.

Rhys shot me a look—

"Nope. Nothing." She shrugged and continued rowing.

Something stirred in the water, sending dark ripples across the glassy surface.

"What was that?" my brother whispered.

"It's the week of the summer solstice," Beth replied.

"What's that supposed to mean?" he asked, his eyes darting over the water.

"Some say the land is haunted by the spirits who died here. They say the lake was made from the tears of the Great Spirit."

"Perfect." Rhys clutched the sides of the boat.

"Is this where Katia and Coronado met Aiyana?" I asked.

Beth nodded. "Katia led Coronado, his men, and their families to Quivira in 1541."

"Katia led them?" I asked. "I thought it was Coronado."

"When Coronado saved Katia from the Spanish prison, she agreed to bring him here and make him her immortal mate. They claimed they were looking for the land of gold, but Katia can make all the gold she needs. She was searching for Aiyana."

There went my theory that we could buy my mother out of this. I glanced down at the briefcase full of gold ingots at my feet, wondering if Katia gave it to her or if my mother stole it.

"Aiyana had appeared to Katia in a dream, told her if she came to Quivira she would teach her to commune with the Great Spirit—and how to take an immortal mate."

"How would Aiyana know about any of that?" my brother asked.

"Aiyana was another immortal like Katia, and while Katia used alchemy to achieve immortality, Aiyana was granted immortality from the Great Spirit herself. Aiyana taught Katia everything she knew—they were like sisters—she even taught her Caddo."

Beth dug the oar deeper into the water. "When Coronado killed Alonso, Katia was heartbroken, but when he killed her daughter, she was devastated. Marie's soul couldn't be saved, but the Great Spirit agreed to bring Alonso's soul back to her once their vessels had been found."

"Wait." My breath hitched in my throat. "You said the *Great* Spirit agreed to return Alonso's soul?"

"Yes." Beth skimmed the oar on top of the water for a moment and studied my face.

I looked out over the corn in the distance. In my vision, I'd seen Katia turn to the *Dark* Spirit—and Aiyana tried to stop her. This was a part of the story the community didn't know about.

I couldn't get Aiyana's face out of my mind. That haunted look in her eyes when she realized she couldn't enter the sacred circle.

"What happened to her . . . to Aiyana?" I asked.

Beth continued rowing. "Aiyana couldn't bear to stay after all the blood that had been shed here. She took her tribe out west to start anew, leaving Quivira in Katia's care. They returned briefly in 1861 when they found out Coronado and the Arcanum planned to attack. But there was a great battle in the corn, most of the tribe died trying to protect us. That's when Katia enchanted the corn."

Something didn't feel right. I guess Katia and Aiyana could've patched things up. I mean, five hundred years is a long-ass time to hold a grudge, but it was hard to believe Aiyana would help Katia with anything that had to do with the Dark Spirit.

"I can't believe I'm asking this." Rhys leaned forward, raking his fingers through his hair. "But if the ritual takes place . . . if it's real . . . what will happen to our mom? Will she still be our mom, or will it just be Katia in our mother's body?"

"I guess she'll be a mother to all of us." Beth smiled, but it didn't quite reach her eyes. "It's an honor."

Her words hung heavy in the air. I remembered my mother saying the exact same thing to me in her studio when she gave me the last protection mark.

I couldn't imagine anything worse, living forever, watching everyone and everything die around me, but maybe for Mom it *was* an honor, being able to spend eternity with the one she loved.

"Ahoy." A man's voice called out across the water.

"Hi, Henry." Beth waved as she eased the canoe alongside a long, crooked wooden structure that looked like it was about to commit dock suicide. If the Larkin lodge looked anything like this, we were in for a treat.

A man picked up the lantern resting at his feet, illuminating a ravaged pockmarked face arranged into a scowl.

"Henry's the caretaker of the Larkin lodge."

"This gets better and better," Rhys murmured as he heaved our bags onto the dock.

I slipped my boots back on and climbed out after him.

"Oh, and, Ash?" Beth called from the boat. "Your markings are really beautiful."

All of the hairs stood up on the back of my neck. Slowly, I turned around, running my fingers against the last tattoo on my collarbone. "You see them?" I whispered.

"The circle with a dot in the center," she said as she struggled to hold up the heavy briefcase. "That's the symbol Katia uses on her gold bars."

I reached out and took it from her, clutching it against my chest.

"Don't worry," she said as she pushed away from the dock with her oar. "Your secret's safe with me."

She knew about the protection marks. She knew about the gold.

"Beth, wait," my brother yelled as he rushed to the edge of the dock. "You're just going to leave us?"

"I'll pick you up at dawn," she said as she turned the canoe around and started rowing back toward the Grimsby lodge. "There's something you need to see."

18

HOME SWEET HOME

THE LANTERN SWUNG from side to side as Henry led us up a gently sloping cobblestone path, slick with moss and sprawling ivy. I scanned the surrounding towering pines and cedars and, beyond that, the corn. Always the corn.

Henry stopped and raised the lamp, illuminating the beautiful arched door at the base of an enormous A-frame house with wings jutting off on either side. Here, in the dark, it looked like a cedar-shingled spaceship. There was a flag out front—a simple circle with a golden crescent moon and a star. Henry opened the door, lit two more lanterns that rested on the entry table, and thrust them into our hands.

Rhys dug in his heels, but I pulled him over the threshold.

The moment I stepped inside the house, the scent overwhelmed me: hints of pine, geranium, rising bread, fresh rain, and wet cedar. And deeper than that, my mother was everywhere, like a faint imprint of sunshine. I wondered if—

"She's not here," Henry said, as if answering my thoughts.

I looked up at him with raised eyebrows as he led us inside.

I wasn't expecting it to be so open; the main room was vaulted like an atrium with huge windows covering the wall overlooking the shimmering lake. The décor was sparse—a few elegant and functional pieces. I walked through the dining room, running my fingers along the enormous wide-planked farm table, eyeing a number of portraits and photographs that hung on the walls—their faces as familiar as my own, but nameless.

Henry showed us the kitchen. "You got bread, almond butter, jam, lemonade," he said as he opened the old-fashioned icebox. The light from the lantern shot up his arm, illuminating the scar on his inner wrist, a brand identical to Beth's.

"You're a Mixed," I blurted.

The tendons in his neck flared.

I thought about Dane's scar and the strange overwhelming urge I had to touch it.

Henry glared at me. "I'll do my best to stay out of your head, but you'll need to watch your thoughts around me."

It took me a few seconds to register what he was saying, but then I remembered Dane telling me that all the Mixed had certain quirks. Henry must be a telepath.

I felt a deep flush spread over my face.

"If anyone even suspects an inappropriate relationship there will be punishment. *Severe* punishment," Henry said. "It won't even matter who his daddy is."

"Who's his dad?" I asked.

"Spencer Mendoza."

Just the thought of them sharing the same blood offended me.

"My father was a Larkin, my mother a Mixed," Henry explained as he rolled down his sleeves. "I was caught bringing flowers to my half cousin Anna Larkin. They let me live, but I wasn't unmarred." Henry shifted his weight. "A Larkin girl mingling with not only a Mixed, but a Mixed with Coronado and Mendoza blood? Out of the question. Doesn't matter that the vessels have been found. It's forbidden. Always has been— always will be." He moved into the living room to light a lantern hanging from an iron stand. "Do you hear me, girl?" He turned to stare at me.

I nodded, just to get him to stop. I didn't want to talk about my "mingling" in front of my brother.

"What really happened to the rest of the Larkins?" Rhys asked warily.

Henry's knuckles turned white as he clutched the lantern. "The Larkins started disappearing a few years after Nina and Thomas walked the corn. By this time last year they were gone. We thought all was lost until a few days ago. Katia told us salvation was on the way. She must've suspected a traitor among us, because she kept Nina and Thomas a secret from everyone." He let out a heavy sigh. "She did what she had to do to keep them safe from Coronado."

"Why would she think there was a traitor?" Rhys rubbed his

temples. "And why would you assume Coronado was involved? Maybe the Larkins just didn't want to live here anymore."

Henry squinted at him. "People don't *leave* Quivira."

I clenched my eyes shut. *Please don't tell Rhys about the corn. Not yet. Not now.*

I opened my eyes to find Henry glaring at me. So, it was true—he really could read my thoughts. I looked at him pleadingly.

Henry grumbled at me as he passed, fetching a tall ladder that was hanging on the wall. "Every time a Larkin disappeared, you could see crows flying overhead."

Rhys slumped down in one of the dining room chairs, burying his head in his hands. "God, I hate crows."

Henry dragged the ladder to the center of the room, leaning it against a platform built into the vaulted ceiling. "Before my time, the crows had been known to attack, ripping people limb from limb, but with the Larkins," Henry said as he ascended the ladder to a loft area, "it's like the crows plucked them right off the face of the earth. They disappeared without a trace."

"But not you?" I asked as I followed close behind.

"They say Coronado spared me because I was a Mixed."

"That was lucky," I said as I reached the top, but he didn't offer me a hand.

"Lucky?" His mouth stretched into a thin grim line. "The Mixed are an abomination. After what Coronado did to Katia, letting his kin stay in Quivira was merciful."

Henry opened the door to reveal a screened-in porch with scented candles and blue-and-white-pinstriped cushions. It seemed dainty compared to the rest of the house.

"You're awfully tame for a conduit." His eyes narrowed on me. "Most conduits are . . . well . . . there's something different about you."

I ran my hand over the last protection mark. "So I've heard," I answered, holding his gaze, doing my best to bar him from my thoughts.

Rhys decided to join us, clomping up the ladder like he was carrying the weight of the world on his shoulders. I helped him onto the platform.

My brother and I stood in front of the screened-in window. This appeared to be the highest point of Quivira, offering a unique view. The torches marking the inner perimeter blazed, casting an ominous glow over the corn.

"Why can't Coronado and the Arcanum come in?" Rhys asked. "We were able to walk right through."

"Your blood allowed you to pass, I suppose." Henry scratched at his brand. "Katia's blood."

Rhys squinted into the distance. "But what about all the visitors you've had over the years?"

"You're the first visitors we've had since Quivira was sealed in 1861."

Rhys turned to me, jaw tense. I didn't need to be a telepath to know what he was thinking. All of those cars from the junkyard—all those people. What happened to them?

"Best not to ask too many questions around here, you understand, boy?" Henry's pale blue eyes settled on him.

"What does Coronado want?" I asked in an attempt to steer the conversation away from the corn.

"He wants to stop the ritual. He thought killing off the Larkins would make it impossible for Katia to find a vessel, but now that he's found out he's been tricked, I suppose he's lashing out at the weak. Poor little Betsy Grimsby. His black magic's getting stronger. Watch yourselves, Coronado sure would love to get at the two of you."

"Wait . . . what would he want with *us*?" I asked, pure adrenaline firing through my limbs.

"Coronado could use you as pawns to suss out your parents—the vessels, or just kill you to punish Katia. He'll do anything to hang on to his immortality."

I couldn't stop thinking about our mom telling us how Katia did her a great kindness that day by allowing her to leave Quivira. I never understood what she meant until now. Katia could've taken her vessels right then and there, but she waited another cycle, another seventeen years, in order to let my mom raise her children, to give us a chance at a normal life. Suddenly, I understood why my mother held her in such high regard—why they all did.

We stood there in silence, staring out over the fields.

"Even if you could get through the corn . . ." Henry looked at my brother sympathetically. "Coronado has Quivira surrounded. You wouldn't stand a chance."

Rhys whipped his head around. "How did you know what I was thinking?"

"And Ash is right . . . what makes you think Nina would want to leave with you? Nina and Katia have been connected since the moment Katia cut into your mother's palm. Asking Nina to leave would be like asking her to turn against her very nature."

Henry's eyes bore into us with a sharpness that made me squirm. I had a thousand questions, but I wasn't sure if he could be trusted.

"Don't trust anyone," Henry said as he turned to go back downstairs.

"Wait, you're just leaving us here, too?" Rhys gripped the top of the ladder.

"Sleep anywhere you'd like," he said as he reached the main floor. "I stay in the shed out back."

With that, he left us alone in that strange empty house with nothing but ghosts and shadows to keep us company.

19

WATCH
THE ROPE

IT WAS THE SOUND of creaking rope that pulled me down the ladder, plunging me into the darkness of the east corridor.

"Ash, wait." Rhys juggled our bags with his lantern, trying to keep up.

I opened each door as I went, shining my light inside. One had a nautical theme—red, white, and blue, with little anchors painted along the trim, another was drenched in floral chintz, and then there was a nursery with cream-colored lace. Bedroom after bedroom, spotless and carefully arranged. It was like walking through an abandoned dollhouse.

I wondered what happened to the Larkins . . . how they died.

Along with the sound of my brother's labored breath was the sound of the dead girl's delicate skin scraping against the rough texture of the rope, pulling me toward the last room at the end of the hallway.

The instant I opened the door, I knew this room had once belonged to my mother. Her scent was everywhere.

But there was a new resident, too. Hanging from the light fixture in the center of the room was the dead girl, her sun-kissed waves dragging across the gleaming hardwood floor in a slow, circular pattern.

I walked past her, keeping my eyes trained on the wall in front of me. Rhys couldn't know she was with us or he'd bolt out of the house screaming.

"This was Mom's room," I said as I browsed through her things. Achievement ribbons decorated the walls—swimming, archery, and something called double ball. This was a part of her life I thought I'd never get to see. "It's strange thinking about her as a teenager."

"Don't touch anything. We shouldn't even be here."

I smoothed my hand over her brass bed, the worn patch-work quilt. "She was our age when she got pregnant with us and left Quivira. Can you imagine?"

"You can cut the act now." Rhys stood in the doorway, clutching the bags as he looked toward the stairs.

"What are you doing?"

"I want to make sure Henry isn't coming back to check on us. If we—" He tilted his head, listening closely, and then lowered his voice. "If we keep running in the same direction, we'll make it out of the corn eventually. Do you remember anything about celestial navigation?"

"Rhys . . ." I took a shaky step toward him. I wanted to

tell him about the corn, I truly did, but I couldn't bear to see the look on his face when he found out we were trapped. He'd blame me for bringing him here . . . for everything. I just needed to buy some time, keep him calm, until I figured something out. "I think we should stay."

A deep crease settled between his brows. "Are you scared of Coronado and the Arcanum? Because it's like the boogeyman, Ash—it doesn't exist. This is the kind of thing they tell people so they won't leave. Cult playbook one-oh-one."

I gathered the sides of my dress in my sweaty palms. "It's more than that."

"Are you talking about Betsy?" He tightened his grip on the bags.

"That's not a natural death . . . People don't die like that."

"Exactly." He nodded emphatically. "That's why we need to get the police . . . get some medical personnel out here. These people are stuck in the dark ages."

The air felt heavy, like I could hardly move, guilt gnawing at my insides. "After everything that's happened, everything you've seen, you *still* don't believe in any of this, do you?"

Rhys pressed his lips together, taking a deep breath through his nose. "These people think they're going to become immortal." He tried to keep his voice low and even, but I could tell he was on the verge of a mental breakdown. "Even if Katia's real, how could she do that? They're delusional, Ash. And I don't want to be here when they figure out they've been had."

"What if you're wrong? What if all this is real? And aren't you the slightest bit curious about our dad?"

"I'm curious about the Loch Ness Monster, too, but you don't see me going to Scotland with a harpoon!" He peered down the hall again, then lowered his voice. "Of course I'm curious about Dad, but where has he been if he wasn't here in Quivira? Why hasn't he tried to find us? Why didn't Mom try to find *him*? Something's not right."

"Maybe he's been with Aiyana all this time, waiting for Mom." I swallowed hard. "I just need a little time," I said as I stared past the dead girl, out the window.

I felt him glaring a hole into the side of my head. "Something's going on that you're not telling me. I can tell. I don't know what's happening, but the Ash I know would never run around in that creepy dress and get all crazy over some guy. And what's with that weird black ribbon?"

I pulled the strand from my neck. "I'm sorry," I whispered as I secured the ribbon tight around my wrist.

"'Sorry'?" He shook his head in dismay. "That's it? That's all you have to say to me?" After a few agonizing seconds, he dumped the briefcase and my backpack to the floor. "I guess I'll have to do this by myself, then," he said as he hoisted the duffel onto his shoulder.

"Three days." I got the words out before he could take a step out the door.

The sheer panic in my voice must've given him pause. His shoulders slumped as he turned around to face me.

"That will still give us plenty of time before the summer solstice . . . to get help."

"Why?" he asked. "Give me one good reason why we should risk it."

"This is going to sound crazy."

"Believe me"—he cracked an uneasy smile as he stepped toward me—"nothing would sound crazy to me right now."

I took his hands. "I had a vision of Mom and Dad. I saw them walk the corn seventeen years ago. Katia cut into the palm of Mom's hand and said, 'A vessel at last.'"

Rhys looked me straight in the eyes, like he always did when he was trying to calm me down. "That wasn't real, Ash. It's just your imagination."

I wanted to tell him I was fine . . . like I always did, but nothing was fine. Not anymore. "I'm a conduit, Rhys. The visions . . . the horrible memories . . . the feelings that don't belong to me—they're real and they're only getting worse." It hurt to say it out loud. "If you believe *one* thing, believe that. Believe *me*." Tears stung the corners of my eyes, but I held them back.

"What can I do?" He squeezed my hands before letting go.

"The dead girl." I snuck a glance at her over my shoulder. "She's been leading me here all along. She wants to show me something. Maybe through her I can figure out what's happening to me and find a way to get Mom back . . . and our dad."

He lowered his eyes as he set his bag down. "I'll do it, but not because I believe in any of this. I'll stay because I love you."

"Thank you." I wrapped my arms around his neck and hugged him. I didn't want to let go.

After a while, he gave me an awkward pat on the back. We weren't a very huggy family.

"Okay, then," he said, prying himself away and taking the toiletry bag out of his duffel. "Three days." He stepped inside the bathroom and shut the door.

Feeling completely spent, I slumped down on the edge of the bed, staring at the dead girl. The downward curve of her mouth, the golden sheen to her hair—"Who are you? What are you trying to tell me?" I whispered. "I'm here. Help me." But she just stared out with those dead eyes.

I held my head in my hands, as if I could somehow shake the cobwebs free, when I felt the wreath Brennon had placed on my head at the end of the night. I pulled it off, feeling the distinct ridges of the leaves between my fingers. The realization slowly burned from my fingertips all the way to the tips of my ears. I stood up like a shot, eyes glistening with fear, breath dying in my chest. I dropped the wreath to the floor, staring up at the rope binding the dead girl's ankles.

It was made from corn leaves. Someone at Quivira made that rope.

As Rhys came back into the room, I pretended to look for something in my bag—a sad attempt to hide the terror building inside of me.

"It's in the bathroom," Rhys said, giving me a weak smile. "You always forget to pack your toothbrush."

"Thanks," I said as I slipped inside the old-fashioned bathroom and shut the door. When I looked down and saw my toothbrush resting on the edge of the sink with a thick line of toothpaste already applied, I lost it.

It wasn't just the toothpaste, or Rhys, or my mom, or even Quivira—it was me. Rhys was right. Something in me had changed. I could feel my ancestors, their feelings, their memories, swelling up inside me, taking over.

I'd bought myself a little time, but there were only five days until the summer solstice, until my mother was lost to Katia forever. Or Coronado killed us. I had to get a grip for all our sakes.

I splashed cold water over my face until I felt I could look my brother in the eye without bursting into tears.

I dimmed my lantern as I came out of the bathroom so he wouldn't see my red-splotched face, but Rhys was already curled up on the floor next to the bed with the quilt. I felt guilty for taking the bed, and for a lot of other things, but I knew he wouldn't have it any other way. He was always too chivalrous for his own good. Even with the dead girl still hanging there, I was glad he didn't want to stay in a different room.

I lay back on the bed. The sheets were crisp, like they'd just been dried on the line. There was a hint of rose water, the same thing my mother liked to use in the wash. Surrounded by her belongings, it felt as if her heart had never left this place—that it had been perfectly preserved here among her possessions.

"I'm sorry I yelled at you," Rhys said softly. "It's this place. Can you feel it?"

"I won't let anything happen to you," I whispered into the dark.

"It's not me I'm worried about," he said before drifting off to sleep.

I tried to keep my heavy eyelids open so I could watch the dead girl, study the familiar angles of her face, but my body had a different idea.

20

LET THERE
BE LIGHT

THE SICKENING CRACKLE *of the corn-husk rope pulls me from sleep, down the hall, up the stairs, and out into the night. The sky is the strangest color, a dusky gray rose. Dark blond hair skims the ground as it disappears into a patch of tall prairie grass.*

Tearing through the coarse grass, I try to reach her. As I break into a small clearing, I catch a glimpse of her face—eyes wide and lifeless, she stares back at me as her body's being dragged into the corn.

Sensing a presence, I turn to see a winged figure made of smoke move toward me, but I'm not afraid. The scent of freshly rained-upon soil, salt, hay, cloves, sandalwood, and saddle leather permeates the air. It's the most beautiful smell in the world. I close my eyes to breathe it in, hoping it will imprint on my memory. And when I open them, the smoke has sharpened into the face of Dane.

I reach out to touch him, but he flinches away. I can't help but laugh. Even my illusion of Dane won't cooperate.

My skin is pulsing with light. Faint at first, the golden light soon grows into a soft halo that wraps around me, illuminating the protection marks.

I stand perfectly still, coaxing the golden light forward to reach him. As soon as it meets his skin, I can feel him, just as if I were touching him with my own fingers. Every bit of our connection is alive and electric as it flows through me and into him, back from him to me, and around us.

I feel his spirit, damaged and beautiful. Perfect in its flaws. Suddenly, I become worried that he can see all of me, too; something in me wants to cover up, to hide my imperfections. I feel vulnerable, like a gaping wound with salt water lapping at the edges.

"Do you see the light?"

"There's no light," he answers.

It makes me so sad he can't see or feel what I feel. "Just because you don't see it, doesn't mean that it doesn't exist."

Dane's shadowy figure takes an unexpected step toward me. Even though he's only a hallucination, I swear I can feel his gentle breath on my face. He leans forward, pressing his lips against mine. I can taste him, along with the salt of my tears that stream into our mouths. Sadness and ecstasy consume me.

I open my eyes to find Dane has vanished, along with every bit of light that beamed from my skin. I hear the crops rustle behind me. I turn and step toward the corn. As I peer through the stalks, a feeling of dread presses down on me, crushing me, holding me in place.

The dead girl's hand emerges from the corn, clasping my ankle. "I thought you loved me," she whispers.

"Ashlyn."

I awoke sometime before dawn, sprawled on top of my covers, a thick sheen of sweat covering my body. I stirred; my muscles ached. My feet gritted against the sheets. Looking down, I found them caked in dirt.

I leapt out of bed.

"What's going on?" Rhys mumbled.

"Nothing. Just need to get ready." I escaped into the bathroom and rested my forehead against the closed door.

"This is real," I told myself as I pressed my fingers into the cool wood grain. I stole a glance at myself in the mirror and did a double take.

Threaded into my tangled hair were coarse strands of prairie grass. In a panic, I checked the rest of my body. "Holy shit." I exhaled when I discovered a bloody handprint coiled around my left ankle.

I'd gone outside without a clue of how I got there or how I got back. I'd lost time again. Maybe hours. Was Coronado's black magic trying to lure me into the corn? But it felt deeper than that.

"Are you okay in there?" Rhys knocked on the door, startling me.

"Find another bathroom," I snapped as I pumped water

into the washtub. I stepped into the cool water and scrubbed my legs with a washcloth until they were raw, then pulled the plug, watching the dirty water swirl around my ankles and disappear down the drain.

The dead girl spoke to me. She touched me. She wanted me to find her in the corn. And Dane could take me there.

21

CRADLE
TO GRAVE

TRUE TO HER WORD, Beth was waiting for us at the end of the dock. When she stood to help us into the canoe, I saw that she'd chopped off the bottom of her yellow dress, turning it into an above-the-knee skirt, which she'd paired with black socks rolled down to the same height as my motorcycle boots. I think she was trying to copy my outfit from yesterday, but she missed the mark in the worst way.

"I made muffins," she said with that same goofy smile. "Beet and carrot."

"Thanks." Rhys took one. He hated beets.

I shook my head. I wasn't up for pleasantries . . . or muffin eating . . . or anything other than staring straight ahead like a lobotomy victim.

The lake looked completely different in the rising sun, glittering and serene, like nothing bad had ever happened here.

"These are good," Rhys said through clenched teeth.

"Really?" She took in a shallow breath. "No one ever likes my muffins."

Rhys nodded as he made quick eye contact with me, raised an eyebrow, and swallowed.

They continued to chat while Beth rowed us across the lake, but my mind was elsewhere, drawn to that tiny slice of twilight between nightmare and dreams. What *happened* last night?

As we neared the dam on the north end of the lake, Beth set down the oar in the bottom of the boat and then leapt onto the low stone wall, maneuvering the canoe so we could step out easily.

"Where are you taking us?" I asked.

"I thought you might want to visit your family . . . their resting spot, I mean," Beth said as she tied the boat to a cleat. "After that, we'll head to the fields for the social. No one will even know we were gone."

We set out past the meeting house to a small stretch of woods on the western edge of the corn.

When we came to a clearing cluttered with gravestones, I froze.

Hanging by her ankles from a battered oak was the dead girl.

Beth and Rhys stepped around me.

"The oldest stones date back to 1541," Beth explained as they strolled around the cemetery. "Alonso's wife is buried here."

"His *wife?*" Rhys asked in disgust. He hated cheaters.

"She died almost immediately after arriving at Quivira, while giving birth to their fifth child."

"That's terrible." My brother shook his head. "So did Coronado have a wife, too?"

"No. He was a widower, like Katia. They each had four children from previous marriages. But Marie was Katia's only daughter."

I took a deep breath and stepped toward the dead girl. The girl Katia said I was tied to. I could almost feel her grip around my ankle.

The worn stone plaque beneath her body had nearly been swallowed up by ivy. I pulled it away. MARIE ANNE LARKIN. BORN APRIL 13TH, 1524. TAKEN FROM US ON JUNE 21ST, 1541.

I felt the past slipping over my throat like a noose, pulling me down into the depths.

She moves through the corn, all shadow and light—the rustling of her skirts, the flush of her cheeks, the patter of her heart—the heavy scent of secrets all around her.

As she reaches a clearing, a figure appears in the distance, beneath a tree full of black birds. "Coronado," she says, a smile engulfing her face.

They embrace under the safety of the flowing branches.

His long dark hair mingles with her golden tresses—his deep olive skin pressing up against her alabaster.

"Did you get the information I asked for?" he whispers in her ear.

"Do you love me?" She runs her fingers through his hair.

He pulls away from her to study her face. "More than life itself."

She looks down at the ground, almost as if she's ashamed. "You won't hurt her?"

Coronado lifts her chin, tenderly. "No, but Alonso bears my mark. He must pay for his betrayal."

"And then you'll come for me?"

"Marie." He strokes her cheek. "Yes, mi amor."

"The meeting is set. Midnight at Silk Pond."

He starts to pull away, when Marie grasps his hand. "I'm going to keep trying," she says with a desperate edge to her voice. "If the Great Spirit makes me immortal, we can be together forever."

"If it's meant to be, it will be."

"Don't give up on me."

"Until tonight . . ." He slips his fingers down the length of the black silk ribbon fashioned around her throat.

As she watches Coronado walk away, she presses the ribbon against her lips, her eyes welling up with tears.

"Ashlyn?" Beth placed her hand on my shoulder, jarring me back to the present.

"It's her . . . it's Katia's daughter . . . Marie." I gazed up at her body, seeing the dead girl in a whole new light.

A drop of blood fell from the cut on Marie's hand, splashing onto the stone. Beth flinched.

"Did you see that?" I whispered.

Beth just smiled back at me with that blank expression.

"What on earth do you mean?" she asked as she flitted off to my brother's side.

When I looked back at Marie, she was gone.

"This can't be right," Rhys said, startling me.

I turned to see him standing on the outer rim of the cemetery, his eyes fixed on the ground. "'Nina Lee Larkin, born February 6th, 1977.' The plaque next to hers is 'Thomas Mendoza, born April 25th, 1978.' Our dad," he whispered.

"The stones on the outer perimeter aren't graves," Beth explained as she plucked a leaf from a nearby tree, tracing the veins running through it. "They're commemorative plaques to honor the Larkin girls and Mendoza boys who've walked the corn. I've heard your father was very nice . . . and handsome." She looked up at my brother; I swear I saw her blush. "No one knew that Nina and Thomas were in love," she said as she glanced back at me. "They thought Nina would choose Spencer at the wreathing ceremony. It was a surprise to everyone, especially Spencer."

The thought of my mother choosing Spencer completely creeped me out. "Why did they think she'd choose him?" I brushed the dirt from my knees and joined them.

"Spencer had been sweet on her forever," Beth said as she hopped over a stone and then smoothed down her dress. "Though the Larkin girl is supposed to choose her mate based on scent, there's a fair amount of arranging that went on between the parents. But your mother defied them all and chose love."

"Thank God for that," I said under my breath.

"Oh, there was plenty of gossip." Beth lowered her voice. "People wondered if Nina found out Spencer had been sneaking around with a Mixed, because nine months later, Teresa gave birth to Dane."

"Where do you think he's been all this time?" Rhys asked as he stared down at our father's plaque.

Beth placed her hand on my brother's shoulder. "Maybe he's been with Aiyana in New Spain . . . waiting for Nina."

When Beth took her hand away, my brother glanced at his shoulder, the tiniest smile lighting his face. "Let's say, for argument's sake, that Thomas never made it out of the corn. What then? Who would Alonso's vessel be?"

"Oh, I love games." Beth rubbed her palms together. "I suppose since Ash stood in for your mother at the wreathing ceremony, the answer would be Brennon."

"And he'd just willingly do that?" I asked as I moved closer, being careful not to step on any headstones.

"It's tradition," Beth chirped. "An honor." A breeze moved through the trees and Beth turned to face it, closing her eyes as it moved her fine hair around her face.

Leaning over, I traced my mother's name on the plaque. "Why does the Larkin girl get to choose Alonso's vessel?"

"The female holds all the power in the Larkin bloodline, but true love between Katia's chosen vessel and the Mendoza boy would create the strongest bond."

I then traced my father's name. I thought if the choice had

been mine—if the ceremony were real—I would've chosen Dane. I reached up to touch the black silk ribbon in my hair. "Why can't a Larkin be with a Mixed?"

"They say Katia and Coronado's hatred for each other runs in the blood. And just in case we forget, the Mixed are marked when they come of age." She showed us the brand on her inner arm, a c identical to the one Henry had. c for Coronado.

I stood and studied her mark. "Dane's brand looks different—almost like wings or something. Why?"

"Spencer branded him at birth instead of waiting for him to come of age. As he grew, the brand became distorted."

"How could someone brand a *newborn*? That's barbaric."

Beth shrugged, but I could tell it bothered her by the way she traced her own brand with her thumb. "The only Mixed with Larkin blood is Henry. And when he got caught sneaking around with his half cousin Anna Larkin, there was a lot of debate about whether to let him live or not, but the community finally compromised."

"What kind of compromise?" I asked, looking up at her sharply.

"Spencer took care of it so his line couldn't continue."

"What do you mean, *took care of it*?" Rhys asked. Then his eyes widened. "You don't mean they *castrated* him. As in snip, snip?"

"More like chop, chop," Beth said with that odd lilt.

I kept picturing Henry's anguished expression, the way he

shifted his weight when he talked about the punishment Dane would face if the two of us were caught together.

"The ritual," I said as I took in the sea of plaques before me. "Why would anyone just hand over their sons and daughters like that?"

"It's an honor," Beth replied.

"You keep saying that." My eyes locked on hers. "But what if Coronado murdered them, along with all the other Larkins who disappeared?"

She looked around cautiously, like the dead might be listening in. "When Katia becomes one with her vessel, when Alonso's returned to her, she's going to make everyone immortal." She forced a smile. "We're all going to live forever."

"Do you honestly believe that?" Rhys asked.

"There will be a path to lead us from darkness," she whispered, staring out over the corn.

22

MOUTHFUL OF DIAMONDS

WHEN WE REACHED the fields, Beth skipped ahead to greet people, giving hugs whether they wanted them or not.

"Good morning," a pregnant woman in a long dress and a sunbonnet said as she passed.

"Morning," I called after her a little too late.

Rhys lifted his brows.

"What? We need to try and fit in."

People walked by carrying wooden casks of homemade ice cream. A couple of kids whipped past us, running down the hill, trailing kites behind them—not the cheap Mylar kind with pictures of Spider-Man—*real* kites with long ribboned tails that spiraled in the breeze.

"It looks like a Norman Rockwell painting down there," I said.

"Oh, totally." Rhys crossed his arms. "Other than the fact

it's a creepy cult that worships our five-hundred-year-old ancestor who's supposedly hell-bent on wearing Mom's body like a skin suit, it's *exactly* like a Norman Rockwell painting."

"Not here," I said as I headed down the hill, feeling the dandelions brush my ankles.

"Ash, I said I'd give you three days, but what does this have to do with the dead girl?" Rhys followed close behind. "You seriously want to hang out with these people and play games—pretend like none of this is really happening? Which Kool-Aid have you been drinking because I—"

"I have a plan," I interrupted him before he had a complete meltdown.

"Okay." He took in a deep breath. "Let's hear it."

"Dane." I glanced up toward Beth on top of the hill. She was looking for us. "He can take me into the . . . well, he can help me."

"How?"

My eyes veered toward the corn. "I can't say."

"I see." Rhys tightened his jaw.

"I just need to talk to him—get him alone without drawing suspicion," I said as I waved at Beth, hoping she'd hurry up.

"You could get him neutered if they suspect an inappropriate relationship. But that's beside the point, because you can't trust him. We can't trust anybody."

"You can trust *me*." It killed me to say it, considering I'd been lying to him from the moment we arrived.

He studied me, his moss-green eyes reminding me of our mother. Dragging his hand through his hair, he let out a heavy sigh. "Fine. I'll do what I can to help."

"Thank you," I said as I watched Beth skip back to us, hoping she could be enough of a distraction to keep my brother off my case for a few more days.

The Kansas sun beat down on the fields, conjuring up a thick veil of perspiration, lemonade, and bergamot.

I felt a twinge of nervous energy as I searched the crowd for Dane.

As we walked through the gathering, Beth pointed out the different areas of the field that were appropriated for various games and competitions—archery, some kind of horseshoe game, barrel races, and an activity involving bacon grease, burlap sacks, and watermelons that I didn't even want to contemplate.

The Mendozas, Grimsbys, and Hanrattys had their own sections of the field, marked by elaborate canvas tents anchored by flagpoles, each bearing a family crest.

I was shocked to see Henry perched on the edge of the field with the flag from the Larkin lodge—the circle with a golden crescent moon and a star. He waved. For the briefest of moments, he almost looked like he wasn't a total serial killer, but then he ruined it by trying to smile.

"Oh my stars," Beth trilled as she looked across the field toward the Mendoza camp. "Here he comes."

The thought of seeing him again made my insides feel all

feathery. As much as I tried to stay indifferent, I could feel a smile slipping across my lips.

The breeze blew in my favor, carrying the distinct scent of oak and honey. The scent wrapped around my senses like a soft blanket, but it wasn't the scent I craved.

I turned to see Brennon striding toward us, shoulders broad, a straw bowler covering his neatly combed blond hair.

"Any word on when our mother might arrive?" my brother asked Brennon, giving me a moment to hide my disappointment.

"Soon." He gave Rhys a firm pat on the back. "But you're safe here. I wouldn't let anything happen to you or your sister."

"Wow. I feel so much better," Rhys said under his breath before stepping out of the way.

"I brought something for you." Brennon presented me with a small sprig of flowers—delicate white petals tinged with the softest pink.

I smiled. "Apple blossom."

"May I put it in your hair?" he asked as his eyes darted toward his parents, who were watching our every move from the other side of the field.

"Sure . . . ?" I looked to Rhys and Beth for some help, but they were already lost in their own world, a conversation about bugs, or the weather, or something.

This morning I'd braided a piece of hair from each side of my head and connected them together in the back with the black silk ribbon. Brennon walked behind me, tentatively burrowing the woody stem in the ribbon.

"Lovely," he said.

Dane walked by, and I swore I could feel his gaze on the nape of my neck.

I watched him as he made his way to the backfield. I couldn't help but follow.

Brennon spoke to me as we walked across the field. I knew this because his mouth was moving, but I had no idea what he was saying. All of me focused on getting to Dane. It wasn't just the attraction, though that didn't hurt. I needed answers. I needed him to take me into the corn and I wasn't going to take no for an answer.

23

SHINNY

THE GRIMSBYS AND the Mendozas were playing a game that looked a little like lacrosse but wilder. They were basically running around a giant field and whacking one another with four-foot-long sticks. The girls stood on the sidelines, oohing and aahing every time some poor guy took a hit.

Among the Mendozas, I recognized Tommy from the party last night. His black eye had faded to light purple.

I scanned the crowd and a tingling sensation spread over me the moment my eyes grazed Dane's face.

"What are they playing?" I asked, trying to figure out the strategy.

"Shinny," Beth said as she and Rhys joined us. "You use the sticks to move the beanbag ball around to score points. They play it on the ice in winter, too."

"Why aren't any girls playing?"

"It's too rough," Brennon explained. "The girls play a similar game, with less blood; it's called double ball."

"I bet they do," I said as the girls waved at my brother and Brennon.

Rhys stared up at the sky awkwardly. Good to see some things would never change.

The ball came hurtling our way. Instead of ducking like a normal person I reached out and palmed it. It stung, but I forced a pleasant smile.

"What do you think you're doing?" Rhys hissed as I stepped forward.

"I told you. I need to talk to him." I squared my shoulders as I watched Dane cross the field toward us.

"Okay, but not like this," Rhys said as he tugged at my elbow, but I wouldn't budge. I couldn't take my eyes off Dane. Sweat and dirt never looked so good.

As Dane got closer, I noticed the dark glint in his eyes. "Are you not getting enough attention or something?"

It felt like I'd just walked right into his fist, punching my own lights out. I was such an idiot. Here I'd hoped he'd go back to being the boy I'd met at the junkyard or, better yet, the boy from my dream last night.

This Dane was acting like a complete prick.

Lauren breezed past me onto the field, standing next to Dane, a smug look about her flawless face. "Where are your *clothes*?"

"What are you talking about?" I glanced down at the peas-
ant dress I'd pulled from my mother's closet. I thought it was
a little small, so I wore my black shorts underneath.

She raised an eyebrow. "You're wearing an undergarment."

"Right," I murmured, suddenly feeling naked.

"I think it's stylish." Beth stepped next to me.

"Look," Lauren snickered. "Batty Beth has two whole
friends now."

"Don't call her that," Rhys said in a low tone as he glared
at Lauren.

I was stunned to hear him speak up like that; usually he
only mouthed off to me. Lauren turned her attention on my
brother and I stepped in front of her. "What's your problem?
Am I missing something here?"

"As if she doesn't know." Lauren's bright hazel eyes burned
into me. "You don't scare me, Ash Larkin."

"Okaaay?" I laughed uncomfortably. "I wasn't trying to—"

"Ash, don't bother," Beth whispered. "It's not worth it."

"It's about your nocturnal activities," Dane said, a tiny
smile curling the corner of his mouth.

Whispers erupted behind me. I turned and felt the enemy
flush invade my cheeks. I didn't realize we had an audience for
this. It wasn't just kids. People of all ages pressed in around us
like they didn't want to miss a single word.

Did Dane know what happened to me last night—that I'd
dreamed about kissing him? Did they all know?

Dane rested his shinny stick on his shoulder. "This morning, Lauren woke up with a corn-husk doll lying next to her pillow."

"And?" I raised my eyebrows.

"It's the mark of death." Lauren flicked her wrist, and a delicate light blue fan spread out in her hand. "I know you did it," she said as she fanned herself.

"Please." I burst out laughing. "I don't know how to make a corn doll. I can't even make a wreath!"

There was a part of me that wondered if I could have done it in my sleep. Anything was possible.

"You girls can work this out later. Now, if you don't mind, we have a game to finish," Dane said as he turned his back on me to join the other players waiting on the field.

In a burst of frustration, I threw the shinny ball at the back of his head; Lauren caught it. As she handed the ball to Dane, I noticed her arm brush against his chest. I wanted to rip it from her body.

"What do you want?" Dane turned with an exasperated sigh.

"I want to play," I blurted.

He looked at me, incredulously. "*You* want to play shinny?"

"Sure. Why not? You and Lauren against me and my brother."

"What?" Rhys's eyes went wide.

Dane grinned. "First team to score three goals wins," he said before he made his way up the field.

I motioned for Rhys to join me.

"No, no, no." He waved me off as he backed away.

"Come on." I pulled him forward. "It'll be fun."

"I don't play sports. Remember?"

God, how could I forget? My mom made him join my soc-cer team in first grade. Got his first bloody nose and started puking all over the place, setting off a chain reaction of epic proportions. Took them a week to clean up all the regurgi-tated Cheerios and orange slices from the field.

"Look, nobody here knows about that," I said. "Clean slate. You don't even have to do anything remotely athletic—just keep Lauren occupied while I talk to Dane." I pushed him to-ward her.

As I jogged ahead to catch up to Dane, a bunch of Grimsbys passed, looking like they'd just been in a brawl. "Good luck," a tall, gangly boy I recognized from the party last night grunted as he shook bits of matted grass and dirt from his hair.

"They're going to get slaughtered out there," his friend said as he wiped the blood from his ear on his sleeve.

What did I get us into? I looked down the field to see Rhys trying to talk to Lauren, and Lauren pointedly ignoring him. He was going to kill me for this.

I found Dane at the goal line, making sure the markers were in place—iron poles with loops at the top to hold the lanterns.

"Are these the same things they use to mark the perimeter of the corn at night?" I gave one of them a good shake, and accidentally pulled it out.

"Do you mind telling me what this is all about?" he asked as he took the iron stand away from me.

His change in tone took me by surprise. Maybe all of that was just an act back there. "I need you to take me into the corn."

"Why?"

I wanted to tell him about Marie, but I didn't know if I could trust him with an honest answer. "I just do."

"First"—he stabbed the pole back into the ground with such force, it made me flinch—"you need to tell me how you walked into the corn by yourself last night." His eyes settled on me—they were so full of light and life—I still couldn't tell exactly what color they were.

"I . . . I don't know. It must be a conduit thing. I don't have any control when the memories come over me."

"Dane?" Lauren hollered from midfield. Rhys stood next to her awkwardly, like he didn't know what to do with his limbs.

Dane and I joined them.

"Angus here will officiate," Tommy announced as he pulled some poor kid off the sidelines. "He's a Hanratty—pretty neutral. Right, Angus?"

Tommy pounded his hand down on Angus's shoulder and I could see his Adam's apple bob up and down.

"Are we all in agreement?" Tommy asked.

"Agreed," Lauren and Dane answered in unison.

Rhys and I just nodded.

Dane started to take his shirt off. My voice rose about six

octaves. "No need . . . there's . . . we . . . I know . . . we don't need to . . ."

Rhys saved me. "We don't need to do shirts and skins—I doubt we'll get one another confused. Unless of course, you just want to show us your abs."

"Fine." A smile eased across Dane's lips. "But aren't you forgetting something?" His eyes flickered to my waist and all I could think of was his thumb dragging across the top of my hip bone. A flash of heat rushed to my cheeks. *Get a hold of yourself, Ash.*

"You might need a stick," Dane said.

"Right." I nodded like one of those idiot bobbleheads.

As Dane led me to an old metal washtub at the end of the field full of shinny sticks, he leaned in. "I'll make a wager. You win, I'll take you."

"And if we lose?" I glanced up at him.

"You're on your own," he said as he strode away.

I picked through the pile of sticks, looking for one with a decent grip. Each one had a natural Y shape at one end to balance the ball. I found a solid piece of oak. "Rhys," I called out as I tossed it to him. He didn't even bother trying to catch it. It dropped to the ground with a hollow *thunk.*

"I can't believe I'm doing this for you." He bent over to pick it up like an old man.

"All you have to do is stay on Lauren. I'll take care of the rest." I studied her as she tied her long skirt into a knot above her knees. "I bet she runs like a three-year-old."

161

"No, Ash, *I* run like a three-year-old."

I picked up another stick and whipped it through the air, pleased by the wicked sound it made. Dane took notice. Obviously, he'd never seen me play lacrosse or he would've thought twice about the wager.

"Let's kick some ass," I said to Rhys as we took the field with Dane and Lauren.

The whole community had left the other games and gathered for the spectacle. There were ladies twirling old-fashioned parasols to shield themselves from the sun and boys with hand-me-down trousers being held up by suspenders. Beth alternated between biting her nails and cheering. I spotted Brennon at the back of the crowd, talking quietly to Spencer, who never took his eyes off us. It put me on edge.

Dane and I faced off. The ref threw the ball high into the air; I waited for Dane to snag it, then knocked it away from him and ran it down the field. It was harder than lacrosse— harder to balance the flimsy beanbag on the end of the stick. But I got the feel for it quickly, and muscle memory kicked in.

I glanced back to see Dane standing on the field, looking oddly amused, while Lauren came gunning for me. For a second, I thought I'd grossly underestimated her, but thankfully, I was faster. I slammed the ball between the two markers at the end of the field and the crowd broke into startled cheers.

I turned to Dane, ready to bask in the glow of his newfound respect, but he was chatting up some girl on the sidelines. I wanted to knock that smile off his face.

We met up midfield for another face-off—me against Lauren this time. I won the ball, racing it down the field as Lauren slammed her stick onto mine, trying to get me to drop it. Frustrated that she couldn't shake me, she hurtled her stick between my feet. I fell hard, skidding on my knees.

The ref opened his mouth to call a foul, but closed it when Tommy clasped his hand on his shoulder.

"You're finished," Lauren spat as she swooped up the ball, passing it to Dane.

My knee was a bloodied mess. I ripped a strip of cloth from the hem of my so-called dress and tied it around my knee.

The community exploded as Dane scored a goal. One to one.

I tried to play it off, but I *needed* Dane to take me into the corn. Marie was trying to tell me something . . . *show* me something. I had to win this.

"Are you hurt?" Rhys panted, purposefully not looking down.

"Just a scratch," I said as I got to my feet.

"Are you sure you know what you're doing?"

"No." I laughed.

If nothing else, it felt good to let out some aggression. There were so many emotions rattling around inside of me that were begging for release.

Lauren and I faced off again. Angus threw the ball into the air and dove away from the hot zone. I'd just taken the ball when I felt Lauren's stick come down hard on my shoulder, which made a sickening pop. The pain made me scream—my arm had come out of the socket. But I couldn't give in. I gritted my teeth and managed to keep control of the ball with my one good arm. Halfway down the field, I felt Dane on my heels. Rhys advanced to my right; I used all of my strength to hurl the ball in his direction. I missed the mark, but my shoulder popped back into place.

I slowed to catch my breath, thinking Dane would scoop up the ball and rush it to the other end of the field, but he flew right past it. Lauren waited for Rhys at the end zone, Dane coming up fast behind him. They were lining him up and he didn't even have the ball.

"Watch it!" I called out to Rhys. He was giving me a thumbs-up when they body-checked him from both sides. As he collapsed to the ground, I looked to Angus to do something, but he just stared down at the grass.

The crowd seemed to take in a collective gasp, everyone except for Beth, who jumped up and down, clapping her hands manically like she was trying to save a dying pixie. "Get up, Rhys! You can do it."

Lauren scooped up the ball and took a leisurely jog down the field for yet another goal.

By the time I got to Rhys, he was dazed, but on his feet. His bottom lip was split wide open. I started having flashbacks of the infamous soccer game/puke festival of 2004. I ripped the makeshift bandage off my knee and held it to his lip.

"What are you doing? What's wrong?" Rhys asked.

"It's nothing really. Just a tiny cut. Can I get some water over here?" I called out, hoping he could hold off on vomiting for a couple of seconds.

Tommy grinned as he came onto the field carrying a jug of water. "Ready to call it quits?"

I snatched the jug from Tommy and pulled the rag away to find Rhys's lip had already surged shut. "What the hell," I said under my breath.

"What?" Rhys's eyes went wide. "Is it that bad? Did I lose a tooth?"

"No." I exhaled, trying to keep the shock off my face. "It's fine. Better than fine. It doesn't seem to be bleeding anymore."

"But I can still taste the blood in my mouth." He started to gag.

"Oh God, okay, just swish your mouth out and spit."

Rhys took a gulp of water and swished it around, but then froze. He looked like a very confused blowfish. I put my hand over my mouth to stifle a smile. Rhys thought spitting in public was the grossest thing in the world.

"Just spit it out, you moron." Tommy pounded him on the back and Rhys turned his head, spraying it all over Tommy's face.

I burst out laughing and then Rhys did, too.

"Classic." I grinned as I handed Tommy the jug and slung my arm around my brother's shoulder as we walked back to center field.

Rhys and Lauren took the next face-off.

"You and your girl play dirty," I said to Dane.

"Whining already?" Dane smiled mischievously. "This is why we don't usually let girls play."

"Any tips?" Rhys glanced back at me, shifting his weight nervously between the balls of his feet.

"Just try to get the ball," I said.

"Really? That's your advice?"

I shrugged.

By some miracle Rhys managed to catch the ball on the end of his stick, and we all took off after him.

I came up quick behind Lauren and rammed into the back of her knees, sending her crashing to the ground. Rhys barely managed to slip past Dane to make the goal. We were tied.

Rhys turned to me, huffing in air. "I scored a goal. Ash, did you see that? I scored a goal!"

I held my hand up for a high five, but he missed.

"This is it," I said as we made our way back to center field for the final point.

Dane and I faced each other, both of us drenched in sweat.

He braced his hands against his knees, looking up at me through his dark lashes. "Take that flower out of your hair," he whispered.

My mind went completely blank. The world seemed to disintegrate around us. His smile, his mouth, that sexy dimple, consumed me.

Angus threw the ball into the air but neither one of us

moved. The ball dropped to the ground between us with a dull thud.

I wanted to leave the flower in, just to spite him, but something in his eyes made me take it out of my hair.

As the flower dropped to the ground, I scooped up the ball, running as hard as I could. Dane stuck close by my side. He darted his stick toward the ball, but it was clearly a half-hearted attempt.

"Go left," Dane yelled.

I lunged to the right, and he laughed as he dove after me, grabbing nothing but air. As he tumbled to the ground, I looked back at him in confusion. "Take the shot," he urged.

I slammed the ball across the line and everyone screamed.

Dane got to his feet, then turned to walk away.

"Hey!" I scurried to catch up to him. "You gave me that shot . . . why?"

I grabbed his arm, feeling his raised scar beneath my fingertips. I swore I could still feel the heat from the branding iron.

I felt myself slipping into his skin, disappearing into the mass of scar tissue and pain, until there was nothing left of me.

24

QUAKE

ON THE EVE *of the summer solstice, I kneel in the sacred circle, at the edge of the chasm, a wide crack in the earth. As I peer down into the darkness, I whisper to my lover's bones. "I believe the vessel is finally upon us. She looks the part, and has a fiery spirit. She chose well in the wreathing ceremony—a Mendoza of good stock—warm eyes. Tomorrow, we may be reunited at last—"*

A gust of wind rushes from the depths, rustling the corn. I turn to see Coronado, accompanied by an army of men in full black armor and a number of native warriors trailing behind them.

Venom rises in my bloodstream as I stand to greet him.

He holds up a fist, commanding his men to a halt.

"Katia," he calls with a tense smile. "Over three hundred years and you're still ravishing as ever."

I walk to the perimeter of the sacred circle. "Have you finally come to pay your respects, to face the death and destruction you've brought upon my family?" I motion toward the chasm, but he refuses to look.

"What's done is done, Katia." Coronado takes a careful step forward. "No more blood needs to be shed. Let us make amends."

"The time for amends has long passed," I reply through my teeth. "What brings you here?"

Coronado drums his fingers against his breastplate, a rattlesnake waiting to strike. "You think you've found your vessel."

I feel my carefully arranged face crumble. How could he know that? I've been so cautious. Unless someone among my people has betrayed me.

Coronado raises his chin. "Doing this will start a war you'll never win. The Dark Spirit will devour your soul, leave you ravaged, alone . . . irredeemable."

"How touching." I pace the edge of the circle, aching to charge. "Are you so concerned for me . . . for my soul?"

"For my own." I catch a real glimmer of fear in his eyes. With a flick of his finger, his men bring forth a girl who's bound and gagged. My breath halts in my chest. He's found her—the Larkin girl who is to walk the corn for the ritual tomorrow.

Coronado pulls the sword from his sheath and steps behind her, pressing her trembling body against him.

She looks at me pleadingly, letting out a stifled sob.

Never taking his eyes off mine, Coronado eases his blade across her throat as if he's pulling back the bow of the most beautiful instrument.

She crumbles to the ground in front of him, her blood painting the stalks.

Coronado steps over her, wiping the blood from his blade on his trousers. "Let this be a lesson. Do not force me to kill them all."

"Ashlyn," someone whispered.

I blinked hard and found myself grasping Dane's arm—the entire community gathered around us.

"She's a conduit, all right," someone said behind me.

"Poor girl. It's a miracle she's lasted this long."

"She's as crazy as a bedbug."

Rhys ran to my side, helping me to my feet, but the damage had been done. I saw it on Dane's face. I saw it on everyone's faces.

I opened my mouth, struggling to come up with some kind of coherent excuse, when the smell of burning copper flared in my nostrils. Tommy staggered toward us and dropped to his knees, blood streaming from every orifice.

"Just like Betsy Grimsby," Rhys whispered.

Instead of rushing to Tommy's aid like they did with Betsy in the ballroom, the people of Quivira ran away, screaming, as if a bomb had been detonated.

"Hey," I yelled. "He needs help!" But no one stopped.

Beth was trying to get to us, but the Grimsbys held her back. Dane was caught in the thick of it, helping an old man to his feet so he wouldn't get trampled to death.

I kneeled beside Tommy and shook him, but he didn't

respond. I'd never seen anything like it. I pushed him onto his back and started chest compressions.

"Ash, don't," Rhys pleaded with me. "You shouldn't touch him."

Ignoring him, I kept pumping. When I reached thirty, I tilted his head back and pinched his nose, but when I leaned over to blow, someone gripped me hard underneath my arms and yanked me away.

"He's already dead," Dane said as he released me.

"Ash . . ." My brother looked down at his feet, at Tommy's blood inching toward him. His head lolled to the side right before his knees gave out from under him.

"Not now," I groaned as I rushed over to him, slapping my brother's cheeks, but he was out cold. I tried to move him away from Tommy's body . . . from the blood, but he was dead weight.

Dane saw that I was struggling and helped me carry Rhys to the dandelion slope that led to the dam.

When I looked up to thank him, I noticed him staring down at my knee. My *healed* knee. I quickly covered it with the shredded hem of my dress. I didn't know how to even begin explaining that.

Rhys's eyes finally opened, his pupils looked like tiny drops of ink in a bed of moss. "Crow," he whispered.

I looked up to see a dozen or so black birds circling above.

When I turned back to Dane, he was already gone, rushing to the sidelines to help calm the agitated crowd.

The black silk ribbon slipped from my hair and took flight, curling onto the field.

I knew it was crazy, but I had an inexplicable urge to run after it. I had to dig my fingers into the earth to stop myself.

"Friends," Spencer called out as he marched onto the field, standing next to Tommy's body. He motioned for everyone to come closer. The people of Quivira moved in cautiously.

After helping Rhys to his feet, we stood at the back of the gathering. I couldn't stop from peeking through the crowd at Tommy's body. His skin had a strange bluish tint, his eyes, sunken, his plump face, now gaunt—like every bit of blood had been wrung from his body.

"We lost Tommy Mendoza today." Spencer tilted his head thoughtfully, the perfect balance of reverence and authority. He reminded me of a politician—perfect hair, tan skin, easy smile, but there was something lurking underneath. Something rotting and foul—just like his scent.

"It's Coronado's black magic," a man with beady eyes and a scraggly blond beard called out.

"You saw what he did to Tommy," a frazzled woman cried. "Same thing happened to Betsy. His evil's spreading. He's picking us off one by one."

"Katia's not here to defend us!" A stocky man took off his hat, exposing his sunburned face. "What if her spell is weakening?"

"Enough," Spencer yelled as he tossed a kerosene lantern onto Tommy's body. A deep *whoosh* sent flames shooting toward the sky; the smell of burning hair and flesh hung heavy in the humid air.

The crowd grew deathly still.

"Have you lost sight? Lost faith?" Spencer tried to regain his composure as he paced around the burning body. "We're on the cusp of eternal life, of everything our ancestors hoped for. The corn will hold; it *will* protect us. Katia and the vessels are safe. Nina and Thomas have given us a great gift. This isn't a time for fear, but a time to rejoice." Spencer seemed to make eye contact with every single person in the crowd, and they hung on his every word. "Go back to your lodge. Say a prayer. Be with your loved ones. Tomorrow evening we will reconvene on the eastern shore for the ceremonial bonfire where we will camp for the night." He bowed his head. "And so it shall be . . ."

As the community answered his call, I stared at Tommy's scorched body—at the streams of blood soaking into the field, stretching toward us like gnarled fingers.

25

HONEY TRAP

I SAT IN THE screened-in loft of the Larkin lodge, listening to the wind moving through the cornstalks, rustling the leaves like rasping breath.

I glanced down at Beth and Rhys, who were lying on cushions on the floor, their hands nearly touching, which brought an unexpected smile to my face. A tiny ray of sunshine at the end of a day full of death.

Suddenly, the breeze found me, making the candles flicker. I brought my hands to my throat, searching for the comfort of the black silk ribbon, but it was gone.

A soft brushing sound broke through the whisper of the corn—like the distant flutter of a moth's wings.

I followed the sound down the ladder, through the living area to the front door. I cracked it open. The black silk ribbon blew in; it had been tied to the doorknob. I freed the silk and wrapped it around my wrist, tucking the ends directly under my pulse point. It felt warm, like someone had been holding it tightly. I knew that scent by heart. Strawberries, earth, musk, and sandalwood.

Dane.

Stepping outside, I closed the door behind me and stood at the foot of the walkway, staring out into the darkness. He didn't make a sound, but I knew he was there.

"Thank you," I called into the void, not really expecting an answer.

"You're welcome."

A smile pulled at the corner of my mouth. Stepping off the cobblestones and onto the grass, I crept toward the sound of his voice. The grass was cool and damp beneath my bare feet. I stumbled into some kind of ditch, tripping over what felt like tree roots.

"Oh God." I careened forward, and Dane caught my waist. "It's so dark out here," I said as I righted myself, but I still couldn't see his face.

"You'll get used to it," he murmured.

I liked the way he said it, like maybe he was getting used to me, too. But I knew that kind of thinking was dangerous. Nothing more than a honey trap.

"I could light a fire," he said.

I squinted in his direction, trying to make out his features. "You just go around making fires in people's yards?"

"Well, you're standing in the fire pit."

My face warmed. "Of course I am." I backed out of the pit to stand on the grass again. "Do you use a flint?"

"I can, but that's a little old-fashioned, don't you think? I make my own matches. Trade them for things." As he lit a match, I caught a glimpse of him. Firelight was kind to just about everyone, but what it did to Dane's face was ... *criminal.* His skin took on a gorgeous tawny hue, and his eyes became even more luminous and penetrating, twin flames reflecting in their dark pupils.

As I lowered myself onto the ground near the fire pit, he surprised me by settling next to me, his arm resting only a few inches from mine. I felt raw energy ping between his body and mine; I had to will my arm not to inch closer.

I stole a glance at his face. "Aren't you worried we'll be seen together?"

"Henry's drunk. Your brother and Beth are asleep. We're alone." He looked at me and I felt so light, like I could float away.

I forced myself to sit up straight ... stay grounded. "How did you know Beth was here?"

He smiled. "I've never seen her take to anyone the way she's taken to you and your brother. It's nice. She's been on her own for so long."

"Please tell me you know what the word *hump* means."

Dane cringed a little. "Yeah, some of the kids kind of messed with her after she fell."

"That's terrible."

Dane shrugged, but I could tell that it bothered him, too.

"What happened to her?"

"Head injury. She'd been acting strange before the fall, running around telling all kinds of crazy stories."

"Like what?" I couldn't help thinking about the scar running across her skull . . . that must've been one hell of a fall.

"It doesn't matter." His jaw tensed. "She's better now. She lost a little bit up here, but she always had more brains than everyone else to begin with, so I guess it evened out."

A long silence stretched out between us.

"Strange how I found your ribbon in my pocket," Dane said wryly.

I raised an eyebrow. "Well, *I* didn't put it there."

He looked at me skeptically, then readjusted one of the logs. The light caressed his arm, showing off the long muscles beneath the scar on his inner wrist. That inexplicable urge to touch him came over me again.

I wanted to play it closer to the vest, but I couldn't help myself. "It's kind of hard to imagine you with a girl like Lauren."

"You can't choose your family."

"I guess that's one way to put it," I said under my breath.

He gave me a puzzled look.

"I'm sorry, I shouldn't have said anything." I looked out over the lake. "It's just, incest is frowned upon where I come from."

"Wait, you think—no." He laughed. "Lauren's my half sister. We share a father. That's it. We're not *together*."

"Oh! I mean, oh?"

"So, you've been *imagining* me," he said with a smile.

I wanted to ask him why he was suddenly being so nice to me. Why now, after he'd acted like such a jerk? But I didn't want to ruin it.

His gaze lingered. "Do you have someone waiting for you back home?"

"What, like a boyfriend? No," I answered, trying to kill the blush threatening to take over my cheeks.

"Well, you're not entirely without attachments, Ashlyn." The way he said my name was so odd, so formal. "Do you know what the apple blossom flower symbolizes?"

"Um . . . I know it's used in the heart notes of a lot of perfumes."

"It means promise." He stared at me so intensely I had to look away. The term *bedroom eyes* must've been coined especially for Dane. "Brennon was bred for your bloodline. His parents would be thrilled if you and Brennon were intended, a direct tie to Katia and Alonso—to the vessels."

My throat went dry. "I was just standing in for my mom."

"I understand. But do you *feel* anything for him?"

I opened my mouth, trying to force some words out, but they wouldn't come.

"If you have to think about it—you don't." He looked down, trying to stifle a smile.

"Brennon's a nice guy."

"Ohhh." He clutched his heart dramatically. "That's the kiss of death, isn't it? Being the *nice guy*."

"Don't worry, *you'll* never fall into that trap."

"True."

I looked up at him, trying to decipher his meaning, but I got a little lost in his gaze.

He cleared his throat. "Today, at the field—"

"Yeah, I'm so sorry about your cousin—"

"No. Not that. What did you see when you touched my arm?"

My first instinct was to play dumb, but I was tired of pretending. He'd trusted me with his biggest secret—the least I could do was let him in on how crazy I was.

"I saw Katia and Coronado in the corn. Coronado killed a Larkin girl right in front of Katia. Threatened to kill them all."

I held my breath, waiting for him to run off screaming, but he just looked at me curiously.

He added a stray twig to the fire. "Did this start when you came to Quivira?"

"No. I've seen things my entire life . . . the dead girl . . . always hanging by her ankles and always dripping blood from the cut on the palm of her hand. But it's getting worse."

He nodded, a hint of sadness in his eyes. "I've seen conduits do incredible things when they're in their ancestors' memories—terrible things, too. And you're the first conduit born into the Larkin bloodline. Who knows what you're capable of. It's amazing you're still—"

"Sane?" I finished his sentence. "Believe me, that's debatable." I pulled my hair over one shoulder. It felt so good to talk to someone. Not just anyone . . . *Dane.*

"How have you managed it?"

I ran my hand over my collarbone, over the last tattoo. "My mother gave me protection marks to help stave off the symptoms, but I don't think they're working anymore."

"What kind of marks did she give you . . . where?"

I ran my fingers up my arms and down my legs. "You can't see them, but they cover my entire body." I swore I could feel the warmth of his gaze on my skin. "The dead girl is Katia's daughter, Marie. I see her all the time now. She looks just like me. Katia said I was tied to her, but didn't explain how."

"So, you've *spoken* to Katia?"

I took in a jittery breath. I couldn't believe he was still sitting here, talking to me calmly about all this. I got the impression Dane was accustomed to weird.

"I'm not sure if I actually talked to her or not. On the day my mother disappeared, I had a very real . . . vision . . . of Katia coming to see me. She cut the palm of my hand—but it didn't leave a mark. I thought the cut would give me a scar like my mother's, but it never came."

"Your mother's scar," Dane whispered, his brows pulling in tight.

"Right here." I ran my finger across the length of my left palm.

He traced the imaginary line with his thumb—a tingling warmth spread up my arm like wildfire.

He pulled his hand away. "Why do you want to go into the corn?"

Hope welled up inside of me. It seemed to come out of no-where. "Marie *wants* me to find her. I think she's trying to show me something. Maybe a way to save my parents. I need to see the sacred circle . . . and the chasm."

His spine stiffened. "You know about the chasm?"

"I saw it through the memories."

He tore his eyes away from me, staring out over the dark water, a haunted look on his face. "You have no idea what you're asking me to do."

I swallowed hard, thinking about what happened to Henry—and what could happen to Dane. I couldn't blame him for not wanting to get involved. "I understand," I said as I started to get up.

"Wait." He grabbed my hand. All I could think of was when he touched me at the junkyard and when I touched him today at the field and how much I wanted to feel that same touch all over me.

"Please." He tugged gently, and my body obeyed, settling next to him once again. "I just need to understand why I'd risk everything . . . for *you*."

"That's easy." I smirked, happy to lighten the mood. "You're a reckless gambler."

"*I'm* the reckless gambler?" He laughed. "You never even had a chance. I had to let you win."

His smile was so warm, so perfect, that for a tiny moment, I forgot all my problems. I wondered if anyone else obsessed over that tiny dimple on his right cheek. I picked up a small stone from the edge of the fire pit and began drawing in the dirt—I needed to distract myself.

"Interesting. You chose a rose quartz."

"Did I?" I turned it over in my hand.

"See the light pink threads? Stones have meanings, just like flowers."

I turned my attention back to the dirt so I could stop staring at him.

"What is that?" He leaned into me, his shoulder barely touching mine, as he studied my drawings.

"It's the symbol for fire ascending," I said as I erased the triangular image from the dirt. "And this is the symbol for wet earth." I etched the figure into the soft ground. "They're similar. Just inverted. So, fire points up and earth points down. Common sense, really."

"They're alchemy symbols."

I looked up at him curiously.

"I've seen Katia drawing symbols in the dirt like that. Did your mother teach you?"

I shook my head. "She never wanted me to learn. I picked up what I could," I said as erased the symbol. "My mother's a perfumer."

"What's in the perfume you wear?"

"I don't wear perfume."

He narrowed his eyes and turned away.

We sat in silence, watching the kindling burn. I could almost see the small flame take in a deep breath of air right before spreading its tendrils to engulf a piece of cedar. That's exactly how it felt to sit next to Dane. I kept waiting for the breath to come.

I'd begun drawing again in the dirt when he took the stone away from me, pressing it into the palm of his hand, making it disappear.

"That's impressive," I said as I pulled my legs to the side so I could face him. "What's your secret?"

Dane rubbed his hands together dramatically, making the stone reappear.

"Some people think not knowing is the best part. It's in our nature to want to be fooled. We put up blinders all the time. Illusion is a way to hold on to our innocence. Do you really want to give that up, Ashlyn?"

I reached in to take it back from him, but didn't want to remove my hand. Just the slight touch of my fingertips against his palm was euphoric. That seemed to be exactly where I'd lived since the moment I met him—in the palm of his hand.

"Why do you call me that? *Ashlyn*," I imitated his dramatic tone. "Everyone calls me Ash."

"Ashlyn means secret, which suits you. Besides"—he closed his hand around mine—"Ash is a nickname for a young girl. I don't see you that way."

Instead of looking away in embarrassment, I held his gaze. Something bubbled up inside of me—stronger than courage; the feeling was almost predatory. I wanted him. I couldn't stop staring at his mouth. I would've said anything, done anything, been whatever he wanted me to be at that moment just to feel his lips against mine.

As if sensing my intentions, Dane tried to pull his hand away, but the black silk ribbon had come undone, coiling itself softly around his wrist, binding him to me.

He looked down at the ribbon in surprise, but didn't flinch.

"I don't care that you're a Mixed," I whispered. "My mother told me we're not responsible for the sins of our ancestors."

"That's a nice sentiment." Dane's eyes were soft and wistaful. "But people like us don't get to choose their fate."

"What do you mean . . . people like us?"

A flash of heat lightning ripped across the sky; I could see him bury away his thoughts for safekeeping as he untangled himself from the ribbon.

"Tomorrow night's the annual bonfire." He got to his feet. "We can slip into the corn without anyone noticing."

"So, you'll help me?" A flood of relief washed over me as I stood to face him.

"I'll take you into the corn." He kicked dirt over the flames, leaving me to the dark.

I tried to focus on his retreating footsteps, but all I could hear was the corn rattling, like it was whispering my name.

26

GIRLS'
DAY

TOWERING STALKS LOOM *all around me as I follow the sound*
of crackling rope. She's close, but no matter what I do, no matter
how hard I run, she remains out of reach. A soft light beckons in
the distance, illuminating a circle within the corn. I catch a glimpse
of her pale fingertips, followed by the ends of her honeyed waves as
she's dragged inside the circle. Everything in my body screams at me
to run away, but I have to see her. I have to understand what she's
trying to tell me.

"Ashlyn."

I woke to find Beth smiling down at me, her strawberry-
blond hair glinting in the bright sun streaming through the
window.

"What time is it?" I propped myself up on my elbows, but
even that took a tremendous amount of effort. I was exhausted.

"A little past ten."

I looked around my mother's old room, at the quilt folded neatly in the corner. "Where's Rhys?"

"He's helping Henry chop wood for the bonfire tonight."

"My brother's chopping wood?" For a moment I wondered if I'd woken up in an alternate universe. I laughed. "Okay, I'm definitely dreaming." I flopped back down on the sheets.

Beth pinched me hard on the back of my arm.

"Hey!" I bolted upright, the quick movement making my head throb. "What was that for?"

"Pinch me, I'm dreaming," she said, flitting to my mother's closet to thumb through her clothes, humming that same stupid Backstreet Boys song she was singing when we first met her.

"Hey, if you've never been outside of Quivira, how do you know that song?"

"Dane taught it to me when I was recovering from my fall. It's a good one, isn't it?"

"Sure," I replied, trying to keep a straight face. He must've heard it at the junkyard.

Beth selected a few frilly dresses, draping them over her arm.

"I hope you're not suggesting I wear one of those."

She perched herself on the edge of the bed, eyes dilated, breathing shallow, like she'd just chugged a vat of coffee. "I got invited to the Mendoza lodge for Girls' Day but only if I bring you with me. Please come. *Please*. I never get invited anywhere and I re—"

"Will Dane be there?" I asked, suddenly feeling more alert.

"For *Girls'* Day?" Beth snorted. "No. But I saw him walking along the eastern perimeter early this morning. He looked . . . worried."

I leaned forward. "Like, dreamy worried or angry worried?"

Beth shrugged and moved on. "I've heard the Mendoza lodge is really beautiful and they make these little sandwiches with cucumbers, and we just sit around and chat and play parlor games . . ."

I did my best to tune her out. As tiresome as Girls' Day sounded, the thought of seeing Dane's surroundings, his room, was too much of a temptation to pass up.

"Just give me five minutes," I said as I tried to rally.

"I think you're going to need a little more than five minutes." She pulled strands of debris from my hair and laid them across my lap. Corn silk.

"Not again," I whispered, a dry ache settling in the back of my throat.

I swung my feet out of bed. They were covered in dark rich soil. I had a vague recollection of following Marie's body into the corn, but my last real memory was of Dane walking away from me last night. The remnants of his scent along with the cedar campfire hung heavy in my heart.

"Please don't tell anyone about this," I said, feeling light-headed.

"Okeydokey." Beth turned her attention back to the dresses. "Which one do you want to wear?"

"Neither." I got to my feet. Every muscle in my body ached like I'd just run a marathon.

Beth looked longingly at the dresses, fondling the hem of a lemon-yellow chiffon number.

"But *you* should wear that one," I said.

"Oh my stars! Really?" she squealed. She came toward me like she was going to give me one of her obnoxious bear hugs, but quickly changed her mind. "I'll just start the bath for you. This might take a while."

As Beth and I walked to the Mendoza lodge, along the cobblestone path that lined the lakeshore, we came across Rhys and Henry, who were carrying freshly chopped bundles of wood on their shoulders.

"You look nice." Rhys smiled warmly at Beth.

She twirled for him, laughing as her hair flew around her shoulders. It was just so Beth.

Rhys glanced at my wrinkled black shorts and T-shirt and shook his head. I gave him a sarcastic thumbs-up. Disapproval noted.

"Come on, Beth." I pulled her along.

"One more day," Rhys said as I passed, like I could forget. And only three more days until the summer solstice.

But tonight, Dane was taking me into the corn.

The Mendoza lodge was enormous—twice the size of the Larkin lodge and immaculately maintained. Everything hinted at old-world Spanish charm—from the dark wood furniture, rich carpets, and heavy red curtains in the main living rooms, to the smell of saffron and sea salt wafting from the black-and-white-marble kitchen. I could picture Dane growing up here. It suited him.

Beth pulled me toward the lavish spread at the far end of the room. On a long scrolled table sat crystal pitchers full of pastel-colored drinks muddled with strawberries and platters full of dainty sandwiches and fancy hors d'oeuvres.

"Look," Beth squealed as she picked up a triangle and inspected it. She rotated it, nibbling off wee bites like she never wanted it to end.

"Good afternoon." A middle-aged woman in a prim high-collared lace blouse looked me up and down as she passed. Thick dark hair, widow's peak, clearly a Mendoza.

"Afternoon," Beth replied, her mouth full of cucumber mush.

Though the women of Quivira smiled and exchanged pleasantries, there was an underlying tension in the room. I didn't know if this was because of the recent string of deaths or my presence, but the way they stole glances at me made me wish I'd put on one of those ridiculous dresses after all.

Beth seemed enamored with the whole thing, but I couldn't wait to get out of there.

I noticed a frail woman, wearing a faded black dress, sitting in an oversized chair in the corner of the room, staring straight ahead, rocking.

"Who's that?" I asked Beth.

She let out a sympathetic sigh. "That's Teresa. Dane's mother. She's a Mixed."

"Does she live here?" I asked, tucking in the back of my shirt.

"No, but they try to include her when they can. Spencer said it's the decent thing to do."

"Wasn't very decent of him to knock her up and not marry her," I murmured.

"Ash!" Beth looked at me with wide eyes, then laughed so hard she almost choked on her sandwich.

Suddenly, Teresa stopped rocking and leaned forward a bit, as though in anticipation. Everyone ignored her, but I was drawn to her. I'd expected Dane's mother to be formidable, instead, she was heartbreaking.

"What's wrong with her?"

"She's a conduit," Beth replied nonchalantly.

It felt like someone had bashed me in the chest with a shinny stick. I couldn't believe Dane didn't tell me his own mother was a conduit. Come to think of it, he'd never mentioned his mother at all.

I crossed the room and leaned down to greet her. Her eyes slowly focused in on my face.

"I know you," she whispered.

I could see the resemblance to Dane, the fine features, the lovely olive skin, but her eyes were vacant. She was like a long-forgotten doll.

She reached out slowly, like she was submerged in heavy water, but her fingers stopped short of making contact with my collarbone. "I see your markings. But those can't save you," she whispered, her mouth barely moving.

"What do you mean? Why aren't they working anymore? *Please*, tell me." I held her hands, noticing dozens of cuts and bruises running up her birdlike wrists and disappearing into her black chiffon sleeves. "Who did this to you?" I asked.

"Love makes you blind to the truth." She gripped me, her face suddenly filled with terror, eyes moist with tears. "Immortality is a curse."

My heart thrummed in my chest. "Did Spencer do this?"

"How nice, it's Ash Larkin," Lauren said, walking around me and prying Teresa's fingers back from my wrists. "Spreading joy wherever she goes." She tried to coax Teresa to relax in her chair. "It's all right now," Lauren said softly. "Ash was just leaving." Teresa's eyes went vacant again. Lauren stood up tall, straightening her raw silk dress.

"Someone's been hurting her," I said as I faced Lauren. I didn't care if she was Dane's half sister, she was still a total bitch.

"She hurts herself," Lauren spat. "That's what all conduits do. Destroy themselves and everyone close to them."

"Now, now . . . there's no need for that kind of talk." Brennon's mom stepped forward in my defense with that tight smile. "Ash is our honored guest."

I looked at the women stationed around the parlor. Lou's

eyes were full of pity, while the woman in the prim blouse pretended to be interested in a stain on the edge of the tablecloth.

That's when it dawned on me. It didn't matter that I was a Larkin or the daughter of the vessel; I was a conduit, and everyone expected me to turn into another Teresa. I ran my hands over my arms, over the protection marks. My mom helped me for as long as she could, but time was running out. The best I could hope for on the outside was an institution, and if I stayed here Beth would cart me around to these archaic social events while I was dead inside. Either way, I was screwed. Soon, I would go insane, like Teresa, and none of this would even matter.

"Excuse me," I said, backing away from the parlor, away from prying eyes.

As soon as I stepped into a stairwell, Dane's scent washed over me.

Desperate for an escape, I followed the scent down a flight of stairs and to the second door on the right, slipping inside and closing the door behind me.

Dane had a mahogany sleigh bed with rumpled linens, an old armoire with mirrored front panels, a claw-foot nightstand and a bookshelf stuffed to the brim with classics and old textbooks. On his desk were twenty or so fist-sized rocks, lined up exactly a half inch apart. So, he liked rocks and he was a little OCD, nothing wrong with that. I was a complete slob, so we'd make a perfect match.

My eyes grazed his bookshelf and immediately locked in on an old gemstone encyclopedia. I remembered Dane telling me about a stone last night in great detail—rose quartz. I pulled the book from the shelf. It was lighter than it should be. A rush of adrenaline swept through my bloodstream as I opened it to find it had been hollowed out.

Inside, I found stationery, India ink, a fountain pen, deep red wax, and a seal with the Mendoza family crest.

At first glance, it appeared to be nothing more than a cache for stationery, but the real stash was in another compartment underneath. A pair of scratched-up Ray-Bans, a well-worn map of the United States, a half-empty pack of Chiclets, an old Walkman, and a Backstreet Boys CD.

"Ash! Ash! Where are you? Ash?" Beth tramped down the hallway, calling my name like a town crier.

"What the hell," I groaned, shoving everything back in the book and tucking it away on the shelf.

I cracked open the door to make sure she was alone before slipping out of the room.

"Oh my stars!" Beth exclaimed. "What are you doing down here? Everyone's asking about you. I'm afraid they'll make me leave if we're not together."

"Do we have to go back to the party?" I looked at her pleadingly.

"Oh, are you ready to leave?" She took my hand.

I felt bad for messing up Beth's big break into the social hierarchy, but I couldn't go back. "I just need some air."

"There's another way out down here," Beth said as she led me to a darkened staircase at the end of the hall.

"I thought you'd never been here before."

"That's curious, isn't it?" she replied as she hurried down the stairs to a dead end.

She ran her hands over the wood-paneled wall.

"Beth, I don't know what's going on with you, but this is—"

I heard a chilling pop as the wall swung open, revealing a dark, narrow entryway.

Beth grinned up at me before pulling me inside and closing the door.

"What is this place?" I whispered.

"I'm not sure." Beth fumbled with something, striking a match. She lit a small candle that was resting on a table.

"How did you know that was there?"

"I think I've been here before."

"Yeah, that's a pretty safe assumption." I exhaled, feeling completely sketched out. Sometimes Beth scared me.

I took a few matches from a silver cup on the table and put them in my pocket. I wondered if Dane made these.

As we stepped out of the cramped entry into a large circular room, the smell of old parchment and eucalyptus hit me. Spencer's scent.

Beth drifted around the windowless room as if in a daze. I gravitated toward a huge cross on the far wall, made from dried cornstalks. Beneath the cross was a candle-filled altar with mounds of melted wax forming monstrous shadows against the wall.

At the foot of the altar, lying open on the ground, was an old Bible. I'd read the Bible before, but this wasn't like any Bible I'd ever seen. It was the Old Testament, but much of it was crossed out, with words written over the text along with unintelligible scribbles.

Next to the Bible was a whip with a worn leather handle and a chalice containing a dark red substance that smelled of mandarins and the sea.

"What the hell is this place?" I whispered.

"I don't think we should be in here," Beth whispered as she backed into a table, sending a barrage of oily blue-black feathers to the ground. Crow feathers.

Beth's hands shook as she scrambled to pick them up. Her breath came in rapid bursts.

"Beth," I soothed. "Calm down. You said there was another exit. Concentrate. Where is it?"

Beth grabbed my hand and led me behind the altar wall, to another narrow hallway—another dead end.

She felt along the wall, trying to find a way out when we heard footsteps approaching from the outside. We ran back through the chapel to the narrow hallway we'd come in. Frantically, Beth tried to find the right panel, when the door behind the altar creaked open. There was no time. I blew out the candle. Leaving us in complete darkness.

A match was struck—the smell of phosphorous and kerosene did little to mask Spencer's eucalyptus scent.

As he stepped into the circular room, I heard him slipping off his shoes, followed by a soft pooling of fabric hitting the ground.

Beth clung to my arm as I tried to edge down the hallway. I peeked around the wall to see the back of Spencer's perfectly sculpted naked body kneeling before the altar, his only flaw the thick scars crisscrossing his back.

He clutched the handle of the whip in front of him. He appeared to be praying.

"Forgive me, for I have sinned."

He dipped the end of the leather strings into the dark red substance and swung it fiercely over his shoulder. The sickening sound of the leather strip splitting his skin made me cringe. The scent of fresh blood filled the small space. "Let this blood cleanse me and keep me strong." I was stunned to see his wounds heal right before my eyes. The dark red substance must've been the blood of an immortal—Katia's blood.

"Tonight, I will fulfill my duty." He brought the whip across his back with even greater force, slicing it wide open, only for it to heal right back up again. "I have sacrificed everything for you. Betrayed everything I love."

Beth cowered in the far corner of the passageway, pressing her hands to her ears, flinching each time the whip struck his skin.

"And so it shall be," he whispered. "At the harvest of the end of the world. The reaper will come forth and sever the wicked from among the just." His words became more fervent with every blow. "Sever the *wicked* from among the *just*," he groaned. "I am wicked, but I am just!"

Beth took in a sobbing gasp.

Spencer stopped and turned to look over his shoulder. I ducked back into the hallway. I wasn't sure if he saw me or not.

Beth clamped a hand over her mouth, her eyes wide with terror, as he stepped toward our hiding spot.

He came closer.

Closer.

He'd almost reached the entryway when a loud, insistent rap came from the other door.

Spencer halted. He turned and crossed the room, shrugging back into his robe.

Beth fumbled with the wall, desperately pressing on wood panels. As soon as Spencer opened the door behind the altar, Beth found the right one.

Before I had a chance to see who was calling on him, Beth had pulled me out of the hallway and up the stairs.

"Holy shit, did you see that?" I hissed.

"No." She squeezed my arm. "And you didn't see anything either. Understand?"

We nearly collided with Lauren Mendoza at the top of the stairs.

"What are you doing down here?" Her eyes darted behind us.

"We were looking for Brennon's room." Beth smiled sweetly, the lie rolling effortlessly off her tongue.

I could see Lauren bristle as her eyes dragged up and down my body like a razor blade.

"I don't know what you're up to, but I'm watching you." Her cheeks were flushed, making her olive skin even more luminous. "If you hurt anyone close to me, you and I are going to have problems."

Did she know about Dane and me? Would he have told her? Is that why she hated me so much . . . she didn't want to see her brother get hurt?

She leaned forward, whispering in my ear. "I'm glad you got a chance to meet Teresa. To see what you'll become."

I felt the black silk ribbon stir against my neck as a venomous feeling rose up inside of me. My eyes settled on Lauren's neck—on her pulse throbbing under her beautiful skin. Something inside me wanted to stop it from beating.

"Thank you for a lovely time," Beth said, taking my arm and pulling me outside, breaking my dark fixation.

27

BONFIRE

I'D NEVER BEEN to a cult bonfire before, but it seemed to be nothing more than a barbecue. Of course, Henry went straight for the booze. That seemed to be a favorite pastime around here. What did they care if they rotted out their livers? They expected to become immortal in a few days.

Kids crammed around small fire pits scattered around the field, jockeying for position, trying to char their mystery meat skewers. It all seemed pretty harmless, except for the mammoth sculpture at the center of the field made of carefully arranged logs and willow branches. I didn't know what the figure was supposed to be, but it loomed menacingly against the violet sky.

I spotted Dane on the other side of the sculpture. It looked like Spencer was giving him a stern talking-to.

"We'll set up camp in a bit," Beth said as she dropped the bedding carelessly to the ground and hugged me. "Don't tell anyone what you saw today," she whispered. "There will be a path to lead us from darkness."

Why did she keep saying that?

She looped her arm through my brother's and led him into the thick of the Grimsby camp.

"Stay close," Rhys called over his shoulder. "We have a big day tomorrow."

Hopefully, tonight would bring answers, because I needed to figure something out. Fast.

When I looked back across the field, Dane was gone, but Spencer Mendoza's eyes had settled on my skin like a rash. I knew there was something off about him the moment I met him, but I didn't realize how deep it went.

As he began to walk around the sculpture, I took off in the opposite direction.

"Miss Larkin?" he called.

Reluctantly, I waited. As soon as he approached, that eucalyptus smell with the rotting undertone nearly gagged me.

"I haven't had a chance to formally introduce myself. I'm Spencer Mendoza. I understand you're already acquainted with my nephew, Brennon . . . and Dane."

I kept my face as expressionless as possible.

"You look so much like your mother. Except for the hair." He'd reached out to capture a strand when I took a decided step back.

"I had a nice chat with Teresa today," I said, but it didn't seem to bother him in the least.

"Ah, poor Teresa. There's nothing more pitiful than a conduit who's run her course."

He spoke of her like a nag who needed to be put down.

"Oh, forgive me." Spencer smiled. "I forgot you're a conduit as well." He leaned in close, close enough for me to smell the blood from the chalice mixed with his own. "I trust you've had a pleasant stay in Quivira."

What did he mean by *had*? I felt the ribbon straining against my neck, rage rising up inside of me.

"There you are," Brennon said behind me.

Thankful for the rescue, I grasped his arm, but then I thought of the apple blossom—the promise. I didn't want to lead Brennon on, but I needed him to keep up appearances. I didn't want anyone to suspect Dane of wrongdoing.

"It's time," Spencer said with a dark glint in his eyes.

As he walked away, the drums began to beat, slow and steady. The community quickly took their places, waiting with bated breath. Brennon led me to the front of the sculpture.

Strange electricity filled the atmosphere.

"Friends," Spencer announced as he paced around the giant sculpture with a lit torch. "We've been waiting for almost five *centuries*. There's much to celebrate, but we must also remember our loved ones who were taken from us along with the brothers and sisters, sons and daughters who've walked the corn in order for this to come to pass. Nina will be the one to bring us light, but there can be no light without darkness." My brother and I exchanged uneasy looks from across the gathering.

Spencer threw the torch onto the bed of kindling, igniting the sculpture, bringing to life the shape of a man. I didn't have to ask who it was supposed to symbolize. The look of rapturous hatred on the community's faces as they watched Coronado burn in effigy reminded me of a crazed mob straight out of a horror movie.

Suddenly, the wood at the base of the sculpture settled with a loud groan. Coronado's jaw had come unhinged, sending a hiss of flames shooting from his mouth into the night air. A sick familiar feeling rose up inside of me. *Not now. Not here.*

My muscles quaked, my knees buckled. I felt the past clinch around my heart like heavy chains.

"You will not come to my home and threaten my people." I glower at Coronado and his army closing in around me. "You have no power here. Not anymore."

"That may be true." Coronado steps aside. "But she does."

Aiyana walks toward me through the corn. The sight of her nearly takes my breath away.

"Sister."

"Katia, this must stop," she says, her eyes shining like black shale in the dying light.

"Is it true? Did you bring my enemy to my door?" My breathing becomes shallow as I stare over the Arcanum positioned throughout the field. "Did you betray me . . . tell Coronado of my plans?"

Aiyana's eyes cloud in sorrow. "Coronado has wronged you, but you cannot unleash the Dark Spirit into the world without paying the price. I fear for you and your future generations. Let me help you through this, I can break the blood bond between you and Coronado, here and now."

My nostrils flare. "But can you bring Alonso back to me?"

She stands tall and strong, her long black hair whipping around her. "The answer is still no."

"This I cannot live with." Raising my hands to the sky, I call upon the Dark Spirit, "Kahnah'k'an'day hahawca'suh daka'ah."

Coronado and his men hold their ground, but Aiyana's warriors begin to waver. They know what's coming for them.

As the Dark Spirit gathers strength, a screaming wail rings out over the corn.

Some of the men charge, some flee, but none will escape. The deadly force seeks them out, ripping through armor and bone, tearing them limb from limb.

Aiyana spreads her arms like wings, releasing a flood of black birds, which encase her and Coronado like a cocoon.

It's a powerful spell, but I am more powerful now than Aiyana ever was.

I stretch out my fingers, summoning a ferocious wind.

As I force them back through the field to the outside world, I let out a primal scream.

And then there's silence.

The only sound I hear is blood dripping from the leaves of the stalks, soaking into the fertile soil.

As Aiyana and Coronado stand on the outside, looking in, I turn my back on them.

Tears stream down my face as I step over the hundreds of bodies of the slain Quivira tribe, and Arcanum littering the fields.

I take in a deep breath, letting the Dark Spirit fill the void inside of me.

With each step, my path becomes crystalline.

I drag my fingers along the stalks, feeling raw power flow through me, the energy spreading through the corn, bending it to my will. "Let these fields be a barrier, protecting us from the outside world." The stalks quake as I pass, a deathly recognition of our accord.

There will be darkness and I will feed the darkness.

And then there will be light . . .

"Ashlyn," someone whispered.

"Hey there, lovely," Brennon said as my eyes fluttered open. I lay on blankets in front of one of the smaller campfires, Dane on one side of me, Brennon on the other.

I tried to sit up, but it felt like I had an anvil embedded in my skull. "What happened?"

Dane answered, "You passed out."

I sat up like a shot, ignoring my brain sloshing around in my head. I stared off into the corn, thinking of Katia stepping over all those bodies. How heartbroken she was. Aiyana betrayed her trust, bringing Coronado to Quivira. And when Coronado threatened to kill her people, her followers, she felt she had no choice. Katia enraptured the corn to protect them. I felt her breathing life and death into the fields, like the corn was an extension of her body.

"The smoke must have gotten to you. It happens," Brennon said.

"Here, this might help." Dane passed a bottle to me, but he didn't make eye contact. I noticed a deep scratch on the left side of his neck. He adjusted his collar when he caught me staring at it.

I took a drink that burned all the way down my throat. I wanted to play it cool, but my face contorted involuntarily. "What *is* this stuff?"

"Rye." Dane leaned into me, his shoulder grazing mine, which sent a flood of warmth through my entire body. "Neil Hanratty makes a batch every year for the solstice. I swear each batch gets stronger." He coaxed the bottle away from me and took a deep swig.

I kept waiting for him to send some kind of signal, but he gave me nothing. I wondered if he'd forgotten that he'd agreed to take me into the corn; maybe I dreamt the entire thing.

I snatched it back and took another drink, not because I wanted more, but because his lips had just touched the bottle. I wanted to capture his warmth, his kiss. And then I wanted to slap myself for being such a tool.

Feeling dizzy, I fell back onto the blankets.

As Brennon reached out to take my hand, I flinched.

"Are you okay?"

"Yes," I answered with a forced smile. "I'm just still a little out of it."

Lauren passed our campfire, staring daggers into me.

Brennon got to his feet, smiling sheepishly as he brushed grass from his trousers. "I'm going to find you some water. A girl can't live on grain alcohol alone."

When he left, I sat up and looked at Dane expectantly.

"Patience," he whispered as he stared ahead into the fire.

I looked down at his hands holding the bottle and I couldn't stop thinking about his thumb stroking my hip bone and the feel of his scarred skin beneath my fingertips. I closed my eyes, hoping the sensation of the wind rushing over my sun-burned shoulders would give me some reprieve from him, but he was everywhere. His scent. His movement. His breath. I was drawn to him, like a moth to a flame—only in it for the burn.

The wooden sculpture creaked and groaned, drawing everyone's attention.

"Now," Dane whispered as he got up and walked away from the camp.

As the sculpture collapsed into a heaping pile of embers, I followed Dane to the edge of darkness—and never looked back.

28

TORN

DANE WAS STANDING before the corn.

Without looking at me, he held out his hand behind him.

I laced my fingers through his; that euphoric warmth spreading across my skin.

"Don't let go," he whispered.

He stepped forward and the stalks parted as if he'd brought the summer breeze.

I braced myself for the electric current to hurl me back into oblivion, but he pulled me right along with him.

The hazy glow from the torches lining the inner perimeter did little to combat the darkness of the field. Our footsteps were muffled, and the corn around us seemed to lack dimension. It felt as though we'd stepped into another world.

I tightened my grip around his fingers. Even here, surrounded by unknown danger at every turn, I couldn't stop thinking about his skin against mine.

Gradually, the row widened, so we could walk side by side. He brushed his other hand along the stalks.

"What do you feel?" I asked.

The muscles in his shoulders tensed, like my question caught him off guard.

"When you touch the corn."

"I guess it's an energy. If you listen closely it almost sounds like it's breathing."

He was right. The air moved through the stalks like rhythmic breath—in and out—out and in.

"It must be hard keeping a secret like this."

"We all keep secrets." His eyes settled on me, and my blood seemed to shimmer in my veins.

A long silence stretched between us, but it wasn't uncomfortable. Something about being here with him, in this moment, felt serene, like nothing could touch us.

"I've been thinking about something you said last night . . ."

I waited for him to ask what it was, but he remained focused on the path in front of us.

"You asked why I wanted to go in the corn." I tucked my hair behind my ear. "At first, I thought it was just to find a way to stop the ritual—but what if this is what my mom and dad want? Maybe there's a way for Katia and Alonso and Nina and Thomas to all be together—to coexist."

Dane looked at me with a soft, puzzled expression. "How much did you drink?"

"I know it sounds crazy." I shook my head and laughed.

Dane was probably only adjusting his grip, but it felt as if he were caressing his thumb against my palm. "Would you want to live forever, Ashlyn?"

"God, no," I blurted. "I've had a hard enough time dealing with the life I've got."

Dane let out an unexpected laugh. Just like he had when we'd first met at the junkyard.

"But maybe with the right person?" I shrugged. "I don't know. I don't even know what I'm saying anymore. Maybe it's the rye . . . or this place," I said, staring up at the stars. "Quivira really is a utopia."

The muscles in Dane's hand tensed. "It's not as perfect as you think."

I thought about what I saw at the Mendoza lodge today and my buzz quickly faded. "Why didn't you tell me your mom's a conduit?"

"Teresa didn't raise me. The Mendozas did. Spencer built her a cottage on the outskirts of the eastern woods. I'm not even sure she knows I'm her son. Spencer said she used to walk the corn, like me, before she—well, before the conduit side of her took over."

Before she went crazy, he meant.

As the lights from the outside world came into view, the odor of our surroundings did too—sweet, pungent, and on the verge of being sickening. It smelled like stale soda syrup mixed with ammonia. The ground became softer and squishier with every step.

"Are we close to the sacred circle?" I asked. It seemed like we'd been walking for miles.

"Almost." He nearly swallowed the word.

"What's inside the chasm?"

"I wouldn't know." He strained his head to see what was ahead.

"You've never looked inside?"

"I'm not allowed inside the sacred circle."

I smiled. "You don't exactly strike me as a rule follower."

"My blood won't allow me to enter the circle. Don't forget, I have Coronado's blood inside me."

It killed me the way he said it, eyes downcast like he was ashamed.

I stopped walking, pulling him to a halt. But still, he wouldn't meet my eyes. Closing the gap between us, I laced my other hand through his. "I told you. I don't care about that. We are not our ancestors."

He looked up at me, eyes blazing. I felt his warm breath pulsing against my cheek, sending sparks of raw electricity across my skin.

The sound of voices in the distance pulled me from the moment. "Do you hear that?"

Without a word, Dane turned and started pulling me back toward Quivira.

Beyond the voices was a strange chittering sound.

"Wait." I tugged against him. "I thought the circle was this way."

"I made a mistake," he murmured.

"I don't understand." I looked back over my shoulder, straining to bring the voices into focus, when I tripped. But Dane never let go of my hand.

When I looked down the row of corn to see what I'd tripped over, I found the source of the hissing noise—a mysterious mound that glistened like encrusted jewels in the moonlight. Dane pulled me to my feet. As I leaned forward, trying to figure out what made it shine that way, the mound shifted. I realized it was made of locusts, thousands of them. They scattered, revealing Tanner Beaumont's head beneath. The guy from the junkyard. Bloodshot eyes, mouth agape, a locust slipping from his mouth into his nostril.

I clamped my hand over my mouth to stop myself from screaming as men's voices filled the atmosphere, the distinct cadence of Spanish. We must be close to the perimeter. The Arcanum—they must've killed poor Tanner. The wind moved through the field and I swore I caught the hint of my mother's scent. "Mom?" I called out.

Dane started to cover my mouth, when a deep hum followed by a brilliant force of light pulsed through the field, blinding me momentarily.

"Bring her to me and all of this will end." A man's voice with a thick Castilian Spanish accent pierced through the stalks.

For a moment I thought Katia had returned with my mother, that the Arcanum had them surrounded.

But when Dane pulled a knife from his belt, holding it out in front of him, I knew the man was talking about *me*.

As my eyes adjusted to the light, I saw him silhouetted on the outer perimeter of the corn. I pushed forward for a better look, but Dane's arm was hooked firmly around my waist, holding me back. "Don't listen to him. Coronado will kill you."

"Please," I whispered. "I have to see his face." I was scared, but I needed to see the man who'd been terrorizing my family.

Dane was still holding me fast, but he let me inch forward. The locust carpet sizzled loudly as it moved beneath our feet. We held our ground about five feet from the edge of the corn.

I couldn't believe my eyes. It was the man from the memories, but even more handsome, with a rugged stubble covering his fine features. This was the man who'd slit that Larkin girl's throat right in front of Katia, but there was no cruelty in his face now, only sorrow.

"Marie," he whispered, his dark brown eyes welling up with tears. He was reaching his hand through the corn as if to touch my face, when his flesh disintegrated from his fingers, dripping down to the ground like melted wax, exposing the bones of his hand. He jerked it back, cradling his decimated hand against his chest.

The end of the black silk ribbon slithered over my shoulder as if it were trying to reach him. Part of me was drawn to him, and another part repulsed.

212

"I shouldn't have brought you here," Dane said with a desperate edge to his voice as he pulled me back.

"Dane," Coronado's voice boomed. "You are of my blood. Give her to me, or there will be a price."

"She doesn't belong to you. No one has to die." Dane tightened his grip, turning all his attention back to me. "Ashlyn, what did you say to me the night of the wreathing ceremony . . . when you spoke Caddo?"

I couldn't understand why he was asking me this. Why now? As my gaze gravitated back to Coronado, Dane held my chin, forcing me to look him in the eyes.

"He needs to hear this, too. What did you say to me?"

"I . . . I don't know. It just came out."

"I'm warning you," Coronado seethed.

"Please," Dane said in the softest tone, his lips hovering just a few inches away from mine. "Tell me."

I felt so vulnerable, so out of control, especially with Coronado so close to me, but I wanted to tell Dane what I'd said at the wreathing ceremony. I wanted so badly for it to mean something.

"It was something my mother said to me before she disappeared," I whispered, taking in his breath as if it were my own. "When you fall in love, you will carve out your heart and throw it into the deepest ocean. You will be all in—blood and salt."

"Do you believe in a love like that?" His words brushed against my lips.

"Yes," I gasped.

"So do I." A surprised smile seemed to pass over his face. "And that's why I'm letting go."

Dane dropped his hands and took a deliberate step away from me.

Instantly, the energy shifted. A low growl echoed through the corn. The growl quickly turned into a screaming wail; and I knew something was coming for me.

29

RUN

A POWERFUL ENERGY reached through the stalks, grabbing hold of my heart. The tremendous force sent me hurtling back through the corn toward Quivira, the leaves whipping against my skin. I tried to fight it, find my way back to Dane, when something even more powerful rose up in my bloodstream, sinking into my limbs, adding extra weight to every movement.

As the conduit feelings took over, the pulling sensation subsided, until I was standing on my own two feet again—deep within the corn—the sacred circle in my sight. But as soon as I stepped toward it, I felt the past needling its way inside of me, taking over. Muscles clenched, back arched, I tried to hang on to the present, but it felt as though someone were peeling my fingers back from a narrow ledge.

"Run," I whisper.

The boy staggers from the sacred circle into the field, his hands clasped tight over his ears, his cheeks damp with tears.

As he runs, the corn shifts in front of him, opening like a maze. The dark force is toying with him. It waits until he's almost reached the edge of the outer perimeter before seizing him and sending him back into the depths of the field. The boy tries to get up, but something's wrong. The flesh has been stripped from his right leg, exposing bone and torn muscle.

He lets out a gut-wrenching cry as he grabs the stalks and begins to drag himself through the field. The dark energy rolls through the corn again, and he goes flying. He lands with a gaping gash in his side, as though the corn has taken a bite out of him. The dark energy gathers strength until it forms into a single unstoppable wave. The wave rips through him, leaving nothing behind but blood and bits of tissue splattered across the dark green leaves.

"Ashlyn," someone yelled, pulling me back from my nightmare.

I came to, slung over Dane's shoulder as he ran through the corn, the churning field gnashing at his heels.

Dane shoved me through the barrier, back into Quivira, then came diving after me. He landed with a dense blow, clutching his shoulder. I could taste his blood in the air, metallic and sharp on my tongue.

"Are you okay?" I crawled toward him, a dark red stain spreading over his linen shirt.

"It's nothing," he said. "Are *you* okay?"

"Why did you let me go?" I asked, unable to hold back the tears.

"I needed to get you away from there . . . from *him*." He reached out to touch me, but I pulled away. "I thought the corn would move you back faster than I could. I didn't think you'd fall into another vision, I'm sorr—"

"The corn," I whispered, tears streaming down my face. "I saw a boy come out of the sacred circle. Dark blond hair, chiseled features. He looked so familiar, but I couldn't place him. Katia told him to run. She was trying to help him, but the corn . . ." A sobbing choking sound escaped my lips.

"Slow down," Dane said softly.

"He must've been a Mendoza boy . . . one of the unchosen," I said as I stared over the crops. "All those Larkin girls and Mendoza boys who walked the corn. They never made it to the outside world. And all those cars at the junkyard . . . all those people who came looking for Quivira . . . they're dead." I took in a shuddering breath. "The corn is a monster . . . and it's eating them."

"I know." He took my trembling hands in his. "Everyone knows. Sometimes you can hear them screaming."

30

STITCH

I GOT THE FIRST-AID KIT from the bag in my room and flew up the stairs three at a time. I was afraid Dane might disappear.

It was strange, but I wasn't as surprised as I should've been about what was happening in the corn. When Katia turned to the Dark Spirit, she was enraged, fueled by loss and heartache. I felt for her. In her darkest moment, Katia did whatever she felt she had to do to protect her people, her way of life, but in doing so, she created a monster she could no longer control.

When I saw Dane standing by the window, right where I'd left him, I breathed a huge sigh of relief.

"I'm sorry about tonight." He stared straight ahead over the dark water.

"You were trying to protect me," I said as I inspected the cut on his shoulder.

"You don't understand. I almost led you right *to* him."

"But you didn't," I said. "Next time, you won't let go."

His jaw muscles tensed. "There can't be a next time."

"Dane, please, I just ha—"

"It's too dangerous." He cut me off.

He shifted his weight, and suddenly, I understood. A wave of guilt washed over me. It was wrong of me to ask him to do this in the first place. If we were caught together . . . God, I couldn't even go there.

I set my kit on the coffee table and lit another lantern, hanging it on the iron stand. "Why did you want me to tell you what I said in Caddo at the wreathing ceremony? Why did you want Coronado to hear it?"

Dane took an unexpected step toward me. "I wanted to show him that you're not Marie . . . or a pawn in his sick game. I may have his blood, but I have Mendoza blood, too. I wanted him to see us as human beings. Love can be a powerful thing." His eyes locked on mine with an intensity that made me lose my train of thought. I couldn't stop thinking about his mouth so close to mine, the way he held me in the corn.

I cleared my throat as I maneuvered one of the chairs in front of the table. "Have you ever been in the Larkin lodge before?"

"Why would you ask me that?" His body went rigid, his brows knitting into a hard line.

"Brennon said you had a lot of intention offers." I motioned for him to take a seat on the chair.

"Oh." He let out a gust of pent-up air. *"That."* A coy smile played across his lips as he began to unbutton his shirt. "Well, if you're trying to ask me if I've ever taken anyone else into the corn and then gone over to their house to play doctor, the answer would be no." He shrugged out of his shirt.

I had no idea what my face was doing, but inside it was complete hormonal anarchy.

He sat down in the chair. I adjusted the lantern so it would shine directly on his left shoulder, then sank to the edge of the coffee table, carefully nestling my knees between his. I tried to concentrate on the contents of my kit—vials of various medicines, sutures, dressing, and a sparkling scalpel—but I couldn't keep my eyes off him for more than a few seconds at a time.

"You're lucky," I said as I doused a gauze pad in antiseptic. "You'll need a few stitches, but it looks like a clean cut."

He followed my eyes and laughed. "Lucky? I'm an idiot. I think I fell on my own knife and then lost it in the corn. That's what I get for trying to impress you."

"Is that what happened?" I tried to play it off, but it felt like there were sparklers going off in my chest.

"You can't make a wreath but you know how to use all this?"

"My mother wanted us to be able to take care of ourselves. And Rhys—" I chuckled. "Not so good with blood. We joked that she was preparing us for some kind of apocalypse, but maybe it was just Quivira."

He studied me as I cleaned the cut. "What was it like for you . . . growing up?"

"We always thought our mom was a little crazy, the way she talked about this place, but we loved her so much, it didn't matter."

"What about friends . . . hobbies?"

"I played sports, Rhys played chess," I said, tearing off another piece of gauze from the kit. "It sounds weird, but it always felt like I was waiting for something—waiting for my life to begin."

I wasn't sure if his legs were narrowing in on mine or if mine were spreading farther apart, but when our legs touched, a shivering ripple rushed beneath my skin.

I tried to focus on preparing the sutures. "Aren't you the slightest bit nervous that a seventeen-year-old girl is going to stitch you up?"

"I think I'm in good hands." He stroked his thumb against the side of my knee. "Tell me. What does it feel like when you disappear into your visions—the conduit memories?"

"Like standing on the edge of a precipice . . . sort of like the feeling I get when you touch me."

The corner of his mouth curled into a smile.

I looked down, a deep blush creeping over my cheeks. I couldn't believe I just said that. *Pull yourself together, Ash.*

I started to prepare an injection of a local anesthetic, but he shook his head.

"I don't need that."

"It's just lidocaine." I held up the bottle, but he didn't even glance at it.

"Okay," I said as I set it aside, pretending not to notice his touch. "It's going to hurt like hell."

After taking a deep breath, I inserted the suture needle into the edge of his torn flesh, pulling it all the way through to the knot at the end.

He hardly flinched.

"You said you've been seeing memories of Katia and Marie. Can you tell me about them?"

It still felt strange talking about this, but there was something about Dane that made me want to open up. "I saw Coronado's face when he found out what Katia's blood could do. I saw Coronado talking Marie into telling him where to find Katia and Alonso on the summer solstice. But the memory that sticks with me the most . . . the one that haunts me . . . is when I saw my mother and father in the sacred circle. Katia cut into my mother's palm and said, *'A vessel at last.'*"

He flinched.

"Sorry." I held the wound shut with a lighter touch and kept stitching.

He looked down at my legs. "What about your knee at the field?"

So he did notice. "At first I thought it was because my mother pricked her finger when she was giving me the last protection mark, but I think the same thing might be happening to my brother. The cut on his lip at the shinny game—it closed up almost immediately."

"That makes sense." His shoulders relaxed again. "When Nina walked the corn, she was pregnant with you and your brother. You have some of Katia's blood in you, too. My guess is when Katia came to get your mother in New York City, it ignited something in you as well. You're twins. The smallest trace of an immortal's blood can be very potent."

"You'd think all of this would bring Rhys and me closer together, but I've never felt more distant from him." I sighed as I tied off the last stitch. "He's always had a bad feeling about Quivira. I'm the one who wanted to come. Even now, with everything that's gone down, something about being here feels right."

"Does he have any idea what's happening to him? What's happening at Quivira?"

I shook my head. "Just being here freaks him out enough. If he knew what was really going on with the corn . . . or with me . . . he'd . . . I don't even know what he'd do, but it wouldn't be pretty. Rhys agreed to stay until tomorrow—he doesn't know we can't leave."

"What are you going to tell him?"

"The truth, I guess. I don't think I have any other choice."

"You're a good sister," he said as I put a butterfly bandage over the sutures. "The separation you're feeling . . . sometimes people distance themselves from things they know they'll have to say good-bye to one day."

"I don't understand."

"You're a conduit, Ashlyn. Deep down, Rhys must know what that means for you. It would be difficult watching the person you love . . . disappear."

It took me aback. Even Dane knew I was doomed. He knew it better than anyone.

I pretended to reorganize my supplies. "Why don't you leave Quivira?" I asked, desperate to change the subject. "You're the one person who can walk the corn. You could start a new life . . . leave all this."

"And go where?" He tilted his head, like he was amused.

"Anywhere. I've got money. You can have it."

His smile faded as he eased his hands over my knees. "Maybe we could go together. We can bring Rhys and Beth, too."

I felt my heart pick up speed at the thought . . . at his touch. "What about Coronado? Won't he be waiting for us?"

"Not if we time it right. At dawn on the summer solstice, he'll be watching the eastern perimeter, because it's the closest entry point to the sacred circle. We could leave from the old stables on the western edge, slip through their fingers."

For a moment, I got caught up in the idea, Dane and I escaping from all of this, starting life anew; then a crippling thought washed over me.

"I can't leave my mom here."

"Then I'll stay," he said with such sincerity, it made me ache. "Besides . . ." He leaned forward, his hands slowly moving up my thighs. "I always felt like I was waiting for something, too."

He slipped his hands beneath the hem of my shorts, pulling me toward him. "Maybe that something was you," he whispered, his lips hovering mere centimeters from mine . . .

"Ash!" The front door slammed open. My brother's voice cut through the atmosphere like a hatchet.

Dane pulled away.

"We've been looking everywhere for you." Beth grinned, her warm brown eyes twinkling in the lamplight, completely clueless as to what she just walked in on.

"As you can see, I'm fine." I closed the medical kit with a little too much force. I couldn't believe this was happening to me right now.

"What's *he* doing here?" Rhys asked without looking at Dane. "I told you to stay close. You're supposed to be at the bonfire."

Dane stood. "I was just leaving."

Rhys looked down at the blood-soaked gauze. "What happened?"

"I fell. It's nothing." Dane pulled his shirt back on.

"Funny." Rhys squared his shoulders. "You don't strike me as the clumsy type."

Dane smiled at me. "Thanks for a memorable evening."

He stepped outside and my brother slammed the door behind him.

"That's it." Rhys glared at me through his disheveled bangs. "We're leaving."

31

FEVER

RHYS TORE PAST ME, down the stairs, to my mother's room. "I know I said I'd give you three days, but I've had enough."

I looked at Beth pleadingly, but she seemed just as shocked as I was.

Rhys threw clothes into his bag. "From the moment we got here you've changed. This whole thing was never about the dead girl . . . about helping Mom. There was never a *plan*. This was all about *Dane*. God, I'm such an idiot."

"Can we please talk about this?" I twisted the end of the ribbon between my fingers.

He pulled the bag of cash and gold from underneath the bed. "We'll have plenty of time to talk on our way back to civilization." Storming back upstairs and out the front door, he plunged into the prairie grass, making a beeline for the corn.

"Rhys!" Beth scurried to catch up to him.

"And we're taking Beth with us," he said over his shoulder.

Beth stopped in her tracks, that loopy smile engulfing her face. "You'd do that? You'd take me with you?"

"We have to stop him," I whispered to Beth as I pulled her along into the knee-high stretch of coarse grass. "He doesn't know about the corn."

She looked at me in shock.

"Please just wait . . . I can explain everything . . . it's not what you think."

I tried to stop him, but Rhys took a determined step into the corn and was thrown back at least ten feet, knocking the wind right out of him.

"What was that?" He inhaled sharply as he staggered to his feet. "They must've built some kind of invisible fence—like for a dog—but on steroids." He rubbed his shoulder.

Beth raced to his side, her eyes shiny with tears. "I thought you already knew."

"Maybe if we can get past the barrier." He ran toward the corn and it flung him back, again and again and again, until he could hardly pick himself back up.

Tears were spilling down Beth's cheeks now as she stood by, watching him rage against the stalks.

"It's not an invisible fence," I said as I stepped forward. "Not the kind you're thinking of."

"Did you know about this?" he gasped as I tried to help him find his footing, but when I didn't answer he jerked away from me, almost falling over again.

"You *knew* we couldn't leave?" He shook his head in disbelief. "You knew this whole time and you didn't say anything?"

"I'm sorry, Rhys." My voice shook. "I wanted to tell you. I just . . . I didn't want to make it worse."

"Worse?' he screamed. "Do you realize what you've done by bringing us here? We're trapped." He began to pace. "This can't be happening. Somebody must've slipped something in my drink."

"It's real. All of it." I swallowed hard as I turned to face him. "I saw Coronado tonight. I saw the Arcanum. They killed Tanner from the junkyard. Coronado wanted to kill *me*. But Dane saved me."

"Ash," he groaned in frustration. "The visions aren't real—"

"These weren't visions," I said. "The corn is more than a protective barrier. It's alive and it's *eating* people."

"Okay . . . all right." He laughed as he backed away from me. "They've got you brainwashed, too. Use your head. If we can't get *out* of the corn . . . and no one can get *in* . . . how could you have possibly seen Coronado and the Arcanum?"

"Dane," I blurted. "Dane can walk the corn. He's the only one. It's a secret, but he can get us out of here."

"How?" My brother turned on me.

"I . . . I don't know . . . we'll hold hands or something. He said we might be able to slip by Coronado and his men at dawn on the summer solstice."

"Are you serious right now?" He grabbed my shoulders, giving me a hard shake. "Is that what he told you? That we can all walk through the corn together, holding hands, singing 'Kumbaya'?"

"She's telling the truth," Beth said with a faraway look in her eyes. "I don't know how I know about Dane, but I do. He can lead us to the outside world."

Rhys dragged his hands through his hair and let out a frustrated scream. "Every fiber in my body is telling me not to trust that asshole. Didn't Mom always say we should trust our instincts? There's something not right about him . . . about any of this." He stared out over the corn. He was so disgusted he couldn't even look me in the eyes. "There has to be another way." He took Beth's hand and pulled her away.

"Where are you going?" I called out in desperation.

"We're going back to the bonfire. One of us has to keep up appearances. We'll tell everyone you came home with a fever. A fever we need to let you burn out."

32

TABOO

"HE'LL COME AROUND." Dane's voice bled through the stalks behind me.

I turned to find him standing in the corn. "I'm sorry I told your secret, but I didn't know what else to—"

"You were trying to make amends. I understand." He came toward me, his eyes glistening. "I'll take him through the corn when he's ready. For now, I want to help you find answers. You deserve to know what's happening to you." He held out his hand. "Don't worry. I won't let go again."

I swallowed back the guilt threatening to pull me under and stepped forward to take his hand. As soon as I touched him, relief flooded me. He made me want to forget about everything. I wanted to live in this moment for as long as I possibly could.

As we moved through the corn, it felt like we were all alone in the world, but I was never truly alone. The conduit feelings were always with me . . . clawing at my skin, scratching to get out. Before I even had a chance to take in another breath, that familiar feeling rose up, consuming me until there was nothing left to do but fall.

Marie ducks under the thick fringe of a willow tree, clutching a rock threaded with light pink quartz and a folded piece of parchment.

"A'kuay'hdah, hakku nay'si'sa," she whispers to the Great Spirit as she slips the black silk ribbon from around her neck, tying the parchment to the stone. "With this promise, I offer you my most prized possession. This is the ribbon my mother gave to me when I came of age. It's not a trinket of whimsy. My mother imbued it with power and magic to help me find my one true love. All I ask in return is to be granted immortality. This is my fate. Hear my plea." She places the parcel against the dark gray trunk.

As if the breeze is answering her call, the branches sway and dance all around her. A smile flashes across her face and then quickly disappears.

"Fate is a curious thing," a whisper filters through the leaves. "Just like the Ouroboros, the snake eating its own tail, your plea has been answered, but not the way you intended."

"I don't understand. I need this . . . now." Marie stands, searching the leaves for answers. "I fear he'll leave me if I can't offer him an immortal life."

"And so it shall be . . ."

The sound of wings descends upon the clearing. Shadows of black birds permeate the space as they land on the branches of the willow.

Darkness envelops me—the past and the present merging together. Grainy images press in on the edge of my consciousness. A stiff black feather tracing down a woman's bare spine, blood speckling smooth milky skin, clouds of red-tinged water, the black silk ribbon billowing around entwined limbs, the shimmer of leaves.

But it's the sound of crinkling rope that pulls me back to the moment.

"I thought you loved me," Marie whispers as her body is being dragged into the corn.

Blindly, I careen after her, feeling the stalks snap at my skin. A soft halo of light beckons in the distance, illuminating the sacred circle. I stop. As I stare through the stalks, toward the chasm in the center of the circle, I hear a scratching, scraping noise, like something's trying to claw its way out. A chill rushes through me. This place doesn't feel magical, far from it. It feels barren and cold. A place for the dead.

"Ashlyn," Dane whispered.

I opened my eyes to see his face before me. He looked like an angel, with the sun just beginning to rise through the bedroom window behind him.

"Is this a dream?" I asked.

He let out a soft sigh. "I don't know what your dreams are like, but no."

I tried to sit up, but he gently pressed me back against the cool cotton sheets. "I blacked out again," I realized. I wasn't sure how much time had passed. A red welt ran the length of Dane's cheekbone. "What happened to your face?"

He averted his eyes. "It's nothing."

"Wait . . . did *I* do that?"

His silence spoke volumes.

Why would I go after him like that? "Did I give you that scratch on your neck, too?"

"I surprised you, that's all." He brushed it off. "It's *my* fault. You're not supposed to interfere with a conduit when she's having a vision, but you keep running away from me."

I inspected my hands. There was nothing there to indicate I'd punched someone—no soreness, no scratches. "How do you find me?"

"You know how I can feel the energy in the corn? I feel you, too." A hint of a smile passed over his lips as he leaned over to adjust my pillow. "You're surprisingly predictable."

"You're not, though, are you?" I inhaled slowly, taking in his scent. "You can pull me back. How?"

"Maybe I'm your lucky charm. All I have to do is get you to look in my eyes while I say your name." He swept my hair from my shoulder. "What did you see tonight?"

"Marie. She tied a letter to a pink quartz and set it under a tree. She asked the Great Spirit to grant her immortality, but the Great Spirit refused. Marie thought Coronado would leave her if she couldn't give him eternal life."

Dane took my hands in his.

I stared out the window at the lake. "As she was being

dragged through the corn she looked up and said, 'I thought you loved me.'" My skin prickled up in goose bumps at the memory. "I know Coronado was probably using Marie to get to Alonso and Katia, but why did he have to kill her? Just because she couldn't make him immortal . . . or was it to hurt Katia?"

"Coronado is very cunning," Dane said softly as he looked down at me.

"I know he's bad, but when I saw him face-to-face at the outer perimeter, he didn't seem like a *monster*. And when he said Marie's name, I got the feeling he really loved her." I exhaled, hoping to dispel the bitter feeling from my bloodstream, but it lingered.

"What do you think Marie's trying to tell you?" Dane asked.

"I don't know, but the visions keep leading me back to the chasm in the sacred circle. There's something there that Marie wants me to see."

"You'll find it, when the time is right."

"That's the thing . . . time's running out. There's only three more days until the summer solstice. And the memories are getting stronger, and coming more often. Everything's merging together . . . dreams and reality. I'm afraid I might disappear completely."

Dane stroked the palm of my hand. "I've always been able to pull you back. I remember that first night. You were talking about a light."

"That was real?" I looked up at him in shock. "You were actually with me?"

A sly smile played across his lips.

"Did you kiss me?" I raised my eyebrows.

"Maybe." He twined a strand of my hair around his finger.

I glanced down at his lips. "Why didn't you say anything?"

"At first, I wasn't sure if it was *my* dream."

The black silk ribbon unfurled from my wrist to coil around Dane's. He smiled. "I've never seen anything more beautiful than you on that night."

"But that wasn't really me," I said as I pulled my hand away to secure the ribbon around my wrist again.

"It has nothing to do with you being a conduit." He leaned in closer. "It's you. It's always been you."

I reached out and touched the brand on his inner arm, my fingers lingering on the warmth that still lived there. "Does it hurt?"

He stared back at me with an intense expression that I couldn't decipher. "It does right now."

I pulled his arm toward me, pressing my lips against his scarred skin. I kissed it long and slow, pouring all of my intention into that one kiss.

"Would you want an immortal life?" I whispered.

A deep crease settled between his brows. "If you'd asked me that before tonight, the answer would've been no."

"What's changed?"

"Do you really want this to end?" He brushed his hands

from my waist, over my hips, tracing the curve of my body beneath the sheet.

My blood seemed to rush to the surface of my skin to meet his touch.

He leaned in closer. "Have you tried resisting the memories?"

"It's impossible," I whispered.

He caressed my cheek. "You told me that when you touch me, it's similar to the feeling you get when the memories take over."

"Yes," I said, a deep blush settling into my face.

"Maybe you should practice on me."

I tried to laugh it off, but he leaned in so close, my breasts swelled against the pressure of his heart beating within an inch of mine.

He laced his fingers through my hair as he stared down at me, eyes glistening, lips parted. "Resist me," Dane murmured.

I felt drunk with the promise of his mouth. With each breath in, I imagined pulling him closer. His scent wrapped around every inch of my skin, caressing me. He was so close, if I just arched my back I could reach his lips, but I wanted him to be the one to do it—the one to break. His fingers spread out in my hair as he moved closer. The tension was excruciating. The heat unbearable. When he finally pressed his lips against mine I thought I might burst into flames. There was nothing innocent about the kiss; it was dark and deep, something I wanted to dive into and never return from. I ran my hands down the sides of his body, his muscles tensed beneath my touch, and then he pulled away, smiling down at me with that sexy dimple that destroyed me.

"Sleep tight," he whispered as he left me alone in my bed, gasping for more.

Breathless.

33

CONDUIT

"LET'S GO," RHYS SAID as he tossed some clothes on my bed.

I pulled the sheet up tight under my chin. "Where?"

"We're going to see the conduit." He jerked open the drapes.

"Teresa?" I squinted at the sun shining through my window. "Why?"

"Beth thought it would be a good idea," he said as he headed back toward the door.

"You know that's Dane's mom, right? Shouldn't we be asking him first?"

Rhys gripped the doorframe. "It's been arranged. He should be here any minute."

"What?" I grabbed the clothes and started putting them on under the sheet. "But I thought you didn't tru—"

"I don't," he said as he left the room.

Pulling my hair back with the ribbon, I brushed my teeth and raced upstairs.

Beth was wearing the same type of undergarment I'd mistakenly worn to the games. She grinned and waved as if last night had never happened. I knew what she was trying to do by getting us all together. It was sweet, but I'd never seen my brother as upset as he was last night. He was going to need some time.

I peeked around the living room, the loft, the kitchen.

"He's not here yet." Rhys sighed. He still wouldn't look me in the eyes. "You should eat something." He slid a plate of warm, honey-drizzled biscuits toward me.

"Not hungry," I lied as my stomach growled in protest. "I'm going to wait outside."

I couldn't stand the tension between us. I shouldn't have lied to him. I kept telling myself it was to protect him, but maybe I was just protecting myself. I couldn't bear to have him blame me for all this. Sometimes I wondered if I'd just spoken up about the dead girl in our kitchen—if I'd told them she looked exactly like me, maybe none of this would've happened. Maybe Mom would've known something was coming— we could've run. But there was no running from what was happening to me now.

I went around the back of the house and walked across the prairie grass to sit in front of the corn. I still didn't understand why the memories or feelings came on when they did.

All I knew was that they were getting stronger, clearer, more frequent. Maybe seeing Teresa would help me understand myself a little better, what was happening to me, how much longer I had left.

I collapsed back onto the grass, letting the cool dark blades press into me. It reminded me of my mother, and the last time we were together in her studio.

I heard the brush depress behind me. I didn't need to turn around to know it was Dane—his scent, the rhythm of his breathing.

"Sleep well?" he asked as he settled next to me.

For a moment, I wondered if I'd imagined our kiss last night, but he glanced down at my lips like he owned them.

"Did you . . . sleep well?" I asked, desperately trying not to stare at his mouth.

"It was interesting." He smiled, edging his hand closer until he laced his fingers through mine.

Rhys cleared his throat, and Dane stood up like a shot.

"Are you sure you're up for this?" I shielded my eyes from the sun to gaze up at him. "My brother? Your mom?"

Dane held out his hand, pulling me to my feet. "Beth said Teresa knew something about your protection marks. Maybe she knows why they're not working anymore . . . how to fix it. I'll do anything to help you."

It took everything I had to let go of his hand. As Dane and I walked through the tall grass toward my brother and Beth, he whispered, "I'm happy I get to spend time with you, even if it's under the watchful eye of your brother."

I looked up at Rhys and almost burst out laughing. Not because it was funny, it was just so uncomfortable; the four of us being together like this, on a doomed double date.

We walked through the thick forest of pines bordering the southeastern edge of the corn until we reached a large clearing.

"Heartbreak Tree." Dane pointed to a lone tree in the distance—an old weeping willow set in the middle of a field. Its branches spilled to the ground like an overfilled glass of champagne.

"I know that tree," I whispered. "Why do they call it Heartbreak Tree?" I asked as I wandered into the field to find it littered with stones of all shapes and sizes. Some of the rocks had notes tied to them, like Marie's; others were painted with hearts and initials.

Dane followed me. "People come here to deliver proclamations of love to the Great Spirit. They write a note and tie it to a rock and hope their love wish will be granted."

I reached down to pick up one of the stones, but he stopped me.

"It's bad luck to pick up a stone that doesn't belong to you." He brushed my elbow and I almost lost my train of thought.

"Have you ever written a note?" I asked.

He stared off at the tree for a moment, a bittersweet smile washing over his face. "If I had, I *promise* you'd know."

As we approached the tree, Dane held back the thick fringe of branches so we could all step inside.

"It's beautiful," I whispered as I walked the inner circumference of the tree, letting the soft branches graze my outstretched fingertips. The breeze trickled in, making the leaves shiver. It felt like a sanctuary.

The gnarled gray trunk appeared to be split in two.

Beth looked up at the branches. "They say when she died, the tree broke, just like her heart."

"But the tree lived," Dane said, his voice thick with emotion. "It changed and grew, weaving its way through every obstacle." He smoothed his hand against the trunk and looked at me, eyes glistening. "Love is stronger than death."

Beth whispered something to Rhys and his cheeks flushed a deep pink.

"Of course it is." Rhys shook his head in disgust and pulled me aside. "You know what this place is, right? Beth just told me it's basically the *sex* tree."

"Really?" I felt my entire face light up.

"We need to move on." Rhys glared at Dane and then crashed through the flowing branches, getting all tangled up. Beth had to help him get free.

I started to follow when Dane pulled me back by my waist, wrapping his arms around me. "Stay."

The beat of his heart, the feel of his warm breath in my hair, sent tingles across my skin.

"Ash!" Rhys yelled from the other side of the branches.

"I wish." I let out a deep unsatisfied sigh as I pried myself away.

Before I pulled back the branches to step outside, I looked back at Dane—he was leaning against the trunk—those eyes—I still couldn't tell exactly what color they were. "I'm beginning to feel like a racehorse, stuck at the starting gate."

"You're the dark horse," he whispered.

Reluctantly, I left the safety of the branches.

34

CROWS

AS WE PASSED Silk Pond, a dark feeling moved through me. This was the last place Katia and Alonso were alone together—the place of their ill-fated final meeting. I didn't blame Marie for telling Coronado where to find Katia and Alonso. She was a young girl, manipulated by a master. But you can't choose who you fall in love with. I remembered my mother telling me the Larkin women fall too hard, too fast, and too fierce. I looked up at Dane and knew she was right.

As we crested the small hill, a shadow crossed my face. I looked up to see a black bird soaring high above. Was it possible Coronado was watching us right now? Trying to find a way in?

"There it is," Beth chirped as she pointed to a dilapidated cottage nestled in the woods below. As we got closer, trinkets hanging from the eaves became visible, clinking together like dense blocks. I squinted to see what they were made from, and a chill marched over my skin. They were bones. Hundreds of delicate bones strung together like Christmas lights.

"Teresa won't take handouts. She finds her own food." Dane nodded toward the half dozen dishes of food in varying states of decomposition, littering her front steps like a giant unwelcome mat.

I peeked in the filthy front window to see Teresa sitting perfectly still in a rocking chair, staring at the wall in front of her. Expressionless. The same way I'd discovered her at the Mendoza lodge.

Rhys knocked on the door and Teresa's eyes darted to the window, focusing in on my face with a sharpness that cut right through me. Dane took my hand and led me away from the window, up the front porch steps and over the threshold. He seemed just as apprehensive as I was as we stepped inside the dark house.

Through the disarray of dead leaves, broken glass, and bubbled-up wallpaper that curled around the seams to expose the black mold underneath, I could tell that someone had once cared about Teresa enough to try and make this a home for her.

I wondered if this is what would become of me, too. Would I have to be tucked away in a little cottage, or a little asylum?

Dane squeezed my hand as if he knew what I was thinking.

"May we sit?" Beth asked.

Teresa rocked once in her chair. We took it as a yes.

Taking Beth's lead, we filed into the room, sitting on the edge of a tattered sofa.

Teresa turned her gaze to me and began to rock—slow and steady. It was beyond unnerving.

"What are you?" she finally spoke, her voice raspy as if she hadn't used her vocal cords in days.

I remembered Dane had asked me the same question that first night in the corn. "I . . . I'm Ash Larkin," I stammered. "Nina's daughter and I—"

"No," she barked, making my insides jump. Her eyes narrowed into slits. "What *are* you?"

I swallowed hard. "I'm a conduit."

"Is that what they told you? You're nothing like me." She lifted her chin in the air, inhaling deeply. "You have a twin."

"My brother, Rhys." I motioned toward him, but Teresa just kept staring at me.

"It's unfortunate." She sighed. "But without darkness, there can be no light."

Rhys stood up. "This was a bad idea."

I could tell by the way he looked at me that he finally got it. He understood what it meant to be a conduit. What it meant for me.

"Teresa." Dane leaned forward. "We're hoping you can help us."

Teresa's eyes shifted to Dane. "I know you. I know what you are. You're Spencer's bastard."

"Yes." Dane flinched at the word.

I couldn't believe it. She didn't even know he was her son. Would I eventually forget about my mother and Rhys . . . and Dane?

Dane looked into Teresa's eyes. "You'd mentioned Ashlyn's marks when you met her at the Mendoza lodge. Can you tell us anything about them . . . why they're not working anymore?"

"You're marked, too." She seized Dane's wrist, turning it over to expose his brand. Then she took my hand, forcing it into Dane's. "You may carve out your heart and throw it into the deepest ocean but it will remain there at the bottom of the ocean floor, irredeemable."

Dane tried to pry her fingers away from us, when her eyes rolled back in her head and she started trembling. "He's here. He knows what you are. He's not what you think he is."

"Who's here?" I asked. I looked to Dane for reassurance, but he seemed just as disturbed as I was.

"Ash," my brother called out in a panic as he stared out the window. "I think you need to see this."

I broke free of Teresa's death grip and joined my brother by the window to find the trees outside the cottage swarming with black birds.

I looked back at Dane, but he was busy whispering to his mother, easing her back in her chair, trying to soothe her.

"Stay here," I said as I went outside.

Slowly, I stepped down from the porch. The crows stared at

me from the trees, their red eyes gleaming, too many to count. The sound of their talons scraping against the branches set my teeth on edge.

"Scat." I waved my hands, but they didn't budge.

A crow let out a demonic cry and swooped down—Dane pulled me back onto the porch. "What do you think you're doing?"

"He's come for us . . . the last of the Larkins," I said, remembering their presence at my mother's studio. "I can distract them while you take my brother and Beth back to the lodge."

"I'm coming with you."

"You can't." I took his hand. "Rhys is deathly afraid of birds, he'll never be able to make it back on his own."

"Ashlyn, please don't—"

"Let me help my brother while I still can, while I still know who he is." My eyes veered back toward the house—Rhys and Beth were standing by the window. "No matter what happens, I need you to get my brother and Beth out of here."

"We'll all go together."

"No," I said a little too forcefully, and then lowered my voice. "I can't leave without my mom. Promise me you'll get them out."

"I promise," he said softly. "When the time's right I'll take them to the outer perimeter, but then I'll come back for you."

I looked down at the ground, trying to hide my feelings. If Dane knew what was good for him, he'd leave, too. He knew better than anyone what my future entailed.

He looked at me in anguish. "There's something I need to—"

"There's no time," I interrupted. "You said you'd do anything to help me. This is what I need."

He gave me a slight nod. Before I had a chance to change my mind, I let go of his hand and ran into the woods behind the cottage. The wail of the crows barreling down on me from above sounded like hell itself.

I caught a glimpse of a limestone ledge up ahead. I skidded to a stop, and the crows passed over me like a screeching freight train.

As I pressed myself under the ledge, the crows circled back, casting a dark shadow.

They landed somewhere behind me. The smell of rot, algae, and ammonia grew thicker with each step they took as they moved in.

They were so close now—right above me on the ledge—the sound of their talons curling over the edge of the limestone made my skin crawl.

I held my hand over my mouth, trying not to breathe, tears steaming down my face.

My insides clawed at me to run for it, but I was paralyzed with fear.

I clenched my eyes shut, willing them to leave, when Rhys came barreling down the hill. The crows attacked in unison, viciously stabbing at every bit of exposed skin on his arms and neck. I lurched forward, trying to fight my way through the flurry of black wings to help him, when suddenly, the crows dropped to the ground like dead weight.

My brother stood there, stunned, blood flowing from deep puncture wounds on his arms and neck while black feathers rained slowly down on him.

Tentatively, I stepped forward, nudging one of the crow carcasses with the toe of my boot.

"They're dead?" he whispered, eyes wide.

Dane and Beth came running down the hill, but when Dane got a good look at Rhys surrounded by the dead crows, he held Beth back. "You're lucky . . . you have Katia's blood. Otherwise, they would've ripped you apart."

"Is that what saved him?" I reached out to help my brother, but he shook me off.

"I'm fine. Just give me a minute," he said, bracing his hands against his knees, trying to catch his breath. "I don't know what just happened, but we need to get the hell out of this place. Can you do it, Dane? Can you get us out of the corn?"

"At dawn on the summer solstice." Dane nodded. "We'll meet at the old stables at first light—"

"Why not now?" Rhys interrupted him.

Dane's eyes narrowed. "You know you're going to have to trust me if this is going to work."

"I don't really have a choice, do I?" Rhys smirked.

"Then it's set," I said, trying to break up the tension.

Rhys stepped out of the crow circle and began walking back toward the lodge. "Oh, and, Dane?" He peered over his shoulder. "Stay away from my sister until then. If you get caught . . . well . . . you probably wouldn't be up for a long journey." He gave Dane a pointed stare. "Do we understand each other?"

I'd never thought of my brother as being intimidating before, but Quivira had changed us both.

35

RIFT

BETH LOOKED ON, wincing with sympathy pain as Henry cleaned and bandaged the puncture wounds that covered my brother's neck and arms.

"Ladies love scars," Henry said as he concentrated on a particularly raw spot near Rhys's temple.

"Yep." Beth bobbed her head as she gripped the edge of the farm table in the dining room.

Rhys smiled back at her, and my heart melted.

I was proud of my brother for remaining upright throughout this entire ordeal, but my feelings were a little hurt he didn't want me to treat him. Still, when I looked at the three of them huddled together like a little family, it gave me some peace. We all saw what Teresa had become. I had no idea how much time I had left.

"And it's not like you tripped in the woods," Henry added

as he moved the lantern closer. "You survived a *crow* attack. Not many people can say that."

"You were really brave," I said.

Rhys barely acknowledged me.

I'd never felt so out of step with the world. Dane was the only person I felt comfortable around anymore, and I couldn't even be seen with him.

"Henry"—my brother cleared his throat—"I want you to come with us. We're leaving Quivira at dawn on the summer solstice."

"How?" Henry dropped the bloody sponge into the bowl of witch hazel, sending the murky liquid sloshing over the side.

"Dane." Beth smiled. "He's a cornwalker."

"Well, I'll be . . . ," Henry whispered. "Just like his mother." Henry looked back at me with sharp eyes. I wasn't sure what he was looking for, but I tried to bar him from my thoughts.

"But Ash isn't coming with us," Henry announced.

"Of course she is." My brother jutted his head back.

I glared at Henry and then took a deep breath. "Dane will still take you," I assured them. "But Henry's right. I'm not leaving . . . not without Mom."

"Why?" Rhys finally looked at me and I wish he hadn't. "We need to get the police, the FBI, Nancy Grace for all I care—anyone who will listen. We need to blow the lid off this place once and for all. There's nothing you can do for her here. These people are never going to let her go."

"Neither can I."

Rhys sprang to his feet. "They've brainwashed Mom and now they've brainwashed you," he said as he came toward me. "You just want us to stay here with you and—"

"No." I swallowed hard. "That's the whole point. I don't want that for you. Mom's not the only one who's disappearing. You saw it with your own eyes today—with Teresa. I won't be *me* much longer."

Rhys took a step back like he was stunned to hear me say it out loud, but he didn't seem surprised. "Then we need to find a doctor."

I reached for his hands. "Mom did what she could to help me, but the only cure for being a conduit is death. And I don't want die in some cage—in some hospital. I want to be here, in Quivira, where I belong."

Rhys squeezed my hands. "Mom may have wanted to come back here, but she didn't want this for us. You're my sister, Ash. My twin. I can take care of you." He looked at me pleadingly.

"You have Beth and Henry to take of now." I glanced back at the two of them as they tried hard not to listen. "And I have Dane."

He let go of my hands. "You shouldn't count on Dane."

"Why do you hate him so much?" I asked. "What's he done to you?"

"He's using you," Rhys said matter-of-factly, raising his chin.

"Using me for *what?*" I asked, feeling completely spent.

"Besides the obvious? I don't know yet, but I don't plan on

hanging around with him long enough to find out. And neither should you."

"You're wrong about him," I whispered as I descended the
stairs.

"Ash," he called after me.

I paused, looking up at him, hoping for a bit of forgiveness,
some understanding, but his eyes were dark—darker than my
mother's when she dug the bone needle into my flesh.

"You should know, I'm staying up here tonight." He nodded
toward the front door.

"What, you're going to guard the door? You can't stop me
from seeing Dane."

"I know you have your mind set on self-destruction, but if
you care anything for me, for Beth or Henry, you'll stay away
from him until the solstice. He's the one person who can get
us out of this hellhole. If you're caught with him, we'll never
leave."

I ran down the stairs to my mother's room.

As soon as I closed the door, I felt the ribbon stir against
my neck. "Not now." I clenched my arms to my chest trying
to dampen the feelings, but another presence surged through
my bloodstream, like a powerful narcotic. When I thought
of my brother, guarding the door, I started to panic. There
was no stopping me when the memories took over. I punched
Dane in the face last night. If Rhys tried to get in my way, I
had no idea what I was capable of. I'd never been so afraid of
my own body.

I tried to hang on to the present, but my mind raced—Dane caressing my hip, Beth whispering she would protect my secret, Katia's golden blade pulsing in her hand, the grainy image of Heartbreak Tree—until my thoughts turned to nightmares.

The deep hum in my bloodstream would not be denied.

Staring out the window at the dark water, I knew it wouldn't be long.

Without another thought, I opened the window and escaped into the night.

As I ran through the woods, I felt myself losing ground, losing myself, until I finally disintegrated into another time.

36

IN TOO DEEP

AT THE EDGE *of the sacred circle, I peer between the stalks. Dread presses down on me, crushing me, holding me in place. In the center of the circle there's a dark pit, like a gaping mouth into another world. Just the sight of it brings the taste of blood and bile to my mouth. I don't need to get any closer to know the crevice is deep, I can feel it in the pit of my stomach.*

A chill rushes over my skin as I realize I'm not alone.

Something's moving inside the chasm. A sound like jagged fingernails digging into rock—crumbling black shale mixed with the noxious scent of blood.

Whatever's inside that crevice carries a darkness—something that wants to ooze inside of me to snuff out any other light.

I'm so close I can hear the low gurgling sound in the back of its throat, like a dripping wet death rattle.

"Ashlyn," Dane's voice whispered, pulling me back from the edge of terror.

I came to, standing in the corn, naked, covered in blood, clutching a knife.

"It's me. You're safe." Dane pried the knife from my clenched fist. My knees buckled, like they'd been locked in place for hours.

He swept me up in his arms, carrying me through the corn, back toward Quivira.

"What have I done?" I asked in a hoarse voice, staring down at my trembling hands, slick with blood. But there were no wounds.

"You found my knife . . . the one I lost in the corn."

"Did I hurt you?" I felt woozy as I searched his skin for damage, but the only thing I found was a small cut on his hand, a defensive wound.

"You just grazed me," he assured me.

"But all this blood—"

"You're the daughter of the vessels and a conduit. You probably cut yourself and healed back up again before I found you."

"Why would I cut myself?"

"Conduits have a tendency toward self-mutilation."

Confusion washed over me and I buried my face into his chest. "How long have I been out?"

"Almost six hours. You're getting better at evading me, but as soon as you looked into my eyes, as soon as I said your name, you came back." He smiled down at me and for the first time I realized I was naked, in his arms, but too exhausted to care. These episodes were taking everything out of me.

"I don't know what happened," I whispered, "but I was right there, standing on the edge of the sacred circle. I was ready to step inside, when it felt like I was being ripped away."

"I stopped you from entering the circle," Dane admitted, his eyes focused on the ground in front of us.

"Why?"

"I won't be able to reach you once you're inside. Only Katia's blood can pass. You'd be completely on your own."

"But there's something there. I can feel it. Whatever Marie wants to show me . . . it's inside that circle." I held his face in my hands, forcing him to look me in the eyes. "Promise you won't stop me next time."

He stared ahead, his brow knotted up with worry. "I promise," he whispered.

As soon as we emerged from the corn, into a stretch of woods, I felt like I could breathe again. The air no longer held that metallic edge of adrenaline-spiked blood. The oxygen going in and out of my lungs took the conduit feelings far away from me. Almost as if they'd never been there at all.

There wasn't a clear path leading through the dense wooded area, but Dane seemed to know where he was going. We stepped out of the trees and into a small, secluded cove. Slashes of pink and gold painted the surface of the water, reflecting the majesty of the sun rising over the endless sea of corn.

Dane waded me into the salt lake, gently dipping me in. The pearlescent water clouded into soft billows of pink as he smoothed the blood away from my arms, my neck. *Now* I felt naked. My skin prickled up in goose bumps.

"I'm sorry if it's cold," he said.

"It's not cold," I said, meeting his gaze.

I drifted from his arms, completely submerging myself. It was so peaceful below, not a sound, not a care. When I could no longer hold my breath, I came up to the surface to find the air thick with strawberries, musk, sandalwood, and fertile earth.

Everything inside of me reached out for him. Even the blunt edge of the black silk ribbon tied around my neck drifted toward him longingly. I was no longer merely existing or surviving—I'd never felt more . . . *alive*.

"If I gave you my blood, would you be able to follow me inside the sacred circle?" I asked as I swam around him, my heart pounding at the memory of Katia giving her blood to Alonso. "Then I wouldn't have to be alone."

"I don't know if it's that simple," he said as he stood in the waist-deep water, following me with his eyes. "But I'm honored you'd consider sharing that with me."

Dane still didn't understand how I felt about him. At this point, words meant nothing. I needed to *show* him. I didn't know how much time I had left and I didn't want to waste it playing games.

I took in a steeling breath as I planted my feet into the

soft clay floor and stood tall, exposing my upper body to the humid air. It was so quiet; the only sound came from the last few drops of opal liquid that dripped from my navel back into the water.

Slowly, he closed the distance between us. Though he still wore all his clothes, so little separated us now.

It seemed like an eternity before his penetrating eyes met mine again, and when they did, they no longer held any doubts.

Dane reached for the ribbon draped between my breasts, and coiled it around his fingers.

I felt the slight pressure of it straining against my neck, but not enough to pull it from the bow.

"You can pull harder," I said. "You can't hurt me."

"You're wrong." Dane held me close. "I *can* hurt you," he whispered in my ear, "but I don't want to."

He kissed me so delicately it felt like a feather brushing my lips. I twined my fingers in his thick hair, and he kissed me harder this time, his tongue dancing on mine. A surge of warmth radiated down from the top of my head, settling deep inside of me.

He pulled me closer, lifting me from the water, his fingers digging into the backs of my thighs. My body trembled. I wanted him to crush me—consume me, body and soul. I took in a gasping breath when Dane suddenly let go of me, lowering me back into the water.

"Is she *naked*?" Lauren screeched.

Lauren and Brennon stood on the shore, looking on in

disbelief. Dane stepped protectively in front of me. I pressed my face between his shoulder blades, feeling a deep shudder run through him.

"What are you doing here?" Dane asked.

"I could ask *you* the same, but that's pretty obvious," she replied, hands on her hips, staring daggers into me. "Where are her clothes?"

"We lost them," Dane admitted, a beautiful flush creeping over his collar.

"You *lost* them?" Lauren chuckled darkly. "That's rich." She sighed. "Brennon, give me your shirt."

Brennon fumbled with the buttons on his dress shirt and handed it over. Lauren tossed the shirt over the water. Dane snatched it out of the air and helped me put it on. The cotton stuck to my wet skin like cellophane, but it was large enough to cover the parts that mattered.

"Brennon, take the princess back to her castle and don't let her out of your sight until the solstice. And you"—she pointed at Dane—"you're coming with me."

I slipped my fingers through his in defiance.

"I can take her back myself," Dane announced.

"Really?" Lauren laughed. "You're going to take her back to the Larkin lodge looking like that? The whole community's waiting for her there."

"Why?"

"Some kind of emergency," Brennon said.

I sprung out of the water. "Is my mother here?"

"Not yet," Brennon said.

"Is Rhys okay?"

"Your brother's fine," Lauren snapped. "He's been looking for you, though—worried sick." Her eyes narrowed on me. "You shouldn't be here. If anyone knew about the two of you, Dane would be—"

"It's my fault," I said. I couldn't bear to hear her finish the thought. "Please don't tell anyone."

Dane walked me to the shore, his hand resting on my lower back. He pulled me close. "As soon as you're ready, I'll meet you by the corn beyond the prairie grass. I won't interfere again. I promise."

As I watched him walk away from me, slipping into the woods, I felt something break inside of me.

That's when I knew.

I loved him.

I was all in—blood and salt.

37

HENRY

BRENNON AND I WALKED to the Larkin lodge in uncomfortable silence. The warmth of his gray eyes had hardened into brushed steel. As we broke through the trees, he gripped my hand. I tried to squirm out of his grasp, but he wouldn't let go.

"Please don't tell anyone," I pleaded. "It's not Dane's fault."

When I saw the crowd of people gathered on the lawn, my stomach coiled in knots. It felt like I was walking directly into a hornet's nest.

"Where have you two been all night?" Mrs. Mendoza sighed as she led us toward a group of people swarming around the entry, but she held her head high, as if she were proud.

"Sorry, we lost track of time," Brennon announced loud enough for everyone to hear. "Did you see the stars last night?" He grinned at me in that perfect Brennon way and

I almost believed him myself. This was the nicest thing he could've done for me, but I was a little unnerved by how easily he switched on the charm.

Everyone stared at us briefly, then glanced away, almost out of respect. Seeing us in this way, Brennon shirtless, me wearing nothing but his shirt, seemed more than acceptable. It seemed *expected*.

After making sure they got an eyeful, Brennon steered me toward my brother and Beth, who sat slumped on a quiet corner of the lawn.

"We've been looking for you all night." Beth jumped to her feet and hugged me.

"What's going on?" I asked.

Rhys raised his head to look at me and I knew something was very wrong. His eyes were bloodshot, his hands trembled as he pointed toward the walkway. I turned to see people carrying what looked like a mummy on a strange-looking wooden stretcher.

"Another person died?" I asked. "Who?"

"Henry," Rhys murmured, his chin quivering. "Henry is dead."

It felt like I'd been kicked in the throat. "How?"

"The same way Betsy and Tommy died," Beth answered as she placed her hand on my brother's shoulder.

"There was so much blood." Rhys looked like he was going to be sick.

"Blood?" I inhaled sharply. "When did this happen?"

"Sometime during the night," Beth said.

A terrible thought crept into my mind. Could I have done this? I came out of my blackout, in the corn holding a knife, covered in blood. Could it have been Henry's blood? I dragged my hands through my hair, trying to scrape my brain for any memory. Dane told me he'd seen conduits do miraculous and frightening things in the throes of their ancestor's memories. Was Dane just trying to protect me?

"I'm not going to stand watch over you," Brennon whispered through gritted teeth. "We should be happy. We've earned that right. This isn't the old days."

I had no idea what he was talking about, but I couldn't deal with this right now.

"I need to change my clothes," I muttered as I hurried into the house and down the stairs to my room. I wanted to close the door on everything, but when I got there I found Spencer Mendoza waiting.

"What are you doing here?"

"I might ask you the same question. You shouldn't even be here anymore." Spencer circled me like a shark testing its prey. "Where were you last night? And, Ashlyn, don't insult my intelligence by telling me you were with Brennon." The way he said my name was revolting.

"It's true . . . ask any—"

"You think you're so sly," Spencer sneered as he stalked toward me. "But I can smell my bastard son all over you. Katia won't stand for it. You know what must be done."

I felt the ribbon stir against my neck and a familiar dark feeling took over. I didn't even try to suppress it this time, I used it. I charged him, slamming him up against the wall. "If you tell anyone . . . or if you lay a finger on Dane, God help you." The ribbon slithered free of the bow to coil around his neck. As it cinched tighter and tighter, power surged in my bloodstream like a drug. And I didn't want to stop it. I wanted to kill him.

Spencer grunted, bubbles of saliva speckling the corners of his mouth as he fumbled for something in his breast pocket. A flash of steel. He lashed out at me, swiping the blade across my throat—the sharp pain stunned me. I staggered back. The black silk ribbon went slack as the rage poured out of me along with my life.

38

FERVOR

GRASPING AT MY THROAT, I clawed for air, but it was slit wide open.

Blind with terror, I heard Spencer moving around me, digging through my mother's belongings.

Reaching out for anything to grab hold of—my hand grazed Spencer's pant leg, but my hands were too slick with blood, my body too weak to hang on.

As I lay there dying, a tingling warmth spread throughout my body. My skin began to pulse, but it wasn't my skin, it was something deeper than that. I felt raw energy rising inside of me like a powerful wave gaining strength. I wasn't sure if it was real or if I was having an out-of-body experience, so when my lungs filled with air, I reached for my throat, feeling smooth wet skin. Exhaling a ragged breath, I got to my feet, strong and very much alive.

Spencer's eyes went wide as he pressed himself against the wall. He was holding something behind his back. "How? It's not possible . . . it can't be . . . it's *you* . . ."

"Ash?" Rhys called from the top of the stairs.

As Spencer took off running down the hall, I bolted into the bathroom, locking the door behind me. Panicked, I stripped off Brennon's blood-soaked shirt and pumped water into the tub.

I couldn't let my brother see me like this.

Rhys banged on the door.

"I'll be right out," I said, getting into the tub.

"Ash, are you okay? What happened down here? There's blood everywhere."

"It's nothing." I said, frantically soaking the shirt and using it to scrub away the evidence on my body. I wanted to scrub it all away—the symbols, Katia's touch, her scent, Marie's heartache, Teresa's haunting words. And what did Spencer mean when he said, "It's *you*"?

Feeling dizzy, I crouched down, clutching the sides of the white cast-iron tub. I stuck my head under the water, feeling it beat down against my back, trailing into my eyes, my nose, and my mouth, then lifted my chin to the ceiling, heaving for air.

"Ash, you need to open this door, now."

"Just a minute." I clamored out of the tub to face the full-length mirror.

I ran my hands over my throat. My heart thrummed like a sick bird in my hollow chest. He'd severed my jugular. I'd felt myself bleeding out, but there was nothing there. It wasn't just my throat that was left unmarred—there were no marks or blemishes on my entire body. Even the birthmark under my right arm had vanished. Every bit of me . . . erased.

I racked my brain for answers, but none of this made sense. And then it occurred to me—what if none of this was really happening—what if it was all in my head? Or a vision?

I held my head in my hands, pressing my skull as if I could squeeze out the craziness, but it only seemed to make things worse. I threw on a pair of shorts and a blouse that were hanging from the drying rack. I glanced at myself in the mirror, my hair wild, my eyes pinned with shock—I looked just like Marie on the night she died.

I burst out of the bathroom, nearly knocking my brother off his feet. "I need to be alone," I said as I ran up the stairs and out the front door.

Longing for fresh air, I took in a deep breath, but the smell of burning hair and flesh filled my lungs. I couldn't help thinking maybe Henry was the lucky one.

As promised, Dane was waiting for me at the edge of the corn.

"Thank God you're here," I said as I ran into his arms. But as soon as my feet hit the soil, I felt the memories rising up inside of me. I felt myself falling. I didn't have the strength to fight anymore. I dove into the sickness with an almost re-ligious fervor, letting the memories infect every cell in my body.

It felt as if everything were leading me to this moment.

The wave overtook me in one fell swoop . . . and I was gone.

39

BLUE

MARIE TAKES MY HAND as we step through the corn. I feel the warmth of her skin against mine, like she's just been lying in the sun. She looks back at me, a bittersweet smile curling the corners of her downturned mouth.

I pull out the stone hidden in the folds of my gown, and unravel the black silk ribbon.

Hearing the stalks rustling, I turn, thinking it's Coronado walking toward me, but it's not Coronado. Something unexpected grabs hold of my heart.

I felt myself splintering away from the memories, until I saw Dane's face before me.

As I stood on the threshold of the sacred circle, one foot in, one foot out, Dane stared at me longingly. He opened his mouth to speak—

"You promised you wouldn't stop me," I whispered.

Dane's jaw clenched; he had a tortured look on his face.

I gazed into his eyes for what I feared could be the last time and a pang seized me. I swallowed all of the emotion threatening to take me over. It took nearly all of my strength to walk away from him.

As he let go of my hand, I stepped inside the circle, where I knew he couldn't reach me.

I'd always said Dane's eyes were so clear I could never tell exactly what color they were—but today, I could see they were blue.

As soon as the stalks closed in around me, I felt the memories taking hold of me once again, pulling me into the deepest, darkest place.

Marie glances back at me, her eyes glistening in the moonlight. "You found my ribbon."

A wave of nausea rips through me, but I swallow the bile burning the back of my throat. "Great deeds require great sacrifice," I whisper as I slip the ribbon around her throat.

Coiling the ends of the ribbon around my fist, I pull with all my might and bash her head against the hard earth.

As I bind her ankles with the corn-husk rope and drag her toward the chasm, she looks up at me, dazed and gasping, with tears streaming down her face. "I thought you loved me."

I secure the end of the rope around a metal cleat embedded in the stone at the edge of the chasm and cradle her in my arms. "My sweet girl." I brush golden hair away from her damp cheek. "You've betrayed me. But I'm giving you a second chance. Your blood will be the blood that brings me a vessel. One day, we'll be together again, as you were once inside of me."

"You're mad." Marie tries to raise her head, but it's futile.

The golden blade throbs in my hand.

I tighten my grip and brace her against my breast as I slit the palm of her hand.

Warm blood spills, seeping into the earth, penetrating the vines, worming its way into the deepest roots.

I kiss the tremulous breath rattling on her lips.

"A mother's love is the greatest love of all." I pull the ribbon from her throat and nudge her body over the edge.

40

DESCENT

I CAME TO, lying in the sacred circle, my face hanging over the edge of the crevice. The feeling of loss so heavy I could hardly lift my head.

I peered through my disheveled hair to see the weighted rope tied to a metal cleat embedded in the rock ledge.

I grabbed onto it. The grating sound of the braided corn-husks twisting in my hands, the rough texture against my skin, made me want to scream.

I pulled and pulled until I reached the end—where a skeleton dangled from the end of the rope. Clasping the bones to my chest, I rocked back and forth. "Marie," I whispered.

All this time I thought it was Coronado dragging Marie through the corn. But it had always been Katia. She sacrificed her own daughter to the Dark Spirit in order to bring Alonso back. Marie betrayed her by telling Coronado where he could find them on the summer solstice, but she was just a girl in love. She didn't understand. *Is this what love did to you? Turned you into a victim? Or a monster?*

The stalks rustled on the perimeter of the circle. Panicked, I dropped Marie's bones into the chasm and crouched, adrenaline blasting, straining to catch a glimpse of what was out there in the corn, when something icy curled around my ankle and yanked me over the edge.

My limbs flailed wildly as I scrambled for purchase. When I finally made contact with something that felt like vines, I latched on to them with everything I had. My body whipped to a stop, bashing me into the jagged rock. Entwining my legs around my newfound tether, I had started to climb, inching my way toward the surface, when a scattering of rocks sounded beneath me.

Hoping it was just my imagination, I squeezed my eyes shut, listening closely.

The rock crumbled so close to me this time, I forgot how to breathe.

Then something brushed my hair and I freaked. "Who's there?" I screamed as I frantically swiped the air around me. I lost my grip on the rope and swung backward.

Thankfully, the root caught my leg, but now I hung upside down, completely inverted—just like Marie.

I tried not to imagine her pain. How long it must have taken for death to come. She might've cried out for days.

I took in a shuddering breath—the grotesque scent of death

was in the air—algae, decay, sour dirt, and a musky odor that seeped into my pores.

"No more," I cried into the void.

I couldn't take any more of the memories. I couldn't take another moment of heartache, but this wasn't a memory or a dream or a hallucination. I felt another presence in the chasm with me, prickling the back of my neck.

A crunching wet sound followed, like fingernails scraping the side of the rock wall.

"*You* are the vessel," a voice behind me whispered.

I twisted around, staring into the dark. My mind stuttered as a curtain of gray static threatened to overtake my consciousness.

"*You* are the vessel." The voice came from the right this time. I spun around, frantic to see what was down here with me.

"Please, stop," I cried. I felt the light leaving me and the darkness taking hold, stealing away all hope.

"*You* are the vessel." Like a bullet, the words ricocheted around my brain, until they settled deep inside me.

Images flashed in the darkness. The memory of Katia cutting into my mother's palm—*a vessel at last*. But it wasn't my mother's blood she was referring to. It was mine, inside her womb.

"*You* are the vessel."

The way I healed when Katia cut into me—my knee at the field—my slit throat—the cut at the gas station—and how I healed the deer.

"*You* are the vessel."

All of the overwhelming feelings, the intrusive memories, had nothing to do with being a conduit. Teresa told me I wasn't like her. I'd never been a conduit.

"*You* are the vessel."

Katia had been there since I met her, maybe even before I was born, lurking in my bloodstream. This is how I was tied to Marie. Katia killed her to give me life.

I unwrapped my leg from the vine and let myself fall into the depths, hoping by some miracle, I would die.

41

FEMUR

I DREAMED I SWAM *in the salty sea. Sunlight was streaming through the surface, but I felt no need to come up for air. My lungs didn't need air anymore. Joyfully, I did a somersault, then dove down, plunging farther into the abyss.*

Below me, my mother drifted in the deep blue with the silk ribbon dancing around her, like the blackest of ink. She'd never looked more beautiful. Her chestnut hair billowed in front of her face, momentarily obscuring my view, and suddenly everything changed. Every good feeling turned to dread—flooding my mind, suffocating my senses.

The black silk ribbon was squeezing her throat, pinning her to the bottom of the ocean floor— belly bloated, mouth open, dead eyes, her once-beautiful hair knotted like tangled seaweed. A living reef of blood and flesh and bones.

I turned away, kicking furiously toward the surface, but something tugged at me, pulled me down.

I glanced back. My dead mother shot toward me like a comet—arms stretched out, fingers reaching. In a panic, I pushed forward, but that feeling of being held in place seized me again. One end of the black silk ribbon snaked out from her neck and wrapped around my wrist, holding me to her like a tether. I tried to break free, but the harder I fought, the tighter it wound. I turned back and, to my horror, found that it wasn't my mother's face at all. It was my own, staring back at me with a rictus smile.

I came to, lying at the bottom of the crevice. There was no water, but I was fighting to fill my lungs with air. Something hard and jagged protruded from my chest.

I felt my broken body, every breath jolting me with searing pain. With each movement, a strange rattling sound echoed from the brittle rubble beneath me.

I cried out my mother's name, though I knew she was probably dead. She had to be. She'd served her purpose. Katia had no use for her anymore.

I wanted to lie there and wait for Katia to come for me, but then I thought of Rhys. Dane could still bring my brother to safety. I had to get out of the chasm.

Digging through my pockets, searching for anything that might help, I discovered a match I'd swiped from Spencer's hidden chapel.

With trembling hands I reached out and struck it against the limestone wall—phosphorous flared in my nostrils. Snatching a tattered piece of cloth from the ground, I wrapped it around a stick, and set the match to it. The torch illuminated a horrific scene.

The walls of the chasm were stained with old blood and viscera—beneath me, a bed of discarded bones. Even the torch I held wasn't a stick—it was one of their bones; the cloth, one of their wreathing gowns.

These were the Larkin girls who came before me. The unchosen. They never made it to the outside world, because Katia had killed every single one of them and thrown them into the chasm.

Marie fought to find me, to show me the truth. She was trying to warn me about Katia. I wouldn't let her death be in vain.

There was only one way out. I propped the torch against the side of the crevice and piled up the bones. Crawling on top of my ancestors, I stretched out my hand to Marie's skeleton, and climbed her body.

Every movement sent shock waves of pain pulsing through me, but I couldn't give up.

Once I'd reached her pelvic bone, I lunged for the rope, cringing at the crackling sound it made as I pulled myself upward.

Midway up the rope, the torch burnt out, leaving only the glow of the moon to guide me.

With each pull up the rope, the pain hit my torso like a thousand volts of electricity. Every inch was more agonizing than the last.

The remaining few feet were the hardest, seeing the edge of the crevice, having to muster up my last bit of strength to grab the metal cleat and pull myself out into the open air.

Grunting in pain, I dragged my broken body away from the edge of the chasm. The crops rustled along the perimeter, and I had a flash of remembrance. The boy from my vision, the one who stumbled out of the sacred circle and died in the corn—Katia told him to run, but she wasn't trying to help him, she was *feeding* him to the corn. I also understood why he looked so familiar—the dark blond hair, the chiseled features. The boy from the vision was Thomas . . . my father.

Desperate to get away from the memories, I pulled myself out of the circle and through the corn. Dane's scent was all around me. I wanted to call out, but I was panting so hard, I couldn't find my voice. I rolled onto my back to try and catch my breath, but it only made it worse.

The gash in my head had already started healing, but something hard and sharp still sliced into my chest and back.

I gripped the stalks on either side of me, bracing myself as I found enough air for one last primal scream.

"Ashlyn," Dane called as he tore through the field. When he found me, his smile faded into a grim line. "What happened?" he gasped as he kneeled beside me.

"Help me," I whispered in agony.

"Please, tell me what to do." His hands were clenched in front of him, like he didn't know where he could touch me.

"My chest." I winced, guiding his hand to show him where

the pain was. It felt like my skin kept trying to heal around the foreign object, only to be sliced open again. As Dane lifted up my shirt, the color drained from his face.

"That bad?" I grunted.

Terror flashed in his eyes. "It's a bone."

"A cracked rib?"

"No, it looks like part of a femur." He glanced down at my legs in confusion.

"It's not mine," I said. "There are dozens of skeletons in the chasm. Marie . . . all the Larkin girls. When I fell, it must've gone right through me. You need to pull it out."

"I . . . I can't. If I take it out you'll bleed to death. It's a miracle you haven't already. It looks like it's gone straight through your heart."

"You have to do it," I pleaded. "It will be okay."

He looked less than convinced as he stared down at the blood pooling around me. But I couldn't speak anymore; the pain was too intense. My vision started going gray and I desperately tried to hang on to the last bit of consciousness.

Reluctantly, Dane gripped the bone. "Should I take it slow or try to pull it out in one shot?"

I held up my finger.

"Ready?" he asked.

I closed my eyes and rested my head back on the soft earth.

He pulled. The pain was unbearable, like I was being flayed alive. But the bone wouldn't budge; it seemed to be wedged between my ribs.

He stood, placing a palm on my shoulder for leverage. "You better not die on me."

I wanted to laugh, but a searing pain ripped through me as he tore the jagged bone out of my chest. Blood came gushing from the wound.

"No, Ashlyn." He kneeled, putting his hands over it.

"I'm the vessel," I whispered. "I'm immortal—I *can't* die." Tears streamed down my cheeks as I said it aloud. "I never wanted this."

Leaning back on his heels, he looked down at the blood on his hands. "I . . . I'm so sorr—"

"We need to find Rhys," I interrupted. "You need to leave *now.*"

He picked me up in his arms. "First, I'm getting you out of this place." As soon as he took a step toward the outer perimeter a pain unlike anything I'd ever felt before welled up inside of me. It felt like something was crushing me from the inside out.

I screamed in agony.

"What is it? What's happening?"

He took another step forward and I could hear my ribs cracking beneath the pressure.

"Go back . . . take me back inside Quivira," I yelled.

He rushed me through the corn. As soon as we broke through the perimeter, the pain subsided.

Gently, he laid me on the grass. "I don't understand."

"Katia won't let me go. I can feel her inside of me. Please take my brother and Beth and leave."

"I'm *not* leaving you," he said through gritted teeth.

"After the ritual, I won't remember Beth or you or my brother."

"You don't know that—"

"Katia. I've seen into her heart. She killed her own *daughter*. She killed all the chosen Larkin girls and fed my dad and all the other Mendoza boys to the corn. She probably killed my mother, too. She'll never give her followers immortality. They're just breeders to her. And when she transfers her soul into my body, I'll kill anyone who tries to keep me from being reunited with Alonso. Including you."

"Ashlyn, there's another way." Dane glanced up at the moon, sitting high in the night sky. "It's almost midnight on the summer solstice. You and I . . . we can become blood bound."

"N-no," I stammered. I couldn't believe he was suggesting this. I would never wish this on another person. Especially someone I love.

"I'm not just a Mixed. I'm half Alonso's blood, too. It will work." He gazed down at me, lips parted.

"And then what?" I gasped. He didn't understand what being a vessel really meant. He couldn't.

"You and I can walk the corn together as immortals. We can fight her. I know we can."

"No," I whispered, thinking it would be just as wretched for him to be Alonso as it was for me to be Katia. "I can't do that to you."

"You can't or you won't?" Dane asked, his eyes welling up with tears.

A long moment of torturous silence stretched between us.

I watched him staring down at the still-gaping wound in my chest and I couldn't help thinking of Coronado overpowering Katia. "You could take it, you know. I wouldn't stop you."

"I would never do that." He looked shocked, like I'd just slapped him hard across the face. "It's yours to give, not mine to take."

The gash in my chest surged shut. Dane opened a flask of water from his pack and poured the tepid liquid over my chest, washing the blood from my skin.

"Ashlyn"—he gathered my hands in his—"I'll take your brother and Beth to safety. All I ask in return is one more night with you. Just the two of us. At first light, if you still won't bind to me, I'll leave you in peace. I *promise*. At the very least, we can say good-bye."

I watched the last tendril of blood disappear into the soil and I knew it wouldn't be long until I disappeared forever.

And I didn't want to be alone anymore.

42

ALONE
TOGETHER

QUIET BUT PRESENT, Dane led me through the wooded pines on the eastern shore, until we reached the clearing—Heartbreak Tree.

I knew what it meant. Why he brought me here.

As he held the branches open for me, I brushed past him. A prickling rush of heat swept over my body. I leaned back against the gnarled gray trunk, hoping the cool bark would extinguish the wildfire running rampant across my skin, but when he leaned into me, kissing my neck, a euphoric wave washed over me. Blood bound or not, Dane was under my skin. I wasn't sure I'd be able to walk away from him. Not now. Not ever.

"Please bind to me," he whispered in my ear.

"Why would you want this?" I broke away from him before I burst into flames. "Why would you want to be blood bound?"

He caught my hand. The end of the ribbon tied around my wrist coiled around his.

"For you. I'd do it for you. Think about it, we'd live forever, walk the world together, walk through time. If I'm blood bound to you, nothing will be able to separate us. Not even death."

"But we won't be *us* anymore. You won't be Dane and I won't be Ash. We'll be Katia and Alonso."

"I don't believe that." He moved closer. "I've always been able to pull you back from Katia. Together, we have a chance. We can overpower her . . . and Alonso."

"And what if you're wrong?" I untangled his wrist from the ribbon.

"Do you feel this?" He pulled me close, running his fingers lightly down my spine. "How can a feeling like this disappear? There must be a way for us to hold on to each other, through our blood. I won't lose you."

It took every bit of willpower I had to pry myself away from him. "What about my brother and Beth and everyone else? If we fail, they'll never get out."

"I can get them through the corn and make it back in time for the ritual." He brushed my hair from my shoulders.

"I'm sorry, but I can't risk it. I can't bring you down with me." I thought about what it felt like being in Katia's head as she nudged Marie's body over the edge of the chasm and I shuddered. "If things go wrong, we won't be able to take it back."

He grabbed my arms, eyes blazing. "If this is some noble

attempt at saving me, you're too late. I haven't had a chance since the moment I met you. Tomorrow, you'll walk the corn with *Brennon*, and Katia will force you to bind to him. Is that what you really want?"

"I don't want any of this!" I raised my voice, suddenly realizing why Katia had arranged for me to go through the wreathing ceremony with Brennon in the first place. She'd handpicked him as Alonso's vessel.

Dane let go and I turned away from him. I didn't want him to see how scared I was. How hopeless I felt.

As I stared through the shimmering branches into the night, Dane slipped behind me, easing his hands around my waist. "The choice will be made for you whether you want it or not," Dane said softly. "I'm here. I love you," he whispered into the back of my neck. "We were meant to be together."

He traced his thumb against the slope of my hip bone—the same way he'd touched me when we first met. I placed my hands on top of his; the firm pressure of his grip deepening my desire. He kissed my shoulder . . . then my neck, my ear; I turned toward him to find his mouth, when he stepped back. A slow smile spread across his lips with that perfect dimple peeking out. "It's your choice. I've already made mine."

I wanted to refuse him, for his own good, but there was no escaping. The branches seemed to imprison his scent, trapping it there until I felt drunk with his essence.

Thanks to Katia's memories, I knew how to perform the ritual, just as I knew Caddo like it was my native tongue.

"You're sure this is what you want?" I stepped toward him, searching his eyes, but it was too dark to decipher his expression.

"Yes." He pulled me close, his warm breath caressing my face. "I've never wanted anything more than this." He whispered in my ear, "I want to be able to find you, to taste you, to feel you even when I can't feel myself."

The smell of his skin was indescribable, like every good memory mixed with the sweetest bitter sorrow that I would ever know.

He kneeled in front of me and presented me with a knife from his belt.

My blood seemed to ache for his. I took his hand, and dug the knife across the length of his left palm. He sucked in air, trying to hold in the pain.

"A kisctsa rauuir tiaticaa kaukuu'," I chanted as I kneeled to face him, slashing a deep cut above my heart.

I pressed his palm against my chest. It stung at first, but we both held on tight. I could feel my blood slowly overpower his and then flow into him. I breathed in time with him and waited. We were meant to meet, meant to be in this moment. I loved him before I even knew him. It was written in our blood.

I felt both of our cuts heal simultaneously; a wave of raw emotion crashed over me. I was unable to distinguish one feeling from another. They were all intertwined—yearning, fear, lust, despair, but, above all, love.

A brilliant light moved across my skin, enveloping me in warmth. Even though it was like looking at the sun, I watched the light dance across my skin and spread to Dane, but the light never completely left me. I felt our lives surging as one—every cell, fiber, hope, fear, and dream merging with his. We were like a tangled mass of veins and arteries, all leading to one heart, beating for each other.

His body shuddered along with my own at the overwhelming sensation of having my blood pulse within him. He pulled me toward him and kissed me passionately; any resistance I once felt quickly faded with the rushing of blood through our hearts.

I felt like I couldn't get close enough to him even if he swallowed me whole. Without breaking our kiss, he pulled me into his lap. I felt a surge of excitement pulse through him as I slipped his shirt over his shoulders, dragging my fingertips across the now-healed scar on his left shoulder.

"Sometimes I think about the day we met," he whispered. "We would've talked all afternoon," he said as he lowered his hands to the buttons on my shirt. "And when the sun set, we would've walked hand in hand to the sunflower field."

Slowly, he unbuttoned my first button. I smiled into the dark.

"That's where we would've had our first kiss." He moved his hands down to my next button, slipping it from its home. "We would've gone to Windy Point, and never even noticed the stars."

I gently bit down on his lower lip. The third button practically popped open by itself.

He placed his hands on the last button. "And then we would've gone to Crystal Pond and undressed each other in the glow of the rising sun."

With the last button undone, he slipped his rough hands under the tattered cloth and eased my shirt from my shoulders.

We slipped out of our remaining clothes. The thought of finally being able to feel his bare skin against mine was so overpowering that I pushed him down against the cool ground and kissed him, letting my hair fall over him like a veil, my breasts brushing gently across his chest.

The sensation sent a shiver through both of us. He tried to lean forward for another kiss, but I held him back, entwining my fingers through his.

"Ashlyn," he whispered. I released his hands, letting him take command of my body. He traced every curve of me before lacing his fingers through my hair, and in one swift force, he was on top of me. The feeling of the cold hard earth beneath me with his hot skin pressing into me was sheer bliss. I coiled myself around him like a serpent. I wanted to meld into him and never return. It felt as if I were stepping into the sunlight after a lifetime of cold night. It felt all-consuming, electric, destructive, forever, and never.

It was blood and salt.

It was everything.

43

BETH +
RHYS

JUST BEFORE DAWN, Dane and I walked hand in hand through the western woods to the old stables to meet Rhys and Beth. I knew last night wasn't a dream, because my body ached in a way I'd never experienced—a good way. My connection to Dane was something deeper than blood. Deeper than fate. It felt as if nothing could separate us . . . not even Katia.

As we got closer to the west side of Quivira, the scent of blood and lilacs seeped inside of me. I took another step toward the heady scent and I knew something was off.

"Ashlyn, what is it?" Dane slipped his hand around my waist to steady me.

"Lilacs. Where are there lilacs?"

"There are lilac bushes by the old stables, but we're still half a mile away. Why?"

I took off running, following my senses, and Dane stayed close behind. My lungs burned with the caustic scent, my skin was drenched in cold sweat, but I couldn't stop. I couldn't shake the feeling that something horrible had happened.

We broke through the forest in front of a decrepit barn engulfed in lilac blooms. The smell of blood hit me with such force, I could hardly breathe.

I ducked under one of the rotting beams blocking the entrance, to find Rhys crouched over Beth's body. He glanced back at me, a look of pure fear in his eyes. Blood was seeping through a bandage on his cheek.

"All I did was kiss her," Rhys said in a panic.

"Beth." My voice quaked as I ran to cradle her in my arms. Her lips were blue, but she still wore her unreadable smile. The ends of a bright yellow ribbon that she'd tied around her neck hung next to her sallow cheek. Her skin was dotted with tiny beads of blood, like she was sweating it from her pores. She felt light in my arms, like a hollowed-out doll, but I saw the slight rise and fall of her chest.

She reached out to touch me, as if to comfort me. "I remember," she murmured. "I remember everything."

"We have to get her to a doctor." Rhys paced the sawdust floor behind me. "I think she has the same thing as the others."

"I can give her my blood," I whispered, remembering how Katia had healed Alonso.

"Ash, thanks for being my best friend." Beth smiled. "But you don't have to do this. Your blood is sacred and you need your strength. You can overcome her, I've seen it."

"You know what I am, don't you?" I asked, unable to stop the tears from flowing. "You've known all this time."

"There will be a path to lead us from darkness." She gave me one last smile before her eyes rolled back in her head.

"You don't need to keep my secret anymore," I said. "Let me protect *you* now."

"Dane, give me your knife." He handed it to me and I slit my wrist, holding it up to her mouth. She choked and gagged at first, but I held my arm firmly in place, forcing my blood down her throat.

Rhys raced toward me. "What are you doing?"

Dane held him back. "Saving Beth's life."

I felt my life force surging into her, and in return I felt traces of her own flowing into me. Her gentle spirit, her wounded heart: They brimmed over like a waterfall.

My brother stood there, stunned, as the beads of blood retreated back into Beth's pores and the color returned to her lips.

Dane ripped a strip of cloth from his shirt and wrapped it around my wrist like a tourniquet.

"I remember everything," Beth whispered fervently as she motioned for me to come closer. The way she spoke, the look in her eyes, the intensity reminded me of my mother on the day she left. Beth clutched my arm. "Spencer . . . he's the one who hurt me," she said as she reached up and felt the scar running across her skull. "I found out he made a deal with

Coronado—he was giving Spencer his blood. They used Teresa to bring the Larkins through the corn. Men, women, children . . . they're all dead." Dane sank to his knees beside Beth. I felt despair and shame wash over him.

"Someone needs to tell me what the hell's going on!" Rhys said.

This was the moment I'd been dreading. I unwrapped the cloth from my wrist and stood to show my brother my already-healed skin. "*I'm* the vessel."

"That's impossible." Rhys studied my arm. "It's Mom. It was supposed to be Mom."

"Katia wanted everyone to believe that, but she was just a diversion for Coronado. I was never a conduit. I was the vessel all along. Mom scars, I *heal*. Remember the deer on the back of the hunters' truck?"

"So, you're telling me it's true?" Rhys dragged his hands through his hair. "All of it?" He staggered back, accidentally kicking an old horseshoe into the side of the barn. He stood in front of the collapsed doorway, sunlight streaming through the gaps in the wood. "Then where is she? Where's Mom . . . and our dad?"

"Thomas never made it out of the corn," I said, staring out over the fields. "And I don't even know if Mom is alive anymore." It killed me to say it out loud. "Katia let Mom live because I was inside of her. She let her raise us away from Quivira to keep me safe from Coronado, but Katia doesn't need her anymore."

Rhys had a wild look in his eyes. "Then we have to get you out of here before Katia comes back." He glanced back at Beth, who was starting to come around. Dane was helping her into a sitting position, giving her his flask of water. "I'll carry Beth if I have to."

"I *can't* leave." I swallowed hard. "My blood . . . Katia's blood won't allow it. You need to go with Dane. He'll get you and Beth out and then you need to run and—"

"Wait . . . what?" he sputtered. "Just leave you here?"

"I'll be coming back," Dane said as he joined us, taking my hand. "To help her fight."

Rhys narrowed his eyes. "How could you *possibly* help her with this?" He glanced down at our intertwined hands and a look of disgust washed over his face, then shock. "Of course!" Rhys began pacing again. "That's what this is all about. You want to be Alonso's vessel, don't you?"

"I've already made that decision." I squeezed Dane's hand.

"He's a Mixed, Ash. That's never going to happen."

I took a deep breath. I was trying to figure out how to tell him the truth when Dane spoke up. "Ashlyn and I are already blood bound."

"What?" Rhys turned to face me, hands balled up into fists at his side. "You're blood bound . . . to *him*?" He bit the inside of his cheek as he walked toward me. I couldn't tell if he was going to laugh or cry. "So, I was right. He *was* using you. I thought you were smarter than that, Ash." Blood started seeping from the bandage on Rhys's temple.

"Please don't make this harder than it needs to be," I said as I tried to reach for him, but Dane held me back. "What are you doing?"

"There's something you need to know." Dane's voice was low and tense. "I had my suspicions, but this . . . what happened with Beth confirms it."

"Confirms what?" Rhys snapped.

"Your blood," Dane said softly. "You are the one responsible for all the recent deaths in Quivira."

"Me?" My brother began to laugh.

"Betsy Grimsby," Dane said, eyes downcast. "She changed the bandage on your knee before the ceremony."

Rhys crossed his arms in front of him like he was amused by the whole thing. "Okay?"

"Tommy Mendoza," Dane added. "You spit bloody water in his face at the shinny game."

Rhys continued to smile, but the color began to leach from his face.

"But his lip," I argued, "it healed right up at the field. He can heal . . . like me."

Dane shook his head. "*You* healed him. You held the bandage from your knee against his lip. "Look . . ." He pointed to the raw wounds on my brother's neck and face.

"No." I shook my head rapidly. "Those are coincidences."

"The crows," Dane asserted. "They dropped dead all around him. And Henry—"

Rhys hunched over like he was going to be sick. "Henry treated my wounds. He was my friend. And Beth . . ." He looked over at her in despair. "All I did was kiss her—my bandage must've touched her cheek."

"Rhys, slow down," I said. "This is crazy."

"Is it?" Rhys raised his voice. "My blood can't touch anyone without hurting them."

"I've touched your blood and I'm fine," I reasoned.

"That's because you're twins—you're of the same blood," Dane said tenderly. "You're the light and he's the dark."

"You heal and I kill." My brother exhaled.

I wanted to tell him he was wrong, but I felt it in my gut—an awful certainty buzzing beneath my skin.

"Rhys," I said as I squirmed out of Dane's grasp and reached out to him. "We can find a way. I can fix this."

"There's no *fixing* this. *I'm* fucked. *You're* fucked. This place is fucked." Rhys swatted my hand away.

"Watch it," Dane warned as he stepped between us.

Rhys pushed him hard.

"Please don't fight," Beth said as she got to her feet.

Dane was helping steady Beth when Rhys came at him with his fists.

Dane ducked out of the way and then punched Rhys in the face. My brother staggered back; a trickle of blood ran down from his nostril.

We all backed away.

Rhys's face fell. Tears welled up in his dark green eyes before he ran toward the edge of the corn, blood dripping from his nose in a steady stream.

The corn appeared to open up to let him pass. As he tore through the field, his blood left a scorched trail of disintegrated stalks in his wake.

I could smell the salt of his tears, the bitterness of hurt and betrayal. I tried to go after him, but as soon as I set foot across the perimeter, my body collapsed in on itself.

"Ashlyn," Dane pleaded. "Step back inside Quivira."

"What about Rhys?" I gritted my teeth as I struggled to hold my ground.

"We'll find him. I promise."

"I can't leave him." My body began to tremble with the strain of trying to cross the perimeter.

As Beth tried to help move me back, she accidentally stumbled onto the path of scorched earth Rhys's blood had made in the corn. When she realized she was standing beyond the perimeter, a huge smile spread across her face. "Look, I'm standing in the corn."

"You should go," I murmured through the pain. "If you hurry, you can catch him. He shouldn't be alone right now."

"Do you realize what this means?" Beth twirled around. "Rhys's blood can cut through Katia's spell. I kept dreaming about it . . . *a path that will lead us from darkness.* Rhys is the path."

I never knew what she'd been talking about . . . maybe she

didn't either, but it made perfect sense now. Dane told me the corn was a living, breathing thing. When we first came to Quivira, Rhys fell and skinned his knee and a patch of corn disintegrated around him. His blood had been the key to escaping Quivira this whole time.

"It means the others are free to go, too," Beth said with a little jump of excitement.

"It also means others can get *in*," Dane said. "Once a path is cleared, the protection barrier won't hold." For the first time, Dane looked scared.

Beth leapt forward to embrace me. "Rhys hasn't even begun to realize his full power. He will soon. And we'll all be together again, but right now, my place is with you."

I relented, letting Dane and Beth move me back from the perimeter. As soon as I was on the grass once again, the physical pain subsided.

"Rhys will never forgive me," I whispered, fighting back the tears as I stared out over the corn.

"Never is a very long time." Dane kissed my forehead.

44

RECKONING

THE COMMUNITY HAD gathered on the front lawn of the meeting house. Everyone was decked out in their finest clothes, staring at the corn in anticipation, waiting for Katia to arrive with Nina and Thomas. They had no idea.

"How are you going to convince them to leave?" Beth asked. "They don't know you're the vessel."

"I'm going to need that knife again," I said to Dane.

He caressed my fingers as he handed it to me.

Taking in a steeling breath, I made my way to the center of the crowd and cleared my throat. "I have an announcement to make."

Some of the Grimsby girls started giggling at me. I got a few stern looks from the elders, but most of them just ignored me.

"I'm the vessel," I said louder.

"Pay her no mind. She's a conduit." A lady with frizzy

brown hair gathered up her children and whipped around to move away from me, her voluminous skirt nearly knocking me to the ground.

"Oh, sweet girl, you're in a state," Lou said as she stepped toward me, shaking her head in dismay. "Did they let you wander off on your own?"

"I *said* . . . I'm the vessel." I held the knife high above my head and dragged the blade along the palm of my hand.

Lou stayed put, but the rest of the mob pressed back like whatever I had might be contagious.

"Can someone get a bandage?" Lou called over her shoulder.

"I don't need it," I said, trying to hold their attention.

"Sweetheart—"

"Look." I held out my hand. As the blood dripped down toward the earth, the cut began to close up, surging back together, leaving no scar, no mark—my skin looked flawless.

Lou grabbed my hand to study it, the pity slowly draining from her face. "It's *you* . . . ," she whispered. Then she dropped to her knees and began to pray.

The rest of the community quickly followed suit. A few people fought their way to the front to suck my blood from the dark blades of grass, others reached out to touch my feet. It wasn't the same feeling I got when the women prepared me for the wreathing ceremony. It gave me the creeps, like they all wanted a piece of me.

"I was Katia's vessel all along," I said as I tried to shake them off. "You've been lied to and manipulated. *Katia* killed

Marie. She sacrificed Marie to the Dark Spirit in exchange for vessels—for the return of Alonso's soul."

"Where's Spencer?" A man wiped his brow with his sleeve as he searched the crowd.

"No one's seen him or Teresa since last night," a woman with a crazed look in her eyes called out. "Do you think Coronado got them?"

I looked at Dane. He knew it, too. Spencer used Teresa to get through the corn one last time. He wasn't coming back.

"Spencer discovered I was the vessel last night when he tried to slit my throat. He's long gone by now. He used Teresa, who was a cornwalker, to deliver the Larkins to Coronado."

I scanned the crowd, desperately searching for some sign of comprehension on their faces. "Katia will never make you immortal. You were only breeders to her."

They just kept praying.

"Listen to me." I shook Lou, but it was like she was looking right through me. "You can leave!" I yelled as I walked through the gathering. "You can walk out of Quivira and start a new life."

No one moved a muscle. They all stared up at me like I'd just spoken a completely different language.

"If she's the vessel, she needs her intended," a woman with a newborn clutched to her chest called in a panic.

That's when I noticed Brennon, pale, flanked by his parents. He took a reluctant step forward and the flock parted, as if making way for a king. He looked up at me with bloodshot eyes as he reached out to take my hand. "I'm prepared to walk the corn with you. It's my duty. My honor."

I couldn't believe he was willing to go through with this after everything I'd just said. "There's nothing honorable about giving your body to a madwoman."

The people of Quivira only prayed more fervently, as if what I'd just said was sacrilege.

"Brennon, I'm sorry." I released his hand. "But I've chosen someone else."

Brennon let out a huge sigh of relief as Lauren ran to him, embracing him.

The realization burst inside of me. Lauren and Brennon were in love. That's why Lauren treated me the way she did and why Brennon was so cagey around me. His duty to his family, to Katia, had been the only thing standing in their way.

"You should all run while you still have a chance. You will never be immortal."

The community broke out in agitated whispers. "Who is it, then? Who will be Alonso's vessel?"

They weren't listening to me. Finding the vessel, completing the ritual had been their one common goal for so long, they'd become blind to everything else.

Dane stepped forward and took my hand. "*I* will be Alonso's vessel."

Brennon's mom started sobbing. "Katia will never allow it."

"We have to kill him before she arrives," Lou said.

The mob swept Dane up. I knew they couldn't kill him, but a venomous feeling rose up inside me. "Let him go." I glowered. "My blood has already chosen him."

The crowd went silent. They dropped their hold on Dane and backed away in fear.

But they weren't looking at me.

I turned to see Katia standing before the corn.

She was even more beautiful than I remembered. With the sun blazing down on her, she looked as if she were carved from soft gold. Dane wrapped his arm around my waist protectively.

"Clever girl," Katia said with a smile, but I could feel her displeasure.

"But he's a Mixed," someone called out.

"Inferior blood," Brennon's mom cried.

"She's given me no choice," Katia spat. "I should've drowned Coronado's children to begin with." She scanned the crowd. "Where's Spencer Mendoza?"

"He ran," I said, hoping to provoke her, distract her from the ceremony. "He betrayed you. He's been delivering the Larkins to Coronado for years. If you hurry, you can still catch him."

A flash of anger passed over her eyes, but she quickly buried it. "I'll deal with him later," she said as she clutched her golden blade by her side.

The people of Quivira just cowered before her. They'd been suckling off Katia's poisonous teat for too long. They'd even sacrificed their own children for a chance at immortality.

"I know you killed Marie," I blurted.

Katia turned on me with such hatred that my body shuddered beneath her gaze.

"You don't have to do this." I softened my tone. "You can let me and Dane go." I squeezed his hand before I took two careful steps forward. "We're in love. You of all people know what it's like to have that taken away from you."

Katia smiled. "You think love would save you?" Her heady scent intoxicated me as she passed. "The love you feel for each other will only make the binding stronger," she said as she circled Dane, running her hand across his back. "You've done me a great favor."

I started to protest when her eyes settled on me and a blistering pain ripped through my body, grinding me to my knees.

Dane tried to move toward me, but she stepped in front of him.

"Hold still now and I'll let her go."

Dane stood up straight, clenching his jaw.

And Katia released me.

"That's better," Katia whispered as she leaned in and kissed Dane's mouth. He didn't kiss her back, but I felt a torturous mix of desire and repulsion bubbling up within him . . . within me.

Katia then looked at me, a cruel smile twisting the corners of her lips. "He'll do."

When Dane's eyes met mine, I felt his shame, his confusion.

"It's time," Katia said as she slipped back through the stalks.

She knew I would follow. The invisible thread connecting us was embedded deep within my heart now. I had no choice.

As I stepped toward the corn, Beth hugged me from behind, startling me.

"Your mother didn't leave you unprotected," she whispered as she swept her hands down my arms and then retreated to join the others.

Dane laced his fingers through mine.

"I'm scared," I said as I stared straight ahead into the corn.

"You're the bravest person I've ever met, but you don't have to be so strong all the time. You have me now."

Gently, he raised my hand to his mouth, kissing the inside of my palm. Then he closed my fingers tightly around it, into a fist. "Hang on to this," he whispered. "No matter what happens, know that *this* is real."

Suddenly, I realized why I was afraid. I had something to live for. My brother, Beth, and Dane—they were family. I'd finally found something worth the risk, and now that my heart was open, I never wanted to close it again. My life was so full now. Suddenly, I was afraid of losing everything.

The wind swept through the corn, revealing our path.

They say the first step is the hardest, and this time, they were right.

45

PIECES

DANE AND I MOVED through the stalks in silence, following the path laid before us. I was terrified of what awaited me. Everything about this felt like a death march.

Dane kept a close eye on the dozen or so crows circling low overhead. Maybe Coronado was already inside Quivira—I wondered how he could stop the ritual now that Dane and I were immortal and bound?

Sensing my concern, Dane stroked my palm with his thumb. Even now, my blood craved him, my body reached out for him. Dane was a drug coursing through my veins, with an influence just as powerful as Katia's. I felt what he felt, anticipated his every move. His touch was like an anchor holding me to myself, reminding me of who I was.

I wanted to believe we could get through this, but with every step, the darkness spread, sweeping through my cells like poison. I'd seen into Katia's heart. I'd experienced her cruelty firsthand. Katia had been planning this for over five hundred years. What made me think I could defeat her with love? I glanced up at Dane to voice my fears, but I wanted him to hold on to hope for as long as he could. For everything he thought we could be.

I caught glimpses of Katia as she moved through the corn ahead of us, the swing of her skirt skimming the back of her knees, her hair swishing against her bronze shoulders like a wave of black silk. I reached my hand to my throat, thankful to feel Marie's ribbon still with me. It gave me some comfort.

As we neared the sacred circle, the air went thick with warring scents, some as familiar to me as breathing—others completely foreign. Along with sandalwood, cedar, mandarins, and the sea, I swore I caught a hint of my mother's scent, but my senses were on overload. Beyond the wall of sound—the gentle breeze rustling through the stalks—a soft susurration of breath entered my consciousness. I couldn't see the others, but I could feel their presence like a sharp needle softly dragging down the back of my neck.

"Ku' Quivira paatu' huhtaat aat," Katia whispered.

Only my blood shall pass.

As we followed her into the sacred circle, Katia halted.

A feeling of repulsion and fear ripped through me.

"Katia," said a man standing inside the circle. It was Coronado, in the flesh, his hand resting on the hilt of the dagger slung low around his waist.

Katia took out her golden blade, and at least two dozen men stepped out of the stalks, swords at the ready.

"How is this possible?" Katia murmured as she looked past Coronado, out over the corn. Her eyes filled with tears, her breathing went shallow.

"The boy's blood cut through your magic, led the way into Quivira."

Katia's face blanched. "What boy?"

"You didn't know?" Coronado seemed surprised. "The twin. Ashlyn's blood is full of life, but her brother's is pure death. Death for *all* living things, including your precious corn."

I felt a shiver rush through my blood as Katia reached out to the Dark Spirit for help.

"So careless of you," Coronado continued, "but you've always thought yourself invincible—above the laws of man and nature."

As clouds amassed overhead, I could feel Katia's power growing. A sinister wind rustled over the corn, a small taste of what was to come.

"We've already shed too much blood, you and I." Coronado took a bold step toward her. "We were young and foolish. Just like the young lovers you've summoned here today." His eyes settled on me in an overly familiar way, which made my heart beat heavy in my chest.

I looked up at Dane, his face shrouded in fear.

"I took Alonso away from you," Coronado said with a flash

of arrogance. "You took Marie away from me. We've had our vengeance. We can end this right now. Let the lovebirds fly away. Live in peace."

"There will be no peace as long as I'm bound to *you*." Katia's fingers trembled with rage.

Coronado's eyes flickered to Dane. A moment of recognition passed between them, but Dane quickly looked away. I could tell he was trying to stay strong, but I could feel his emotions—fear, sympathy, and an overwhelming sense of guilt.

"I'm glad you're here," Katia said, that rictus smile spreading across her face. "I want nothing more than to watch you die." Raising her hands to the sky, she summoned a vicious wind, which swiftly swooped down through her hands to encircle Coronado in a tight cylinder, holding him in place. "When the binding is complete, your body will wither and rot off your bones. You may have found a way into the sacred circle, but you have no vessel."

The Arcanum pressed forward from the stalks, but Coronado help up his hand, commanding them to stay back.

As Katia closed her eyes and began chanting, Coronado signaled to one of his soldiers, who pushed a hunched figure through the perimeter of corn, into the sacred circle.

It was a woman. She looked almost feral, tucked away against the stalks. But I recognized the graceful movement of her long slender fingers as she traced symbols in the air. "Mom," I whispered as I sank down beside her, brushing her limp hair back from her face.

She looked up at me like a child, blinking slowly a few times, before focusing in on me. "I'm sorry," she whispered. "I didn't know you were the vessel until it was too late." She looked dehydrated and ravaged by exhaustion. She tried to smile, but her lips only cracked. Still, she had a wild look in her eyes. She was very much alive.

"I'm here," I said, grasping her frail hands. My eyes stung from trying to hold back the tears. "Where have you been?"

"Coronado came for me in New York City, took me back to Spain. It didn't take long for both of us to realize I wasn't Katia's vessel," she said as she showed me the cuts on her wrist. "But you and your brother were already here, inside Quivira. She fooled us all."

I thought of her studio on the day she disappeared, filled with crows—her scent all around me when we met Coronado at the perimeter. I couldn't believe I didn't piece it together.

"I can heal you," I whispered as I cradled her arm in my hands. The cuts looked like they might be infected.

"No." She pulled her hand back. "I don't want to heal. This is how I can protect you. This is my destiny. Together, we can end this."

Suddenly, my entire body tensed as I looked out over the corn. There was a darkness building, spreading out over the field like a storm cloud. It's the same feeling I experienced when Katia summoned the Dark Spirit before the battle in 1861. The corn was hungry.

I looked back at Katia, who was swaying to the music of

her own whispering, and a deep ache settled in my heart. As distorted and twisted as she'd become, I understood her. I felt her rage and despair and hopes and fears in every word she uttered.

"What's happening?" Dane asked from behind me.

The dark energy pulsed over the field, screaming out for blood.

"She's going forward with the ritual." I gave him a bittersweet smile.

My mother's eyes darted between Dane and me. She dug her nails into my arm. "You're already blood bound?"

Sensing the tension, Dane said, "I'll give you a moment," before walking to the far end of the circle.

"It was my choice," I said to my mother. An uncontrollable heat rushed to the surface of my skin just thinking about our private ceremony under Heartbreak Tree last night.

Her body went rigid. "You only *think* it was your choice."

The first wave roared through the corn, taking down one of the soldiers and ripping his legs clean off his body.

"What are you talking about?" I searched the field, wondering how many of them were hiding in the stalks and why Coronado wasn't signaling for them to run . . . or charge?

"He's not what you think." My mother's eyes filled with tears.

Teresa said the same thing to me at the Mendoza lodge.

"Dane isn't like his father," I assured her over the horrifying wet screams of the Arcanum as the corn picked them off

314

one by one. "You yourself told me we're not responsible for the sins of our ancestors."

"I was wrong," she said as if she were swallowing thick chunks of glass.

"What are you saying?"

"Spencer chose to have a child with Teresa so he could have a son who was of Mendoza and Coronado blood—a cornwalker."

"He's a terrible man . . . I know this."

"*Dane* is the one who's been delivering the Larkins to Coronado all these years. He was supposed to deliver *you* to Coronado when you first came to Quivira, but he refused."

"What are you talking about?" I looked at her like she was crazy. She *was* crazy. There was no other explanation. Why would she be saying this to me? What did she have to gain? I tried to pull away from her, but she only dug into my skin with more fervor.

"I was there, Ash. When Dane let go of you in the corn, he spoke with Coronado. They've known each other for years. Dane saw an opportunity at immortality and he took it, but he also saved your life."

I didn't want to believe it, but doubt quickly seeped inside of me, ripping me to shreds. The way Dane held out his hand on that first night, asking me to come with him into the corn, telling me we had to hurry, and the savage look on his face when we were interrupted. How he nearly led me right into Coronado's arms the night of the bonfire, then changed his mind.

Rhys warned me over and over again and I didn't listen.

I felt my world crumble. I wanted to burn down villages, cut out people's beating hearts, and rip the stars down from the sky.

My entire body trembled as I turned to face him. I didn't have to ask if it were true. I saw it in the deep flush creeping up the sides of his neck and the way he shifted his weight like he was getting ready to dodge a moving train. "You killed my family," I said as I stalked toward him.

He held up his hands in front of him and tried to back up, but there was nowhere to go. "I . . . I was born into this, just as you were," he tried to explain, his bright eyes clouded with tears.

"So, you knew all along I was the vessel," I cried. "You lied to me. You manipulated me."

Dane pulled me tightly to him; I writhed in his arms and tore myself away. "You were going to take me to Coronado, but you changed your mind. Why?"

"I was in love with you." His voice caught in his throat. "I thought we could be together—"

"You knew I would blood bind to you. You saw a weakness in me and you took it. Because everyone knows the Larkin women are fools for love."

"No, I . . . was . . . I couldn't turn you over to him," he said, his face contorted in agony. "I could never hurt you. Everything I did was to protect you."

"Protect me?" I gasped. I looked back at Katia, hoping

she'd smite him or something, but she was still lost in her own world of longing as she traced symbols in the dirt and chanted aloud.

"Ashlyn, please." Dane sank to his knees before me. "I will spend the rest of eternity trying to make this up to you."

"You have no eternity. Not with me."

"We're blood bound."

"If you really loved me, you wouldn't have taken me to him in the first place. You wouldn't have lied to me. You would've found a way to let me go." Looking out over the bloodstained crops, my eyes filled with tears. "I'd rather be dead than be bound to someone like you."

I felt the shame, hurt, and despair within him and I didn't want to feel that right now. I didn't want to feel him at all. I wanted to open my veins and spill him from my soul.

Not knowing what else to do I lashed out at him in murderous rage, my fists swinging wildly.

"Enough!" Katia turned her attention on me and took control of my body—I felt my ribs cracking but I didn't care. I wanted to feel anything other than this betrayal.

I collapsed to the ground in agony.

Dane moved toward me to help me to my feet while Katia raised her hands to the sky, summoning another terrible wind, which wrapped around Dane's body in a howling vortex, pinning him in place. I didn't know if it was to protect him, or me.

I dragged my body toward my mother. I'd never felt so raw, haggard, and pathetic. The tears wouldn't stop flowing. My heart felt like a thousand-pound brick dragging in my hollow chest.

"It hurts, doesn't it?" My mother's eyes were dark and wild.

"Yes," I answered through clenched teeth, glaring at Dane on the other side of the protective veil. Veins protruded from his neck as he tried to reach me, but it was futile, like trying to walk into a hurricane.

"There is a way out. But the pain has only begun," my mother warned. "You're going to feel like you can't take another breath, like your heart can't stand to beat another second. But in that suffering, you'll find redemption, then freedom, and finally love. As much as it hurts, you must keep your heart open. That is the price you must pay."

"I don't understand."

My mother held me close. "If you want to break the blood bond, you must find Aiyana. There are ways, but make certain it's what you truly want. You will never feel as strongly for another human being as you do to the person you are bound to. Love is love, no matter how you come by it."

I didn't understand what she was saying. Soon, I wouldn't be *me* anymore. The only chance I had of hanging on to some semblance of myself was through Dane and I could hardly stand to look at him. The eyes of my love and now my enemy.

46

VESSEL

"NINA, BRING HER to me," Katia called, her black hair billowing around her face like agitated snakes.

My mother gathered her strength and helped me to my feet. She walked me to the edge of the chasm where Katia waited. I wanted to resist, I wanted to scream, I wanted to dig my heels in and fight, but I could feel Katia taking control of my body—shutting down my will. Raw power pulsed through every cell, luring me in like prey.

My mother whispered, "I loved you before you were even a complete thought in my mind. You gave me a reason to live, to fight, to remember that good still remained in this world. Katia let me go because you were already inside of me. I've been practicing for this moment my entire life—I just didn't know I was practicing for you. You gave my life meaning and I will always be a part of you, but the time has come for you to let me go."

I hugged her tighter, but she broke away from me and stepped back. A wave of pain swept over me, so crushing I thought it might bury me. I was grateful I got to see her one more time, but I knew this was truly good-bye. The next time she saw my face, I wouldn't be me anymore.

My mother smiled. "I didn't leave you unprotected."

Despair and confusion gripped me.

"It's time," Katia announced.

I couldn't believe it all came down to this. All of the struggle, all of the fighting, all of the pain added up to nothing. Katia got what she wanted, and so did Dane.

I felt the black silk ribbon slither from my neck and drift off into the corn. Without it, I felt hollow and cold. Just like Katia wanted me to feel. Just like I deserved. I was never anything more than a vessel.

47

THE KISS

KATIA RAISED HER ARMS to the dusky gray rose sky above
the sacred circle and took in a deep breath. She fixed her eyes
on me. I felt my chest inflate involuntarily, my lungs filling
with tiny sparks of electricity and magic. She exhaled, breathing white flames onto my skin—a celestial fire. I wanted the
fire to burn the flesh from my bones and char my memories,
but I felt no heat from the flames.

The words that flowed from Katia's mouth through mine
felt as natural to me as a nursery rhyme, something that I'd
known since the womb. *"Kirikus icawatka ru', cirasa ru', ka-
awakit ru' rikus kiru kiaarawataar,"* we spoke.

Katia leaned forward to kiss my mouth, taking in a deep
breath of the white fire that danced across my lips. I watched
the flames move through her in a flash, releasing her soul
from her body. Black vapor seeped from her mouth, creeping toward me like a sickness, and her body collapsed to the
ground, like a snake shedding its skin. I felt her presence

probing me, trying to find a place of weakness to get in. My mind told me to resist, but my body wanted to breathe her in, like the most beautiful perfume.

I heard my mother's words in my ear. *Uhurahak a u' a*—Let go and let yourself fall.

When I couldn't hold it any longer, I took in one last deep gasp of air—every memory, every feeling, every dream, every fear collapsed upon me, imprisoning me. I felt like a stranger in my own body. At first I could hear my heart beat, like being in the womb. I felt the euphoric sensation of Dane's presence. But I also felt myself disappearing, receding. Little by little being absorbed into my own bloodstream. Any hope that Dane and I had of being able to keep even a shred of ourselves was a beautiful lie. Nothing remained but despair and emptiness. I felt myself slipping away into the abyss.

I let go.

A ripping sensation etched through my chest—a sound of screeching agony escaped my lungs, as if my heart were being torn from my body with forceps. I came back to my senses to see the black inky tendrils of Katia's soul suspended in midair, hovering between my mother and me. The tremendous force of pure energy my mother summoned as she chanted nearly took my breath away. Despite the chaos around us, my mother looked more radiant than ever, her chestnut hair flowing like that of a goddess, the golden light behind her illuminating her frame. I recognized the words; this was something she practiced at home all the time, but I never understood it until now.

She always said she was practicing hanging on to her soul as the world collapsed around her and now she was using that same power to control Katia's soul, to hold her at bay. But it was more than that . . . it was a resurrection chant.

My mother's attention seemed to be focused on a spot beyond me. I turned, thinking she was looking at Dane or Coronado, but they were still trapped in Katia's spell, looking on, completely helpless. But as I turned back, something caught my eye. Pale, narrow fingers clutching the edge of the chasm. My heart seized as I watched Marie climb out of the crevice. She walked straight toward me, blood dripping from the palm of her hand, She grasped my hand. The feel of her cold, slick skin pressing up against mine was like a dark memory—something buried deep within my soul—something inevitable.

My mother acknowledged Marie with her eyes. The resurrection chant was meant for Marie. No longer a ghost or a vision, she was completely corporal now, made of flesh and bone. And then in one forceful inhalation, my mother sucked in the black tendrils of Katia's soul. My mother's body shook, her eyes bulged, dark veins protruded from underneath her stretched skin.

Marie pried the golden blade from the hand of Katia's discarded body and pressed it into my palm.

The knife molded to my hand as if it were meant to be there.

"It's the only way." My mother struggled to speak. "I won't be able to hold her for long."

Marie tightened my grip around the knife.

My knees buckled.

"No," I whispered, horrified by the realization of what she wanted me to do.

"If you don't do it," my mother said, "Katia will take over your body and soul. Think of Rhys. He needs you."

"I can't," I whispered. I closed my eyes to the horror before me and thought of my mother teaching me to swim in the Sargasso Sea, holding me up above her as the waves came crashing down. Showing me how gentle the world could be through nature and scent. Drying my tears with gold-tinged fingertips. Brushing my hair back from my damp cheeks, telling me how special I was. She taught me how to be brave, how to love—protected me at every turn. How could I end her life when she'd given me so much?

"Do it," my mother grunted in pain. I opened my eyes to see her convulsing, struggling to keep Katia's evil inside of her.

"I can't!" I screamed. "I can't let you go."

"We'll do it together." My mother managed to smile through her pain.

She took my trembling hands within hers, placing the tip of the knife against her chest. Her beautiful moss-green eyes enveloped me with tremendous love and warmth.

Marie wrapped her arms around us both in a violent embrace.

I heard the golden knife slipping between my mother's ribs,

and felt the warm burst of blood as it entered her heart. Her jaw went slack, her eyes darkened, and her body went limp in my arms.

As I held on to her, a great radiance blossomed beneath my mother's skin, until hundreds of tiny drops of light bubbled up, clinging to her like golden beads. I felt every one of them—each bead, a soul. The souls of my ancestors, the souls Katia had collected over the years.

I felt love, peace, and forgiveness beaming from her skin.

The golden beads intensified into tiny molten suns until a huge explosion ripped through her body, throwing me to the ground.

As my mother's ashes rained down on me, I watched Marie grasp the ankle of Katia's discarded body and drag her back toward the chasm. "A daughter's love is the greatest love of all," she cooed as she pulled Katia with her over the edge.

48

ASH

A SONIC BOOM ripped through the fields, collecting all the energy from the atmosphere. In a great show of power, the menacing wind encircling Dane and Coronado was pulled inside the chasm. Dane collapsed to the ground, gasping for air, while Coronado disintegrated into a pile of black blood, skin, and bones. The ground shook and heaved until the chasm surged together, leaving behind only a narrow crack in the earth's crust.

As I lay there, facedown in the barren circle, I stretched out my hand, tracing my fingers over the thin crack in the earth. My mother made the ultimate sacrifice. Coronado and Katia were gone. Marie was finally at peace. I'd never felt such sorrow and relief—it was over.

With great effort, I pushed myself into a sitting position to find Dane digging through Coronado's remains. He stood, wiping the blade of Coronado's dagger clean on the side of his pants.

As I studied him, a tiny bit of static rushed through my heart.

He walked toward me. A deep chill raced through my bloodstream. Something was off.

His eyes carried a dark glimmer that didn't belong there.

His gait.

His scent.

Sandalwood, mandarins, strawberries, and the sea invaded my nostrils—Coronado's scent mixed with his own.

"It's *you*." I exhaled a tremulous breath.

"You're a remarkable woman. Highly intuitive and very brave."

He had Dane's voice, but the phrasing was all wrong.

"How?" I asked in horrified awe.

He rolled up his sleeves, exposing the brand on his inner wrist. "Dane has been marked since birth. He's always belonged to me. But I never imagined it would come to this. It was fate."

That's why Dane's brand looked different from the other Mixeds'. It wasn't because he was branded as a newborn, it was because his mark was Coronado's signet. The crow . . . wings outstretched.

"When he refused to hand you over, I was furious, but when I saw how much you cared for one another, how much you looked like Marie, I couldn't resist his offer. It was worth the gamble. *You* were worth it."

"Dane *offered* himself as your vessel to save me?" I whispered.

"We've all made sacrifices. I would've preferred to stay in my own body, but Katia wouldn't let go of the past . . . of her

327

vengeance. She left me no choice. My soul will always choose life. As will yours."

My chin quivered as I attempted to hold in the tears, to hold in the rage I felt tearing at my heart. "I would never *choose* this life."

"Never is a very long time," he said softly.

Tears streamed down my face. Dane had said the same thing to me when Rhys left Quivira.

"You're beginning to have doubts about hating us . . . Dane and me." He crouched down in front of me. "I saw the look in your eyes when you first saw me in the corn. You feel something for me."

"I can't listen to any more of this." I placed my trembling hands over my ears. I felt so confused, so heartbroken, I didn't know what to do with myself.

"Come with me to Spain."

"I need my brother, I need Rhys," I whispered as I rocked back and forth.

"He'll find you when he's ready. It's in both of our interests that he's found." His eyes narrowed. It was clear he felt threatened by Rhys in some way. "You belong with me . . . with Dane." He brushed my hair back from my face and I flinched. "In time you may grow to love me, too."

I felt sick. "I don't love anyone."

The slightest hint of a smile tugged on the corner of his mouth.

"Besides, you're lying," I said. "I know what it's like to have another person's soul inside of you. Dane is gone. There's only darkness for the vessel."

"That's what Katia wanted you to see . . . to think . . . to feel. The world isn't so black-and-white, Ashlyn."

"Don't call me that," I spat.

He smiled more fully. The tiny dimple peeked out as if to taunt me, and it made me wonder. Was he in there? Could he see me? How could I still *feel* him if he were really gone?

"We all have good and evil in our blood, what we do with it is up to us." He reached out to touch my face. Every cell in my body called out for him, wanting to lean into his touch, to feel his hand against my cheek once more, but I forced myself to pull away.

"Pride cometh before the fall, *mi amor.* Don't let it keep you from happiness."

He stood and started to walk away, but paused at the edge of the circle.

"Immortality can be lonely," he said as he looked at me over his shoulder. "You'll know where to find me. And I'll always know where to find you."

As he left the circle, I watched my mother's ashes dance in the wake of his footsteps. And like those flecks of ash, I felt completely untethered from the world, set adrift in an open sea without a shore.

Lost.

Alone.

Irredeemable.

49

PROMISE

AS I WALKED BACK through the corn, I dragged my hands along the stalks, feeling none of the magic that once lived there.

I couldn't feel Katia or Marie anymore.

I couldn't feel my mother.

But I still felt Dane like a phantom limb.

Every step I took away from him only seemed to deepen the ache. I loved him and I hated him. Even whispering his name felt like fire and ice scraping against my lungs. And now I was bound to him for all eternity, a prisoner of my blood.

Even if I could forgive him for his betrayal, it wasn't Dane anymore. Coronado had taken him over, body and soul. And yet, something of Dane remained. It made me question everything I thought I knew about the world . . . about myself. I reached my hand to my throat to feel the comfort of the black silk ribbon, but it had left me, too. It didn't belong to me anymore. And neither did Dane.

I stepped through the perimeter, back inside Quivira. Beth

was waiting along with the others. They looked at me expectantly, but I had nothing to offer.

"Katia's dead," I said as I walked past their needy eyes and grasping hands straight into the lake, hoping it would wash me of my sins. I let the warm water envelop me, and all I could think of was the time Dane carried me into the water, washing the blood from my skin. I pressed my palm against my mouth, longing to feel the delicate weight of Dane's last kiss, but I only felt my own clammy, murderous flesh. I'd done the unthinkable. I killed my own mother. She gave up her life to save mine, and here I stood, all alone. Unable to live. Unable to die.

I looked down at the milky water, watching it turn the softest shade of pink from my mother's blood. My guilt felt unfathomable, a wild endless thing.

Without a word or a sympathetic glance, Beth waded into the lake next to me and took my hand.

As we both stared straight ahead, I wept.

We stayed like that—side by side, waist deep in the water until dark—until the community retreated to the meeting house, probably trying to figure out what to do with the rest of their mortal lives.

The sky had turned the deepest, blackest blue I'd ever seen. Even the moon and stars didn't dare show their faces tonight.

"You should go home, say your good-byes." I took a deep breath. "We're leaving in the morning."

"You're taking me with you?" She squeezed my hand in excitement.

I attempted a smile for Beth's benefit. "Do I even have a choice?"

"No. No you don't." She hugged me tight. "I'll come at first light. I have a surprise for you."

I listened to her footsteps as they disappeared into the corn—the opposite direction of the Grimsby lodge.

Beth was full of surprises.

A surge of adrenaline rushed through me as I neared the Mendoza lodge. Feeling a need to expose every secret, I let myself in, descending two flights of stairs, to the wood-paneled wall at the end of the hall. I pressed the panels until I heard the familiar sickening pop. The door swung open. The scents of eucalyptus and blood washed over me. The blood from the chalice had belonged to Coronado. The truth was right in front of me all that time and I didn't see it. I was so focused on Dane that I missed everything.

I wondered what made Spencer want to strike an alliance with Coronado in the first place. Was it pure greed, or revenge? What did Coronado promise him in return?

I thought about crossing the threshold, trashing Spencer's sick sanctuary, but I stopped myself. I wanted the world to see who he really was.

On my way back upstairs, I walked by Dane's door. I rested my hand against the cool wood grain. I needed one last look.

As I opened the door, his scent hit me dead on. It was like walking into a cement wall.

I pulled the hollowed-out book from the shelf. The stationery, the red wax, and the seal were missing, but his secret stash remained. I took out the sunglasses—the map—the Backstreet Boys CD and put them in my shorts pocket, but when I started to close the book, I noticed the chart printed on the inside of the front cover. It was a list of all the different gemstones and their corresponding meanings.

I looked up at his desk, trying to identify the stones when I saw that one was missing. I went down the list, trying to figure out which one it was. It was rose quartz. And according to the chart, rose quartz meant promise. Dane talked to me about the significance of rose quartz when he brought my ribbon back to me after the games. It was the same stone Marie left under Heartbreak Tree. And then I remembered something odd.

The first time Dane took me to Heartbreak Tree, I asked him if he'd ever written a note. He said, "If I had, I *promise* you'd know."

Promise.

The missing stationery. The missing gemstone. Was it possible that Dane had left something for me under Heartbreak Tree?

50

NO STONE
UNTURNED

I HIKED THROUGH the pines until I came to the clearing, the silhouette of the weeping willow barely visible against the indigo sky.

With my lantern low to the ground, I stumbled around, trying not to disturb people's hopes and dreams. I didn't need any more bad luck.

I stepped inside the swaying branches of the willow, but I couldn't find any sign of the rose quartz. I sank against the gnarled gray trunk.

I could still smell us here. Our blood. Our sweat. It made me sick, but I wanted to roll in the dirt and wallow in our last memory before it disappeared forever. I remembered Dane explaining the significance of the tree. He said love was stronger than death and that true love would always find a way.

The faintest whisper rose to my ears—the same sound I'd heard on the night Dane came to the Larkin lodge to return my ribbon. This time, the sound was coming from the split in the trunk. I reached in; my eyes welled with tears when I felt the familiar shock of silk wrapped around a stone with a letter attached. Carefully, I pulled it out of the crevice.

"Ashlyn" was written upon the envelope in thick black India ink. I ran my fingertips across the indentations from pen against paper and my heart fluttered.

The envelope had been sealed with dark red wax. In place of the coat of arms I'd seen on other Mendoza correspondence, Dane used his thumbprint instead. I pressed my thumb against it, swearing I could feel his touch there. I slid my finger under the seal, breaking it in two, and removed the heavy piece of stationery, feeling the weight of his good-bye.

> *Ashlyn,*
>
> *This letter is full of words I should never have left unsaid.*
>
> *You once said to me, "Just because you don't see it doesn't mean that it doesn't exist." I need you to remember that now.*
>
> *You were always the treasure, the gold, the glory, and the life worth fighting for.*
>
> *Zuni Pueblo Reservation. Zuni, New Mexico.*
>
> *Aiyana.*
>
> *This is me, letting you go.*
> *Dane*

Aiyana, the shaman of the Quivira tribe. My mother said she could help me break my bond to Dane. Could it be possible? Is this what he wanted?

In that moment, as I held the letter to my chest, I would've given anything just to feel him again—his imprint on my skin, his kiss on my lips, his hair entangled in mine.

My mother told me that love is love no matter how you come by it. But could I ever be at peace with the way Dane came to me? Could I ever be sure he didn't love immortality more than he loved me? Was he in there with Coronado? Could he be saved? If Aiyana knew how to break the bond, maybe she knew of a way to separate them.

Lying there, wrecked, I understood everything my mother had said to me during the ritual. Her warning had nothing to do with the physical pain I would face; it was about the pain of having to keep my heart open while it broke in two. She said I would feel like I couldn't take another breath, that I couldn't bear to feel my heart beat another second. My mother said that if I broke the bond I would never feel that strongly for another human being. But maybe that wasn't such a bad thing. Katia sacrificed everything to be with Alonso, and her love for him drove her to madness. I knew that feeling, and it scared me.

I wanted to bury the ribbon along with Dane's promise, but I held on tightly. I couldn't bear to sever my last tie to any of them.

51

PRECIPICE

I RETURNED TO the Larkin lodge to find our front doorway littered with dishes of mystery meats and cheese balls. They'd been set out like offerings. *Perfect.*

Stepping over the dishes, I went down the stairs and started cramming clothes into my bag. I left my mother's belongings exactly where they were, undisturbed, as if I could somehow preserve her presence there.

I went into the bathroom to get my toiletries, and when I saw Rhys's toothbrush sitting on the edge of the sink next to mine, it brought a lump the size of a boulder to my throat. He forgot it. I didn't know where he was, but I had to find him. I had to make this right.

I took the toothbrushes and reached under the bed for the case full of cash and gold to find nothing but a few lint balls.

It was gone. All of it.

I racked my brain trying to figure out who could've taken it.

Spencer. He'd been waiting in my room the day Henry passed away. I heard him rummaging around as I lay there bleeding out. He must've taken it then.

"Bastard," I screamed as I threw the toothbrushes against the wall.

I slumped down on the bed, grabbing my hair in my fists, when I heard a car horn. For a minute I thought I might be hallucinating, but it happened again. Three short insistent bursts.

I took my bag and ran upstairs to find Beth waving maniacally at me from behind the wheel of a deformed monster truck. She had a bright yellow scarf wrapped around her hair, like something straight out of a fifties' bad-girl movie. In the backseat sat a giant balding Saint Bernard.

"Is that Goober?" I asked as I stumbled outside.

"Is that his name? I'm pretty sure this is his automobile," Beth said as she got out to peruse the food. "But I don't think he minds. Do you, baby? Do you, pretty baby?" she called out to him, and he wagged his whole back end. "Ooh, this one's from Lauren. It's ham salad. She molds it to look like a slice of watermelon. Look, she rolls it in parsley and she even puts raisins in it to look like the seeds. It's her signature dish," Beth said as she put it in the backseat.

Goober immediately dug his face into it.

I grimaced. "I wouldn't let him eat that."

"Too spicy?"

"No." I shook my head. "First of all, Lauren made it. Could be poisoned."

"That's more of a Hanratty thing—the cheese balls." Beth smiled. "Besides, I already apologized to her."

"What the hell for? She was terrible to you. She got Brennon . . . her happily ever after."

"The cornhusk doll," Beth said in a sweet singsong voice as she slung my bag in the backseat.

"That was *you*?"

Beth tried to suppress a grin. "She was being so grouchy to you."

Apparently, Beth had a wicked side.

"Where did you learn how to drive?"

"Dane read the manuals to me when I was recovering. To pass the time. It's not hard. This one means go and this one means stop," she said, pointing to the pedals on the floorboard. "It's fun! And look at the wheels—they spin like windmills."

"Oh my God! Is this our car? Our Escalade?" I gasped as I ran my hands over the hot, butchered metal. "Tanner said he wanted to turn it into a convertible, that it would be good for hauling trash. I can't believe he actually did it. Poor Tanner," I said as I thought of his head rotting in the corn.

As much as I wanted to jump in and go, I had to be somewhat practical about this. I had Beth to take care of now. "I'm sorry, but we can't."

"But I thought—"

"Spencer took it . . . all of it. No cash . . . no gold . . . no gas."

"Oh, looky here." Beth heaved a giant pickling jar full of coins into my arms.

"Where did you get this?"

"Dane gave it to me. He wanted me to have it . . . just in case. I think he's been collecting it for years."

The mere mention of his name opened up a fresh wound.

"It won't get us very far." I swallowed my emotions as I handed the jar back to her.

"If it's just money you're worried about, you can always make more," she said as she put it back in the car.

"Okay?" I burst out laughing. "So, you're a counterfeiter, too?"

"I'm not sure what that is, but I don't think so," she said with that unreadable smile. "Nina left you the formula."

"The formula for what . . . disaster?" I mumbled.

"For making gold, silly." She grinned, slapping me on the arm.

My heart leapt into my throat. "What . . . what are you saying?"

"The formula. It's written all over your skin."

The realization grew inside of me like a slow-spreading fire. All the money we had growing up, the gold ingots, the secrecy of her work, the strange metallic smells, the fine gold dust that always clung to her fingertips.

How hadn't I seen it before? The marks on my skin weren't just protection symbols. My mother wanted to make sure I'd have the means to support myself and my brother. It was her final gift to me.

In a daze, I climbed into the passenger seat and Beth

squealed. "Oh my stars! Are we really doing this?" She revved the engine. "We look so hump-able in this car."

"*Kissable*, Beth," I corrected her gently. "We look totally kissable."

"Where to?" She smiled as she grinded the gear into place. "New York . . . *Spain*?"

"Just drive," I whispered.

As we drove through the corn, following Rhys's scorched path, I wrapped the black silk ribbon around my throat and tied it into a bow—the way Marie and I had always worn it.

I pulled the CD from my pocket and slid it into the player.

"This is Dane's song!" Beth trilled as she sang along and bobbed her head to the awful synthetic beat.

A boundless smile seized me from deep within. Tears sprung to my eyes as I breathed in the wonder of the universe.

Maybe it wasn't so black-and-white. Maybe I didn't have to belong to anyone but myself.

As I looked back over Quivira, to the disappearing lake, I closed my eyes.

I didn't want to erase it from my memory. I wanted to take in every scent, every detail, so I could conjure it up whenever I wanted. Quivira was a part of me now, as was my mother, Rhys, Beth, Dane, Marie, Coronado, and Katia. If I listened closely I could hear my mother whisper, *"Uhurahak a u' a."*

And there I was, once again, at the edge of a precipice. I knew what I wanted. I knew what I had to do.

I simply let go and let myself fall.

ACKNOWLEDGMENTS

THIS STORY has been with me for a very long time. It brought me the most unexpected career and a slew of people that I love.

My editor, Arianne Lewin—I keep going back to our first e-mail correspondence. I said something idiotic, like I was looking forward to getting my ass kicked. To which you replied, "One day you will laugh at the idea of wanting your ass kicked."

Still. Not. Laughing.

There were tears, and there may or may not have been a cornhusk doll involved at one point, but I'm a stronger person because of you. I'm a better writer because of you. I'm forever grateful you cared enough about my book to give me the "what for."

My assistant editor, Katherine Perkins—thank you for all the time and care you put into *Blood and Salt*. And for agreeing to meet me for chocolates whenever I felt weary.

Thank you to everyone at Putnam who helped bring this book

to life—my fabulous cover designer, Kristin Logsdon; interior designer, Annie Ericsson; and copy editor, Anne Heausler.

My agent, Josh Adams—thanks for believing in me—fighting for me. Much love to you and Tracey and my entire Adam's Lit family.

Lorin Oberweger—my mentor and friend, thank you for challenging me in the gentlest way and never letting me censor my writing.

Gina Carey—my muse. You are that wayward ray of sunshine.

Bess Cozby—thank you for being such a wonderful friend and for putting up with my heathen ways.

Jodi Kendall—thanks for your love and support and the fabulous author photo.

Rebecca Behrens—I can't remember, am I Kate or Allie? Thanks for figuratively holding my hair while I puked through this entire process.

Michelle Schusterman—meet you at 8th Street!

Nova Ren Suma—you've inspired me in so many ways. Thanks for taking me under your wing.

My Putnam editor sister wives—Heather Mackey, Jessica Spotswood, Brandy Colbert, Rachel Hawkins—thanks for welcoming me into the fold, but most of all to Maggie Hall, my number one editor sister wife. We've been there for each other every step of the way. I couldn't have gotten through this without you.

My NYC write night posse—Bridget Casey, Kristi Olson, Kathryn Holmes, Edith Cohen, Ghenet Myrthil, Erin Slattery. XO

The Freshman Fifteens—so lucky to be a part of this amazing

group of writers. Special mention to Jasmine Warga, Lee Kelly, Kelly Loy Gilbert, Jenn Marie Thorne, and Virginia Boecker for being true confidantes. Shout-out to the Fearless Fifteens who made this such a fun journey. Sabaa Tahir for that phone call—you know which one. And Adam Silvera for the best hugs.

Thanks to Courtney Stevens for those early morning pep talks. Emma Dryden for your professional support and friendship.

Gabriella Perriera and my first writing group, Quill and Coffee.

There are so many authors who've been kind to me along the way and offered early encouragement for no other reason than because they're awesome—Veronica Rossi, Donna Cooner, Erin Morgenstern, Holly Black, Melissa Marr, April Tucholke, Megan Shepherd, Gretchen McNeil, Kendare Blake, and Carrie Ryan.

My husband, Ken Peplowski—thank you for being my very first editor and for nurturing my love of words and literature.

My family—Maddie Liggett and Rahm Liggett. Thanks for sharing me with this imaginary world and for letting me hijack parts of your personality. I wrote this for you.

My parents, John and Joyce, and my sister, Cristie—you always told me I could do anything I wanted in life. Thankfully, I believed you.